STEALING THE STORM

STEALING THE STORM

Book Two of the Areyat Isles

AARON ROSENBERG

CRAZY 8 PRESS

DEDICATION

For Jenifer, Adara, and Arthur. The real magic.

What is Eldros Legacy?

The Eldros Legacy is a multi-author, shared-world, mega-epic fantasy project managed by four Founders who share the vision of a new, expansive, epic fantasy world. In the coming years the Founders committed themselves to creating multiple storylines where they and many others will explore and write about a world once ruled by tyrannical giants.

The Founders are working on four different primary storylines on four different continents. Over the coming years, those four storylines will merge into a single meta story where fates of all races on Eldros will be decided.

In addition, a growing list of guest authors, short story writers, and other contributors will delve into virtually every corner of each continent. It's a grand design, and the Founders have high hopes that readers will delight in exploring every nook and cranny of the Eldros Legacy.

So, please join us and explore the world of Eldros and the epic tales that will be told by great story tellers, for Here There Be Giants!

We encourage you to follow us at www.eldroslegacy.com to keep up with everything going on. If you sign up there, you'll get our newsletter and announcements of new book releases. You can also follow up on FaceBook at:

facebook.com/groups/eldroslegacy.

Sincerely,

Todd, Marie, Mark, and Quincy
(The Founders)

ACKNOWLEDGEMENTS

First and foremost, massive thanks to the crew at Eldros Legacy, who offered me a chance to write in their world and then liked that first book enough to let me do it again. I'm having a ton of fun with Sundra and Ruhi and all the people around them. It's also been exciting having the freedom to basically create the Areyat Islands myself, within the larger structure of the world.

Thanks also to all my friends and family. I post writing updates on my social media because it helps motivate me to know that people are watching my progress and cheering me on.

Third, thanks to all the pirate writers, fantasy writers, and mystery writers who've come before me. I've always said that any good writer has to be a voracious reader, since everything you read influences your own work—not in the sense of stealing from prior works but in the same way that we absorb everything else around us, using it as a foundation upon which we can build our own styles, preferences, creations, etc. I've read a lot of great books by great authors, and I know those have helped shape my own writing.

Finally, thanks to you, the readers. I write because I love to tell stories, but there's no point telling stories without an audience. I just hope you enjoy reading them as much as I enjoy writing them.

MAPS

Ekiladitar Ocean

Areyat Islands

1. Surpakat
2. Bahut Saare
3. Suraksha
4. Phasal Kaatana
5. Enkar Bindu
6. Riyaasat
7. Ooncha Need
8. Dveep Kile
9. Khet Parivar
10. Sharan
11. Khajaana

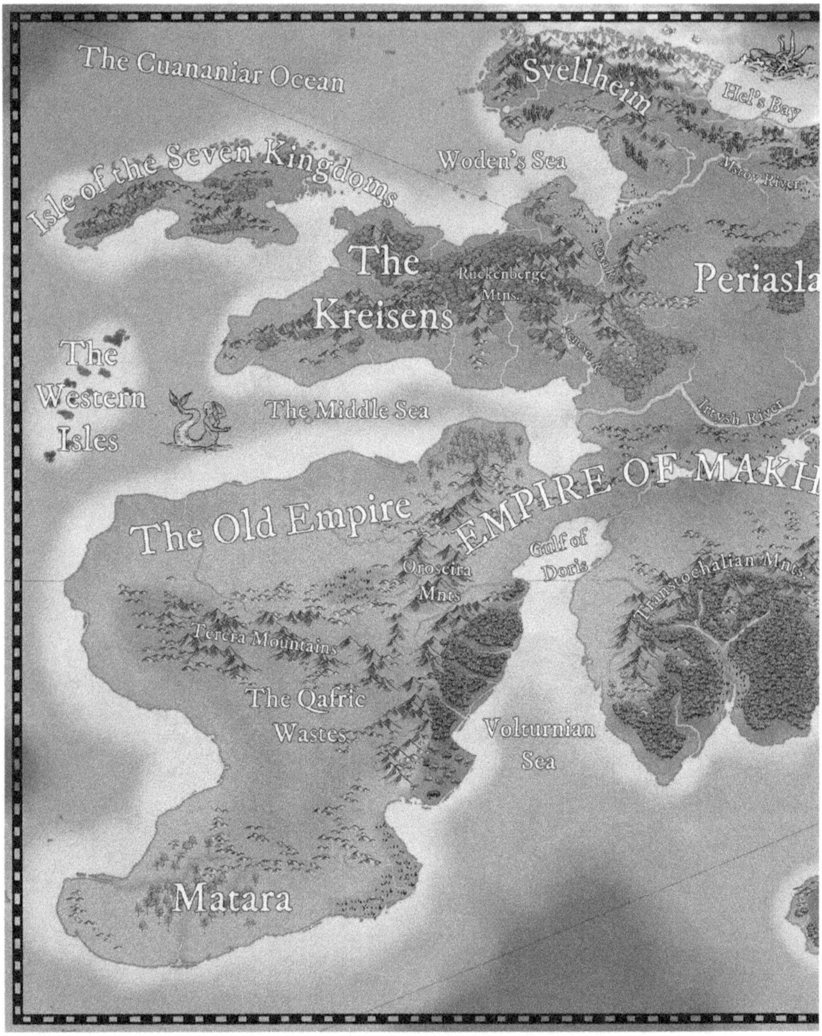

The Guananiar Ocean

Svellheim

Hel's Bay

Isle of the Seven Kingdoms

Woden's Sea

The Kreisens

Ruckenberge Mtns.

Periasla

The Western Isles

The Middle Sea

Trosh River

The Old Empire

EMPIRE OF MAKH

Oroscira Mtns.

Gulf of Dork

Thaprochatian Mtns.

Terera Mountains

The Qafric Wastes

Volturnian Sea

Matara

Euskalleria

Kolyvan Mountains

vl

Bashkal River

Virana Desert

Amaranth

Tanala River

AIRA

Inya River

Medina River

Sea of
Beloye

Ambhromar Ocean

Areyac Islands

Beloye
Terra Incognito

The Continent of
LATHRANON

0   100   200   300   400   500
Miles

By Sean Stallings

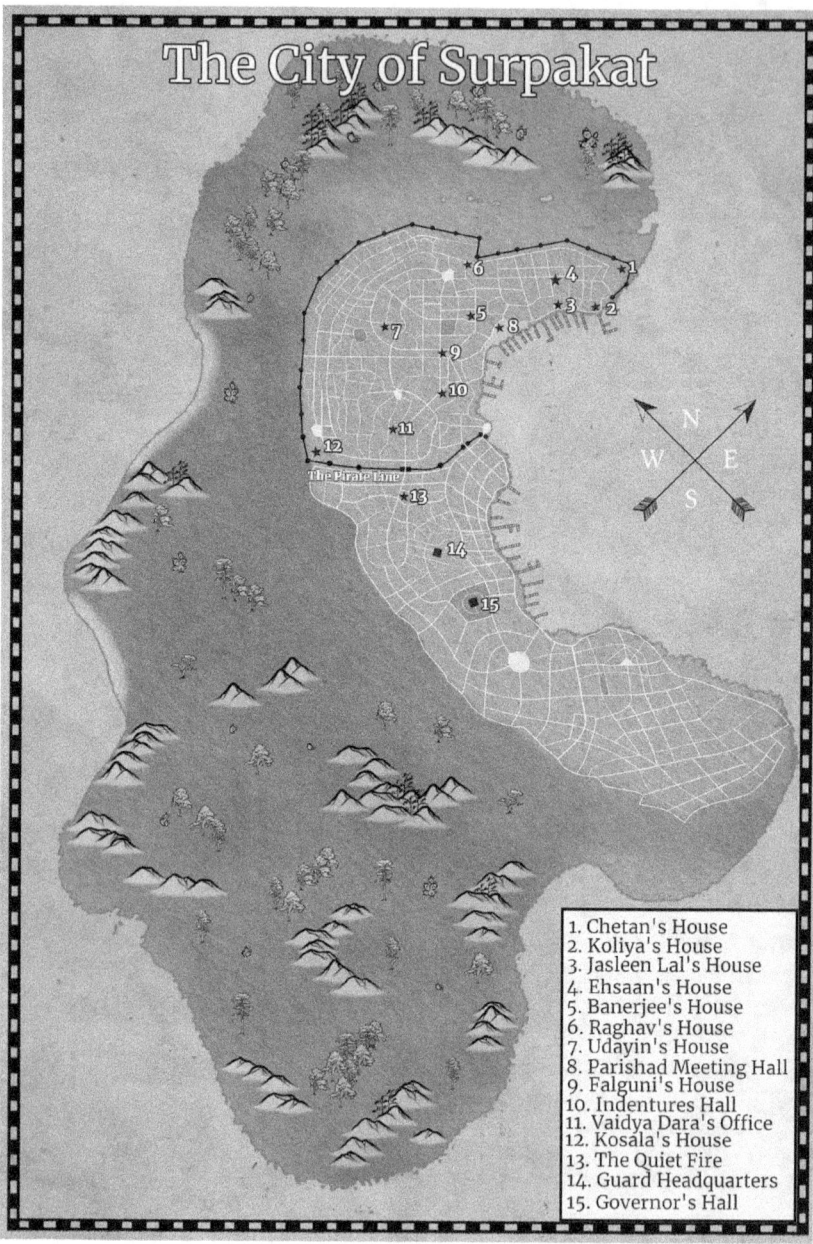

The City of Surpakat

The Pirate Line

N
W E
S

1. Chetan's House
2. Koliya's House
3. Jasleen Lal's House
4. Ehsaan's House
5. Banerjee's House
6. Raghav's House
7. Udayin's House
8. Parishad Meeting Hall
9. Falguni's House
10. Indentures Hall
11. Vaidya Dara's Office
12. Kosala's House
13. The Quiet Fire
14. Guard Headquarters
15. Governor's Hall

CHAPTER ONE

RUHI

Ruhi found herself approaching the docks as the sun prepared to rise.

She'd walked this way, taking a roundabout route, to put herself near the city's edge, right by the water. Surpakat was so quiet at this hour, the sailors still sleeping off last night's carousing, either in taverns or on their ships, the merchants just waking to open their shops and warehouses and start their day. She remembered what that was like, traipsing downstairs to let in the workers and open the logbooks and get ready for the day's business.

Things were different now, of course. *She* was different. And not just because she wore a man's guise, complete with fake beard and enchanted amulet. Back then, she had just been Ruhi Naidu, the merchant's daughter, the tomboy who handled his books and joked with the workers and often hauled bags of meal or rice or dried fruit right alongside them. Her biggest cares had been balancing the day's accounts and keeping up her end of the work while walking that fine line between becoming too familiar with the workers and being too aloof. And, of course, trying to keep her father happy while also not exasperating her aunt too much.

Now here she was on this pirate island, indentured to a pirate lord, disguised as a man, living with someone she called "brother."

And, at the moment, witnessing what she suspected was a band of men up to no good.

They were skulking. That was her first clue. Around here, most people walked like it was a challenge, daring you to question their right to be there. Not this crew. They were being furtive, sticking to the shadows, half bent over. Sneaking.

Like people who didn't want to get caught.

Then there was the fact that they were carrying something long and lumpy between them. Ruhi wasn't sure what it was. Not a body, since three of them had it tucked beneath one arm each. A lance? A masthead? A flag? Whatever it was, they were being careful, both not to let it get damaged and not to let anyone see it.

Though she had places to be herself, Ruhi was intrigued. And, since she still had time to kill, and they hadn't noticed her, she chose to follow the men and see what they had planned. Good thing Sundra wasn't here to see! She'd chided him over his impulsiveness often enough—if he caught her doing something like this, she would never hear the end of it. But something about the men had her curious enough not to care.

She did care about getting caught, however. After all, there were at least ten of them, and only one of her. People here were a lot rougher than she was used to, and interrupting some secret activity could easily get her beaten, or worse. She was no one of consequence, after all—plenty of pirates would just as soon knife her and shove her body into the ocean as let her see something they wanted kept quiet. Ruhi shuddered at that reminder and shifted farther to one side, putting herself deeper into the protective shadows of the buildings she was tromping past.

She'd been nearly to the docks when she'd spotted them, and the men continued in that direction, finally leaving the last few shacks and sheds behind to step out onto the long, wooden piers themselves. Ruhi hung back, close enough to see but far enough to hide, and watched as they approached one ship moored at a pier's end. The rising sun made it easy to see what awaited them there, the first light of dawn catching on the helms and spears of the half dozen guards stationed before the boat.

"Halt!" she heard one cry out. "Who goes there? This area is off limits, by order of the Parishad!"

The men stopped only a few paces away and parted, letting one of their number through. Ruhi hadn't noticed the woman before; she'd been carefully hidden within the group. She moved with some authority now, however, upright and bold, and the bright green of her dulpatta was vivid even from this distance.

"Stand down," Ruhi heard her say, though the rest of her words were spoken too softly to make out. Whatever they were, they had an immediate effect. The guards saluted, then shouldered their spears and marched away, down the pier—straight toward Ruhi's hiding place!

She ducked back quickly, crouching behind a bale of dried wheat. The jangling of armored feet approached, matched to the rattle of spears—and then passed her by. Still, Ruhi gave it another minute, letting the echoes fade, before she dared glance out again.

Two of the men were clambering up onto the ship, climbing the ropes hanging along its side. Once over the railing, they wrestled the gangplank down to let the rest board. The woman spoke to the three bearers briefly, then departed, forcing Ruhi to hide again. When the coast was clear once more, she saw that the men were all onboard with the gangplank pulled back up. They'd untied the mooring rope and cast off, and were now busy unfurling sails and easing the boat away and into open water.

Meanwhile, one of the three was climbing the rigging, the bundle tied across his back. When he'd reached the mainsail's yard arm, he hopped onto it, agile as a monkey, and crossed to its center, where he hooked the bundle somehow before unfurling it.

Ruhi had been right. It was a flag. A banner, at any rate. The skull and crossbones of a pirate, though this one had gold hoop earrings and gold teeth, a dagger clenched between them. She didn't recognize the design, since each pirate captain personalized their banner somehow. But she'd definitely remember it if she saw it again.

The ship had cleared the docks now, and Ruhi finally straightened, stepping away from her shelter. She wasn't entirely sure what she'd just witnessed. After all, the guards had left without a fight or even a protest. But something wasn't right, otherwise why all the sneaking about? And who was that woman, that she could order them away?

Regardless, the sun was now up over the horizon, the sky lightening in swathes of rose and gold and mauve—and that meant she was late. With a muttered curse, Ruhi turned away from the rapidly vanishing mystery and hurried back up the road, away from the water and toward the homes and businesses beyond. Perhaps someday she'd find out what all of that meant.

But not today.

CHAPTER TWO

SUNDRA

Sundra Aruvar was in the courtyard, playing at swordfighting with Sumana. He'd just completed a handsome parry and turned that into a quick but effective thrust, the slim, green switch he'd plucked from a nearby tree extended in a perfect line, his form excellent as ever. The day was warm and bright, the smell of jasmine from his mother's plants was thick in the air and mingled with the scents of ginger, chilies, mango, and fresh nan rising from the kitchen. Sundra himself felt light as air, as carefree and happy as a young Kunwar should be.

All that changed the second he heard their father call.

"Sundra!" His name carried across the grounds, emanating from the open windows of Father's office. Sundra froze, recognizing that exasperated, vaguely disappointed tone. What had he done this time?

Facing him, his little brother snickered. "Someone's gonna get it!" Sumana sang.

"That's not—" Sundra started, but his words faded in horror as he took in the scene before him. Somehow, where he'd held a willow switch before, now his hand clasped his own talwar, the long, slim sword's curved blade wickedly sharp—and its tapering point pierced clean through his brother's chest. "NO!"

Desperately he tried to drop the sword, but the smooth metal handle clung to his flesh. And Sumana—Sumana gazed up at him with those wide, trusting eyes, both hands coming forward to grasp the blade impaling him.

"Why, Sundra?" he cried out, blood beginning to pour from his mouth. "Why?"

Sundra couldn't answer, could only stare. Somewhere behind them, their father's voice was growing louder, closer, and Sundra felt a sharp pang of fear, guilt, and shame at the thought of the elder Aruvar seeing his firstborn stabbing his youngest. There had to be something he could do! Some way to fix this!

"There isn't," a dry voice replied, and Sundra's head whipped back around from where he'd been twisting to peer over his shoulder. Sumana was gone. Instead, there before him, pierced by his blade, stood a grown man, and one Sundra recognized at once.

It was Jivaka Pawari.

"You did this," the paunchy, older Sirdar reminded, gesturing at the sword protruding from his chest. "At least take responsibility for your own actions. Be a man, for once."

And with that, Sundra woke up.

For a moment, he wasn't sure where he was. This was not his room on the family estate—the light was different, and the smells and sounds, everything a bit brighter and more raw, sharper and less refined. The same could be said about his bed, he thought. While not uncomfortable, it was far smaller and rougher than his own, the footboard simple, carved wood without any gilt. A plain, whitewashed wall was immediately to his left, the bed snug up against it, and he spied a matching bed across the room against the right side, a simple but bright woven rug laying atop the wide, wooden planks between them. Though warm and cheerful, the room was a good deal less elaborate than his own, more rustic, and with a vaguely nautical flair.

That brought his memories rushing back, and Sundra sat up, sweeping his hair back with both hands. Ah, yes. Now he remembered.

The other bed was empty, and Sundra frowned, clambering to his feet. Where was his "brother"? Where was Ruhi? The angle of the sun through the curtains suggested that it was already mid-morning, which was considerably later than they normally got to sleep in, and then Sundra recalled the other salient fact and laughed aloud—

It was his day off!

Not just his, actually. Kosala, the raja who employed them both, graciously allowed all of her staff a day off each week, theirs to do with as they wished. Astonishingly, despite everything that had happened—being contracted to the sadistic, young raja Uda-yin, getting accused of his murder, witnessing the death of the equally young Vihaan, getting accused of that as well, discover-ing and revealing the true culprit—they had been in Surpakat less than two weeks, and this was the first "free day" they'd received in Kosala's service, just under a week since all that drama.

Astounding how time flew when you were trying to prove your innocence and save your own life!

That explained why no one had come looking for him to get back to work in the stables, Sundra realized as he stretched, shak-ing off the last dregs of sleep before crossing to where a pitcher of water and a shallow basin waited atop a small table. It didn't answer the question of Ruhi's disappearance, but she was an early riser by nature, he'd discovered, and no doubt had simply chosen to be about her own leisure rather than waiting for him. For an instant, he worried about someone learning the secret of her gender with-out him to stand guard, but she was smart. He wasn't even sure it mattered, really—Kosala was a woman, after all, and not the only one they'd seen here with freedom and authority.

If there was one thing the pirates did right out here, it was set aside some of the older and more foolish social mores. Of course, they set aside a lot of other important rules and strictures, too, like the sanctity of human life, so it wasn't all good.

Anyway, he was sure Ruhi was fine. She could take care of herself. Meanwhile, he had the day to himself.

What to do with it? He could maybe go flirt with Tanvi, the pretty girl he'd met last time he'd delivered a message to the governor's office. Or cadge some food off Kosala's cooks, Madhav and Laila. Perhaps see what Meera was up to, or find a few people to dice with. Even go pester Pillai, or just walk along the docks, admiring the ships.

"Well," he declared, grinning as he headed to the door, "looks like I've got the whole day to decide." And he fully planned to enjoy it.

⬠ ⬠ ⬠

In the end, he didn't wind up leaving the house and its grounds, but that was fine. Sundra had a nice, relaxing day hanging out with some of the other workers, playing at dice, eating, trading stories— though he was careful not to reveal anything about his family and their wealth—and just relaxing. It was perfect.

Right up until sunset, when Ilan, one of the other household staff, came to find Sundra where he was hanging out behind the house with Naaz and a few of the others.

"You should come quick," Ilan advised breathlessly. "Someone's asking for you. Well, shouting, really."

"What? Who?" Sundra demanded. "Who's here?"

Ilan shuddered slightly. "Some big brute in a black vest and a red turban, says his name is Shivaji? And that he's going to talk to you, whether you like it or not!"

⬠ ⬠ ⬠

Sundra hurried through the house, down the long inner courtyard and around the central pool to the front hall, but someone laid a hand on his wrist just as he reached for the front door, already hearing raised voices outside. It wasn't Ruhi, however, but another familiar young woman.

"Don't," Meera warned. "The raja is already out there. Let her handle him."

He scowled but couldn't bring himself to be angry at Meera. The young housekeeper was just too nice. She was also one of the few here close to him and Ruhi in age, and both pretty enough to attract his interest and amiable enough to appreciate it. Still, he'd have stormed outside anyway if not for what she'd said.

If Kosala already had the matter well in hand, interrupting might anger her. And that was something Sundra didn't want to risk. So, despite fuming a bit, he nodded and released the handle, though he didn't back away. Nor did Meera try forcing him. After all, if the thuggish pirate was here for him, he had a right to know why.

"Where are they?" That was Shivaji shouting, Sundra recognized his rough voice and coarse tone easily enough. "Get them out here! Now!"

Sundra felt a pang of worry upon hearing the "they." Where *was* Ruhi? Was she in trouble? But he consoled himself thinking that, if Shivaji had already gotten to her, he would only be demanding Sundra's presence now.

"What you need to do, shri, is back away. Now." That was their employer herself, Kosala's tone as calm and clear and ringingly final as ever. The female raja was never one to mince words, not when she could let her manner, her rank, and her might speak for her. Like now, when her warning was accompanied by a steely hiss Sundra recognized as a sword clearing its scabbard.

"Not without speaking to them," came the sullen-sounding reply. Shivaji had never been one to show much sense. Or restraint.

"You will speak to no one here without my leave," Kosala snapped back, her patience clearly at an end. "And I do not grant it. Now leave before I take offense at your presence. If you return on some other day, and make a polite request, perhaps I will reconsider."

There was a noise somewhere between a grunt and a growl, then a thump, followed quickly by a metallic clang. "You heard the raja." It was Sanga, Kosala's second, and Sundra knew the rangy pirate had unsheathed his talwar as well. "Go while you're still able."

More growling, but no words followed, and Sundra thought he could make out the duller, softer thud of boots on cobblestone. Once that sound had faded, he tugged the door open. Their unwanted visitor had already departed, and Kosala and Sanga turned in the act of tucking their weapons back away. "What was that all about?" Sundra asked them, stepping out onto the smooth wood of the porch. But then he saw a figure approaching, and he tensed. Had Shivaji decided to take his chances after all?

Chapter Three

RUHI

Ruhi was surprised to see several people standing out on the front porch as she approached, and even moreso when she recognized them. "Something wrong?" she asked, remembering to deepen her voice as she spoke.

"Where were you?" Sundra demanded, pushing past the other two and hopping down to reach her.

She straightened so she could peer down at him, if only by a little. "Out." She put all the scorn of a superior, older brother into the syllable. Out of the corner of her eye, she saw Sanga smirk at her reply. "What's going on?"

"Shivaji stopped by for a chat," Sundra answered, his handsome features set in firm, scowling lines. "You just missed him."

"Shivaji? I thought we were done with him!" The big pirate had been a thorn in their sides since they'd first met, particularly Sundra's, as the two had taken an instant dislike to each other.

"Evidently he disagreed. But he's gone now." Never had her "brother" looked more like the prince he truly was than now, suffused with righteous anger.

Too bad they were on a pirate island, surrounded by pirates, none of whom could ever know his royal blood.

"Indeed, I don't take kindly to people turning up at my home, demanding to speak with my staff," Kosala agreed, as regal as ever in her handsome black-and-red sherwani, beaded black choli, and ash-gray gharara over tall, black, leather boots. "So I sent him packing."

Ruhi finally joined them on the porch, Sundra trailing her. "Why was he looking for us at all?" she wondered aloud. "He can't still be angry at us—we proved who really killed his master."

Shivaji had been the Raja Udayin's right hand—which meant he was the one who'd enacted all of the sadistic raja's "corrections." When Udayin had died, rather spectacularly, Shivaji had blamed Sundra and sought revenge. That was all over now, or so she'd thought.

Indeed, Kosala was shaking her head, her thick, black braid whipping about behind her. "Not revenge," she corrected. "Greed."

That answer didn't exactly clear things up, but the raja had evidently said all she'd intended, because she brushed by them now, stalking down the corridor and disappearing into her study, the carved, wooden door closing firmly behind her.

Sanga lingered, however, and it was clear he'd taken pity on her and Sundra's puzzled expressions. "He wants his former master's belongings," the tall, rangy pirate explained, his open vest flapping against his bare, muscled chest. "His wealth, his land, his belongings, but mostly his ships. With those, any pirate could be counted a lord and request a seat on the Council."

"I can see why he'd want all that," Sundra admitted, leaning against one of the thick, circular columns holding the porch up. "But what's that got to do with us? We don't have any of that!" Which was true enough. If they had, they'd have already sold them off, paid off their indenture, and been freed.

Sanga only nodded, shifting back to perch on the side railing. "Nobody has them," he agreed. "They're all being held by the Parishad at the moment. When someone as important as a raja dies, there's a week of reflection, out of respect. Once that's done, though, anyone who thinks they have a right to the dead's belongings can put in their request, state their reasons, plead their case. And then the Council decides."

Ruhi had heard how the Parishad, the Pirate Council, distributed wealth and property, and in some ways it made sense. After all, these were pirates, not nobles—they believed in earning for yourself, not inheriting. And from what Sanga'd just said, she thought she knew why Shivaji had come here.

"He wanted us to put in a good word for him," she guessed and was pleased when Sanga nodded. "He thought maybe the Council'd listen to us."

"They would," Sanga corrected. "I doubt they'd just go along with whatever you said, but your words would definitely have some weight here." He waved a hand to include both her and Sundra. "You two're the ones who were accused of their murders first, after all. And you're the ones who caught the real killer."

"You said 'their,'" Sundra pointed out. "So the same thing's going to happen with Vihaan's belongings?" Another nod confirmed it, which made sense. The two rajas had died within days of each other, after all. "What happens if we say *we* should get all their stuff, since we're the one who got justice for them both?"

That wrung a laugh from Sanga, a note of genuine amusement without a trace of mockery. "Like I said, they're not just going to go along with you. Sorry." He shrugged. "They'll want to reward loyal service and promote talent, like always. But both rajas were rich, so"—he grinned as he stood—"I'd say expect a few more petitioners, at least."

"Great," Sundra muttered as the tall pirate departed, leaving him and Ruhi alone out there. "I'm so looking forward to that."

CHAPTER FOUR

SUNDRA

Sundra was in the yard the next morning, putting Chaaya through her paces, when Sanga emerged. The mare whinnied as the tall pirate approached, but more in warning than in fear, and Sundra gentled her with a soft word and a calming hand on her neck. Still, he was relieved when the other man stopped more than an armspan away.

"You're wanted," Sanga stated, and sighed audibly at Sundra's raised eyebrow. "By the Council. Now."

"Ah." The significance of the summons quashed any glib replies Sundra might otherwise have made. Instead he beckoned Naaz over, passing her Chaaya's reins once she reached them. The horse nickered in greeting and whuffled gently, lipping Naaz's hair and winning a giggle from her.

"Don't worry about the lunges for today," Sundra instructed. "Just walk her a bit more, make sure she's stretched well, and then you can rub her down and let her relax."

He'd been training Naaz in actual horsemanship, beyond her usual stable duties, and the girl was a quick study, her quiet, shy nature concealing a sharp mind and a kind heart, particularly toward animals. She nodded now, patting Chaaya's flank as Sundra rubbed the horse's nose in temporary farewell. Then, pausing only to wash his hands in a basin by the door and rub them over his face to clear away the dust, Sundra followed Sanga back inside and through the house.

Kosala and Ruhi were already waiting by the front door, and a moment later, the four of them had set forth, out of the house and down the lane to the road. Kosala's estate was along Surpakat's back wall, just above the Pirate Line, the wall dividing the city's older section above and its newer portion below. Following the road beside that barrier brought them to another avenue. Wider than most in this half of the crowded, twisty pirate capital, it cut up even as it angled over, toward the docks.

"You smell like horse," Ruhi muttered as they walked behind Kosala, and Sanga chuckled where he brought up the rear.

"So do you," Sundra replied, "but I was working with one. What's your excuse?" That brought a scowl from his "brother" and a snort from Sanga, and he grinned.

His next words, however, were projected forward, to their employer. "Any idea what the Parishad wants with us?" He was guessing it was much too soon for them to have already made a decision concerning Udayin and Vihaan's possessions, or to be asking for his and Ruhi's thoughts on the matter.

Kosala nodded. "Yes." But she gave no further answer, which was frustrating but not surprising. As Sundra and Ruhi had already learned, the female raja liked to keep her own counsel. He glanced at Ruhi, who only shrugged. So she didn't know either. That was something, anyway.

It was evidently a quiet day in the pirate town—they only had to skirt three fights on their way. Though the last, a barroom brawl that had spilled out from one of the dockside taverns, had spread across the entire street.

As they picked their way through the tumult, one drunken lout spied Kosala and stepped toward her, arms wide and a lascivious grin stretching his bearded, weathered face. As he charged forward, however, Sanga stepped up beside the man and brought the hilt of his sword down atop the unwanted suitor's head. The man dropped to the ground, stunned, and they continued their walk unmolested.

At last their road ended, spilling out onto a wide stretch of bare sand and stone. The docks were directly across, the sea plainly visible beyond, but they were headed for the long building facing that expanse, its bottom stone but its upper floors whitewashed plaster broken by thick wooden beams. The second floor had a wide balcony, its glass doors open to allow air and light into the room beyond, and Sundra knew that was their destination. They had been in the Parishad's meeting room before.

Inside, they passed through the first-floor taproom to the broad stairs and up those, where four city guards stood before the closed doors.

"Weapons," one of them ordered, and Sanga started to protest, as he apparently did every time, but Kosala waved him off, preventing the frequent back-and-forth by immediately offering the sheathed sword and dagger from her belt. That didn't stop her from trying to pass without relinquishing her remaining daggers, however, and Sundra thought he heard Sanga mutter something about, "Oh, sure, it's fine for you to do it!" under his breath.

He and Ruhi had no weapons, of course—indentured servants were only allowed such under exceptional circumstances—and a moment later the guards stepped aside, opening the doors and ushering them all through.

The room beyond was as impressive as ever, with its rich carpeting and its gold-tiled ceiling, scalloped arches supported by thick columns against clean, white walls with a bright, mosaic border in between, the smells of furniture polish and wood mingled with the salty tang of sea water. But Sundra's eyes skipped past the decor, sparing only a brief glance at the docks visible through the windows, before turning to the massive, oak table at the room's center. Ten tall, gilt chairs stood around the highly polished expanse, with smaller seats in rows along the two sides walls. The latter were empty, but people already occupied several of the former, and he recognized them all.

Chetan nodded in greeting, much of his former animosity toward Kosala now faded after their mutual attacks from Khatri. The sturdy raja looked as weathered as ever, his clothes and gear well-made but also well-used—much like their owner.

Beside him was Koliya, the big, burly pirate lord, who pounded the table at their entrance. "At last!" he exclaimed loudly. "Now we can get started!"

"Let them at least get settled, hmm?" a tall, slim man on the table's other end suggested, his voice quiet but his eyes clear.

That was Ehsaan—he and Falguni, the sharp-featured woman beside him, were two of the rajas Sundra knew the least about, though he remembered hearing something before about how careful the former was, and how sharp-eyed the latter. Next to them was the quiet, prim Tarabai Banerjee, who he'd barely heard speak. Then there was an older woman, her silver hair catching the late morning light, the shadows deepening the lines on her face but her bright-blue eyes still glittering. That one, he knew, was Jasleen Lal, a legend among the pirates and along the coast where she'd marauded for more than thirty years. Her daughters, who served as her lieutenants, stood on either side of her.

Kosala took her place at the table, Sanga moving to stand behind her. Unsure what to do with themselves, Sundra and Ruhi waited before the assembled rajas, the rulers of all the Areyat Isles. They didn't have to wait long. As soon as Kosala was seated, Jasleen lifted her cane, pounding its heavy silver head on the table. Not that she'd needed to—unlike previous Council meetings, the only people here were the rajas themselves, each one's seconds, and Sundra and Ruhi. Even Surpakat's new governor, Girish Malhotra, was absent, and the only city guards were the ones outside the doors. This, then, was no regular session.

"I'll get right to the point," Jasleen declared, her voice shaking. "My stormer is missing. I want you two to find him."

Sundra stared at the aged pirate lord. "Excuse me?" he said, sweeping into a bow to avoid giving offense. "I'm sorry, you want us to find a missing mage?" That, after all, was what "stormers" were. Mages. Specifically, thalakurioi, mages of the sea and the storm. But what could that possibly have to do with them?

Still, the senior raja nodded. "Yes," she confirmed. "Exactly." She leaned forward, laying both withered hands flat on the table, her daughters reflexively moving in closer for support. "Two weeks now, Makiya has been missing, though I only just learned of it. He's not the type to wander off. Been working for me over a decade." She grimaced. "And Antara's careful, it's not like she'd just let him go, anyway. Something must've happened. I need you to figure out what."

Ruhi was staring beside him, but Sundra had dealt with the idle whims of fellow nobles all his life, and gathered his wits after the initial shock. "We are at your service, of course," he offered now. "But we know nothing of mages, my brother and I. Nor have we ever met this Makiya of yours—"

"No chance you would have," Koliya exclaimed, chuckling. "Jasleen keeps him locked up tight at Dveep Kile when he's not at sea. Like a fancy necklace, only takes him out to see how he shines." He was grinning at the older pirate, and their fellow rajas, as he said this, clearly hoping for some reaction. When he got none, he grumbled and fell silent, sulking like a small child.

Ruhi, however, picked up his comment, if not his tone. "Even more reason we would be little help here," she argued. "We have never been to this Dveep Kile, or anywhere in the Areyat Isles besides Surpakat, and we weren't even here two weeks ago." No, they'd most likely been en route at that time, on the *Kalinga*, after being captured off the *Aden Star*.

Jasleen tutted away her objections. "You'd never really met Bhadra Khatri before, either," she replied. "And you caught him neatly enough. Keen eyes, the pair of you, and good instincts. Fresh perspective, too. That's what we need here."

Now Ehsaan spoke up. "It is not just Jasleen's thalakurios who concerns us," the raja revealed. "One of my mages perished recently, under strange circumstances."

"A missing mage—or a murdered one—is always cause for concern," Tarabai put in, her voice proving sharper and more shrill than Sundra had expected.

Now Kosala joined the conversation. "A strange set of coincidences, across several of our holdings," she declared, nodding at Sundra and Ruhi. "That is why the Parishad asked me to assign you to this problem. I assured them you would give it your utmost attention."

There was nothing else to do now but bow in return. "We will, absolutely," Ruhi agreed. "We will not let you down."

CHAPTER FIVE

RUHI

Kosala wore her customary half-scowl, half-sneer—like she'd caught someone doing something they shouldn't—as she and Sanga rejoined them after the meeting had ended. "I hope you know what you're doing," the raja said quietly. "You've all but promised to solve a mystery that's got all of them scratching their heads."

Interesting that she hadn't included herself in that number, Ruhi thought. But then, Kosala hadn't seemed overly concerned about the situation. Most likely she didn't use weather mages. Certainly she'd never mentioned having any in her employ, nor had there been anything about them in any of the recent household accounts—and Ruhi was the one who tallied those.

Still, their employer was right, it was a daunting task. And Sundra's expression agreed that she should have been more cautious in her reply. Not much she could do about it now, though.

There was something Kosala could do to help, however. "We're going to have to speak to various people about this," Ruhi pointed out. "It would help if we had some sort of proof that we were doing so on the Parishad's orders."

The pirate lord nodded at once and turned back to her peers. "Oy, they'll need a writ," she declared loudly before any of the others could leave. "Showing they're poking around on our behalf."

Falguni had been conversing quietly with Jasleen and one of her daughters but immediately dropped back into her chair. "Quite right," the narrow-featured raja agreed. She held out a hand, and her second stepped forward to set a handsome, portable writing desk in it. The finely wrought wooden case contained paper, pen, ink, blotter—everything Falguni needed to quickly write something out on a page, which she then marked with her seal. Jasleen had remained beside her the whole time, and the older raja added her seal as well, as did Chetan and Ehsaan.

"That should do," Falguni stated, holding out the page, which Ruhi stepped forward to accept.

The sheet of parchment stated that the bearers, Rawal and Sundra Chera, were acting on the Parishad's behalf and should be respected as such. Ruhi bowed, folding the letter and sliding it into the waist of her shalwar. She'd have preferred to secure it beneath a mekhela, but Kosala's staff weren't provided with accessories like the beaded belts, and she'd had neither funds nor opportunity to do any shopping for herself. This would have to suffice.

As they exited the building, Sanga leaned in. "Any idea where to start?" he asked softly. On her other side, Sundra shifted, clearly eager to hear the answer as well.

Fortunately, one had occurred to Ruhi. "Yes, actually," she replied. "I thought we'd start by asking another thalakurios"—she tapped Sundra on the arm—"along the docks. And let's hope the *Kalinga* is still there."

"The—? Ah." Her brother's expression brightened as he understood. "Good idea!"

Kosala had been following the exchange—the raja didn't miss much—and nodded. "Let me know what you find out," she instructed before heading back toward her house, Sanga beside her.

The minute they were apart, Ruhi turned toward the docks, Sundra already a step ahead.

"Hey!" he called out to the nearest man, a big, burly sort, busy hauling a large bushel of something. "The *Kalinga* still in port?"

The man tensed, then shrugged. He looked vaguely familiar, and Ruhi squinted, studying his features. Sundra, however, stared outright before clapping his hands together. "Druv!" he declared. "Druv, is that you?"

The dockhand nodded, but it was a hesitant, fearful gesture, and his eyes stayed firmly on his work. Sundra was rarely one to be denied his pleasantries, however—he bounded over and seized the other man's hand, shaking it vigorously.

"Good to see you again!" he told the man. "Rawal, you remember Druv, don't you? He was the cook aboard the *Aden Star!*"

"Ah. Yes. How are you?" That was why he looked so familiar! Poor Druv nodded but actually looked miserable at being recognized.

She could hardly blame him. Most of the sailors from that ship had been brought here to Surpakat and indentured, just like them. Those with valuable skills should have been in high demand, though, and Druv not only had sailing expertise but was a solid cook. To find him here, lugging bales and bundles instead, spoke of a significant downturn in his personal fortunes, one his worn, stained clothes confirmed. Poor man!

"We should go," she told Sundra, trying to spare their former acquaintance any further embarrassment. "He doesn't know where the *Kalinga* is, and we're interrupting his work."

Sundra finally seemed to pick up on her tone, and on the former cook's unease, and nodded slowly, sympathy clear on his face. "Yes, all right. Good to see you again."

Reaching into his pouch, he pulled out a dirham—Ruhi had no idea where he'd gotten it—and clasped Druv's hand, transferring the coin to him in the process. "Take care, Druv," he said as they turned away.

Ruhi and Sundra didn't speak for a minute after that, not until they spotted another sailor, and then only to ask again after the ship they sought. This time with better results.

"Dock ten," she answered, pointing to their left, and Sundra waved his thanks before veering in that direction. If he noticed the rough and ready nature of both their surroundings and the people working there, he did not show it.

Ruhi still didn't know enough about ships to distinguish between one type or another. Fortunately, Sundra did—he'd mentioned in the past that he'd been sailing many times, as his family back home was wealthy enough to have their own barijah. Thus she was content to let him lead for now, and he did so without hesitation, taking them straight to a ship that did indeed look familiar.

As did the female pirate perched on one of the dock's sturdy supports, right by the ship's gangplank. She was peeling a mango with a short, sharp knife, and laughed when she saw them approaching. As before, she wore a short, open vest and a simple choli, though the bodice was a vividly bright orange-red.

"Well, this is the first time anyone's ever come back!" the woman—Chhavi, Ruhi remembered—declared. Popping a piece of mango in her mouth, she grinned around it. "I gather indenture agrees with you? You both look well. Nice trim."

That last was to Ruhi, with a sharp, knowing look at her beard, and she blushed. The other woman had seen through her disguise during their time on the pirate ship, despite the enchanted medallion Ruhi wore, but for whatever reasons had chosen not to reveal it.

"Thank you, we are tolerably well, yes. And you?" Sundra replied, his tone and stance instantly adjusting to what Ruhi referred to as "flirt manner." Which, unfortunately, happened any time he was around a remotely attractive woman.

At least he didn't behave that way with her, which was something—he was always very careful to treat her like a man and his brother, which she certainly appreciated. This other side of him she found irritating, even though she had to admit it usually had the desired effect.

Like now, as Chhavi laughed again. "I'm glad," she answered, and sounded as if she might even mean it. "So what brings you here, then? Not trying to escape, are you?" That last was said with a look of mock horror, since they all knew it to be impossible, thanks to their bracelets of indenture.

"No, nothing like that," Ruhi assured her anyway.

"Ah, then you've won your freedom and you're here to book passage home," Chhavi suggested next, nodding over her fruit and knife. "Good timing, as we're out to sea again with tomorrow's dawn."

Even Ruhi had to laugh at that one. "Sadly, no—or at least, not yet," she admitted, raising her arm to reveal the bauble in question and smiling at the pirate's satisfied smirk. "We're actually here to speak with your weather mage, if he's about." She proffered the signed writ. "The Parishad sent us."

"Oh?" Now the pirate did look surprised, as she reached for the paper. Her glance went to the bottom, and the seals affixed there, before she tilted her head back. "Captain!" she bellowed up at the ship.

A second later, a tall, slender man stuck his head over the railing. "What ho?" he asked, his eyes going to them at once. "Visitors?"

"From the Parishad, to see Nalan," Chhavi explained, waving the paper.

The man, Captain Khandereo, vanished for an instant, reappearing at the top of the gangplank. His long legs made short work of the descent, and soon he was standing beside them, reaching out to pluck the page from his sailor's grasp. He was dressed as elaborately as ever, Ruhi saw, in a fine sherwani and a handsome silk shalwar topped by a deep-blue turban adorned with a single, large pearl, but his boots were still the same sturdy, black leather, and his pair of short swords hung from his sash.

"Interesting," he stated after a moment, offering the page back to Ruhi. As in their previous encounter, his manners were far nicer than she'd have thought of a pirate captain. "Well, we are at the Parishad's command, of course. Nalan!"

The name was repeated up above, and again, as pirates relayed the call, before someone shouted back from belowdecks. A few moments passed, then a short, sturdy man with a shaven head and a long, drooping mustache emerged.

"What?" His reply hardly seemed respectful, but Khandereo ignored that.

"These two are here to speak with you, on orders from the Parishad," the pirate captain stated. His tone, though mild, left little doubt that this was not a request, and the weather mage huffed but stomped down to join them, though he stopped at the bottom of the gangplank, balanced easily atop the swaying board.

He was bare-chested save for an angavastra draped over him, its fabric a swirl of blue and gray that put Ruhi in mind of a brewing storm. Appropriate, that.

"What does the Parishad want with me?" he demanded, glaring at Ruhi and Sundra. She noted that neither Chhavi nor Khandereo were making any effort to leave, but that couldn't be helped. Besides which, the weather mage was blocking the gangplank at the moment.

"What can you tell me about a thalakurios named Makiya?" she asked instead. She was careful to use the proper title for them, in the hopes the show of respect would help soften the man.

But Nalan merely shrugged. "Why?"

"Do you know him?" Sundra put in.

The man hesitated, glancing at his captain, who nodded. "Of course," he admitted. "All thalakurioi know each other."

Getting this one to talk was like pulling teeth. And unlike some other situations, Ruhi couldn't get away with touching him, so she couldn't use her Gift. Besides which, she wasn't even sure such a thing would work on a full mage.

"What is he like?" she asked instead, forcing any irritation from her voice.

"Decent," Nalan said finally. "Better with waves than wind. Probably because he can't stand heights." His smirk said he'd probably teased the other mage about that failing more than once. "Adequate with a storm. Not strong on lightning, though decent aim."

"When was the last time you saw him?" Ruhi asked next.

The mage frowned, but his distant look said that was from trying to remember rather than from annoyance. "A few weeks, maybe," he stated. "Last time we put in at Bahut Saare, he was there, too, though not for long. Why? What's this all about?"

There wasn't any way to hide the truth, not if she wanted to continue the interview. "He's disappeared," Ruhi explained. "About two weeks ago. The Parishad tasked us with finding out why."

"Disappeared?" Nalan started—but to Ruhi's eye, he seemed perhaps less startled than he should have. "I don't know anything about that."

She desperately wanted to reach out, latching onto his wrist and weakening his reluctance to talk, but knew that would look strange. And she couldn't afford questions about her behavior, not when scrutiny could lead to uncovering her own secret.

Still, she was sure the man was hiding something. And, without her Gift, she had no way of telling what.

"Did he have a feud with anybody?" Sundra asked, and Ruhi could have kissed him for picking up the questioning so easily. "Anyone he owed money, anything like that?"

The thalakurios shook his bald head. "If he did, I don't know anything about it. We were never close."

"Anyone else asking questions about him?" Ruhi tried. "Now, or a few weeks ago?"

Again Nalan denied any knowledge. "Look, I had no idea anything was wrong until you showed up," he insisted. "So no, nobody else poking around asking about him, no weird notes, no cries for help, nothing." He paused, started to say something, stopped, tried again. "You think he's all right?" That concern, at least, sounded genuine.

Unfortunately, Ruhi didn't have a clear answer. "That's what we're trying to find out," was the best she could manage. That, and, "We'll let you know when we do."

The weather mage's answering nod was short, brusque. "Thanks. So, we done?"

Ruhi was still nodding when he turned and started back up the gangplank. "That's Nalan for you," Chhavi told her. "Not exactly a sparkling conversationalist."

"Clearly. Well, thanks for the help with him." Ruhi meant that, and help with keeping her secret—she could see from the female pirate's face that she knew it too. "We should let you get back to work."

"I suppose." Chhavi offered her and Sundra the last slices of mango, wiping the knife clean on a rag before sheathing it. "See ya next time, maybe." She started toward the ship, as did Khandereo, after the pirate captain had executed a grandiose bow.

"Quite the cast of characters," Sundra remarked when they turned to exit the docks.

"They are," Ruhi agreed. "I just wish they'd been more useful in this instance. Or more forthcoming, in Nalan's case."

"You think he knows something?"

"Maybe." She shrugged. "But whatever it is, he's not talking, and we can't force him."

She just hoped, whatever it was, it wouldn't blow up in their faces.

CHAPTER SIX

SUNDRA

Without any clearer idea, Sundra suggested they return home—how strange it still seemed, referring to any place other than his father's house as that—to eat and think. Ruhi agreed. But they'd not made it far beyond the docks before they spotted a slender town guard among the crowd.

Though not particularly tall, she stood out, partially thanks to her jacket of overlapping metal scales, partially from the pointed, metal cap atop her head, but mostly from the long, chisel-tipped spear she held like a staff, tapping its blunt base upon the ground with each step.

Sundra tensed reflexively, thinking of the various run-ins they'd had in the past. He'd even been given a personal tour of the jail at one point—as an inmate. Though admittedly that had been both brief and intentional, to speak with Kosala while she'd been imprisoned there.

Right now, however, he and Ruhi had nothing to hide, he reminded himself. Not only that, they were actively employed in an investigation for the Parishad itself. Accordingly, he straightened and did nothing to alter his path as they approached the guard.

As they drew closer, his pace did increase, but not out of fear, and Sundra felt a smile spring to his lips. This particular guard, a trim, athletic woman with clean features and sharp eyes, was one they knew. And even liked, as long as they weren't the subject of her attentions.

"Captain Pillai," he called out when they were near, and her calm nod confirmed that she'd already spotted them as well. "Good to see you."

"Shri Chera," she replied, stopping her own walk so the three of them were now standing together, off to one side of the street. Which was good, since the streets here were narrow enough that people might have to push past them otherwise. Thanks to Pillai's obvious occupation, however, most were careful to give them a wide berth, with only a modicum of curses and insults in passing. "Both of you as well." Something about the tightness of her mouth told Sundra that wasn't entirely true, but her eyes had slid away from him as she spoke, making him think perhaps something else was bothering her.

"Everything all right?" he asked, and heard Ruhi groan softly beside him. Yes, fine, he could have been more circumspect. That wasn't always his strong suit, though. Besides which, he knew the guard captain valued honesty and direct speech.

Like now—her eyes snapped to him, and she frowned, but after a second, she shook her head, causing the chain links along the back of her neck to swish and jingle. "Yes, of course. No, not really. I don't know." Her sigh was louder than Ruhi's, as she leaned upon her spear. "I wish I did."

"Anything we can do to help?" Sundra meant it, too.

He did like the no-nonsense Pillai. Of course, Ruhi claimed it was the woman's apparent immunity to his charms that intrigued him, and maybe there was something to that, as well. But she'd helped them when they'd been suspected of murder, giving them the benefit of the doubt when she hadn't needed to. That had to count for something.

Ruhi nodded. "We're happy to, if we can," she agreed. "Even if it's just being someone you can talk to who doesn't work for you."

That was a good point. All the other town guards answered to Pillai, which would probably make it difficult for any of them to come to her with problems—and even harder for her to speak about such things with them.

Sundra remembered those lessons from his father: "You cannot be friends with a subordinate. Treat them with respect, value their opinion, reward them with your trust and your honesty, but never forget that they work for you, and certain lines cannot be crossed."

Given what Ruhi had told him about her own upbringing helping her merchant father run his warehouse, he suspected she'd had similar advice.

He was a little surprised, however, when the woman with them nodded. "Thank you," she said. "I appreciate that. And maybe you're right. An outside opinion... it's Chennama." Sundra shrugged, confused, and she explained. "She's the new lieutenant governor. Chennama Macola."

The previous governor, Dalpat Laghari—Meera's father—had been under the thumb of Bhadra Khatri, and had helped him frame Kosala, and thus indirectly Sundra and Ruhi, for Udayin and Vihaan's murders. Laghari had been allowed to live, but had been exiled from the Islands. His own former assistant, Girish Malhotra, had taken his place, which of course meant they'd needed a new lieutenant governor.

"We don't know her," Ruhi was saying. "You don't approve? I know you said the governor was a good man."

"He is," Pillai confirmed at once. "Very. Maybe too much so." She shook her head. "This job, it makes me... suspicious, I guess. I'm always dealing with the worst in people, you know? So that's what I tend to see. And maybe what I expect. Girish... he's not like that. He sees the good in everyone. It's admirable—but I worry sometimes that it's a little naive too. That he misses the negatives as a result."

"And you think that's what happened with his choice for an assistant," Sundra summed up. "That there's something wrong with her, and he missed it."

Pillai shifted her stance, shuffling her feet in a move that was oddly unsure for her. "Maybe? I don't know. She worked for Dalpat and Girish before, so she's certainly qualified. And she seems good. Very competent. Very organized. Very smooth. I think that's what bothers me. She's so smooth, really good at talking to people, at winning them over. Girish is a little awkward at times—and I know some people say I am, too." Her lips quirked in a quick, self-deprecating smile, but then she turned serious once more.

"Chennama's everybody's best friend, a total charmer." She shrugged, her jacket rustling from the motion. "Maybe I just don't trust people like that."

"I'll try not to take that personally," Sundra joked, and was pleased to see a second smile flicker into view. "But I know what you mean. I've been around people like that my whole life. And some of them really are as nice as they seem. Others, though—you're right, that smooth surface can conceal some nasty rot."

"Have you talked with the governor about this?" Ruhi asked, and Pillai's response to that was a quick, sharp jerk of her head.

"No, of course not!" she protested. "What would I even say? 'Sorry, your new lieutenant's just too nice, she must be up to something'? It's just my gut right now. And unless I've got a real reason to investigate, I shouldn't even be pursuing this."

Sundra stroked his chin. "In my experience," he started, and laughed at the eyeroll he got from Ruhi and the quirked eyebrow from Pillai. "All right, all right. From what I've seen and heard, being around ambitious people my whole life? If she is up to something, you'll know it soon enough. All you really have to do is wait, and keep your eyes open. Eventually, she'll act, and then you'll have your proof."

The captain was regarding him fully now, an experience he always found slightly unnerving. "For a poor younger son who left home to seek his fortune, you seem to know an awful lot about people in power," she observed, and Sundra fought the urge to cringe. Damn it!

"Our father's a merchant," Ruhi put in, coming to his rescue as usual. "When things were good, his customers were among the wealthiest in the city. After he fell on hard times, they all deserted him, of course. But we still remember what those people were like."

Either the bitterness in her voice was impressively feigned or she'd really experienced such a reversal of fortune. Sundra wondered which. Neither of them had spoken extensively about their past, after their initial meeting aboard the *Aden Star*.

Pillai's eyes held a measure of sympathy. "I'm sorry," she offered, straightening. "That couldn't have been easy."

She adjusted her grip on the spear, lifting it and resting the shaft against her shoulder. "Thank you. You were right, being able to talk with someone about it helped. I trust this won't go any further, though? Like back to your employer?"

To say she and Kosala didn't get along was putting it mildly— both were strong women used to being in charge and giving orders, so they tended to butt heads when they met, like a pair of cats warring over territory.

Sundra nodded. "Of course." And after a second, Ruhi echoed the gesture. After all, this had nothing to do with the raja. No reason to involve her—or to betray Pillai's trust.

"Thank you," the captain repeated. "I'd better get on with my patrol." And, with a dip of her head and a wave of her hand, she was off, her gaze entirely upon the road and crowd before her.

"That was interesting," Sundra commented once she'd left and he and Ruhi had resumed their own trek toward home. "I wonder if we'll meet this Chennama at some point?"

"I'm sure we will, attending a Council meeting if nowhere else," was Ruhi's reply. Which made sense—the Governor presided over such meetings, and one might expect his assistant to accompany him, just as Sanga and other seconds came with their rajas.

"Then I guess eventually we'll be able to judge for ourselves," Sundra stated. He had a feeling he'd agree with Pillai's assessment, however, and could see that his so-called brother felt the same. The guard captain was a good judge of character.

She'd believed them, after all.

CHAPTER SEVEN

RUHI

The next day, Ruhi was nose-deep in the estate's account books. A quick, light rap on the doorframe startled her. "You about done there?" Sundra asked, stepping into the room. Though the dust on his clothes said he'd just been outside working the horses, his face and hands were noticeably clean.

Ruhi leaned back, stretching. "For now, yes," she admitted.

She'd just reconciled the past week's numbers, which would have been a lot easier if Sanga didn't repeatedly forget about purchases or sales, causing him to come by throughout the day so she could adjust the numbers each and every time. Or if there weren't odd entries from somewhere beyond the property that she'd asked about once and simply been told were "additional elements" that still had to be factored in.

"Why?" she asked.

Her brother shrugged. "I thought we'd head over to the Quiet Fire for lunch," he suggested. "And maybe see what Padmini says about all this."

That was actually a very good idea—both parts. The tavern

owner had become a staunch friend and valuable ally during their previous troubles, and her clear head and good sense might catch something they'd missed. Besides which, she'd been here in Surpakat for years, which meant she knew this pirate city far better than they did.

Also, while Madhav and Laila were kind people, and good cooks, they lacked Padmini's flair for food. Just thinking about some of the dishes the older woman served had Ruhi's mouth watering, and she pushed back from the desk, rising to her feet with an alacrity that made Sundra grin.

"Let's go," she told him. "Though we should—"

"Already did," he assured her. "Come on."

Kosala had proven to be a surprisingly lenient employer, at least in the sense that she let her people have some freedom and some privacy, provided they did their work well and didn't abuse her trust. She wouldn't object to their going elsewhere for lunch, especially if most of their daily chores were already finished.

It was a fine day out, clear and warm but with a pleasantly bracing breeze off the ocean, and it didn't take them long to reach the Quiet Fire. The tavern was just below the Pirate Line and along the main road cutting through that barrier, so not far at all. And this side of the line was not only newer but more sedate, with fewer actual pirates and more tradesmen and merchants as well as more frequent guard patrols, all of which made her feel slightly safer.

Inside, the tavern was busy as usual, many of its tables already full, but the high-paneled ceilings, supported by tall, white columns spaced down the middle of the big room, kept the noise subdued.

Padmini was by the front as they came in and gave them her usual smirking smile, which Ruhi had come to realize was a genuine sign of affection.

"Ah, my two favorite snoops!" she declared, reaching out lightning-quick and tugging on Sundra's chin and Ruhi's false beard. Not hard, though, and only for an instant, as she laughed at their expressions.

"Hungry? I only have enough alleppy meen left for three bowls, and one of those is mine." She was already leading them to a table tucked under the upstairs balcony, a quiet corner that seemed to be her own preferred spot.

"Sounds perfect," Sundra said with his usual gallantry, and Padmini laughed again, the sound a sharp bark but the amusement clear. She even simpered a bit when he pulled out a chair for her, though she swatted at him a second later.

"If I sit, who's going to fetch the food?" she scolded, though she was smiling as she stomped off. A moment later she was back balancing a platter with three large earthenware bowls, each steaming and giving off a rich, spicy scent. There was also a basket of fresh roti, a pitcher of water, and three cups.

"Eat," she insisted, plunking the dishes down in front of them and plopping into her chair. "Talk after."

Ruhi was happy to comply. The curry was thick and rich, large chunks of fresh fish floating to the top, the delicate flesh balancing the spicy gravy, sweet coconut, and spicy-sweet raw mango. She'd downed most of her meal before she knew it, and Sundra was already leaning back in his chair, using roti to mop up the last bits of gravy in his bowl.

"Good?" Padmini asked, and smiled at their eager nods. "Good. Now, tell me—what brings you here besides the food and an old woman's company?"

So they told her. Ruhi did have a momentary qualm about revealing the Parishad's business without permission, but they'd trusted Padmini with their lives before, and she had proven her worth. Surely this was no different.

When they'd finished recounting the brief interview with Nalan, the tavern owner scoffed. "Course you wouldn't get much from him," she declared, though she kept her voice low enough for it not to travel beyond their table. "One stormer's not gonna turn on another."

She rose to her feet abruptly, clearing the table and disappearing with the dishes, then making a quick round of the room, refilling pitchers and baskets and fetching a few additional items, collecting payment from others.

"He made it sound like they weren't close," Ruhi commented once their host had rejoined them. "Maybe we should ask another, though."

"Good luck with that," came the reply. "What did he look like, this mage of yours?"

"A few inches less than my height, a little on the heavy side," Sundra answered at once. "Bald. Long mustache, barely waxed. Patched pants, bare feet. Nice angavastra, though. Handsome pattern on that."

It was a surprisingly astute description, and he smirked at Ruhi's expression. "What? I can be observant!"

"When it's a pretty girl, sure," she shot back, but Padmini cut off any further teasing.

"That stole," she said. "Nice, hm? All blues and grays, like a storm cloud? Now, where've you seen that before?"

She waited, eyeing them both as they racked their brains and finally shook their heads. "You haven't," she confirmed. "And you know why?"

"Because storm mages are rare?" Ruhi guessed.

"That, yes," the older woman agreed. "But not just that. They're not allowed here in Surpakat. Yours, where'd you speak with him? On the ship?"

"On the dock," Sundra corrected. But Ruhi frowned, and he immediately amended, "No, that's right—he stayed on the gangplank the whole time."

Padmini nodded. "Smart. If he'd set foot on the docks, there'd have been trouble. For him *and* his shipmates." She took a long, loud gulp of her water, as ladylike as ever, which was to say not at all.

"So he can't be here?" Ruhi asked. "Why not?"

Their host snorted. "Cause they're too valuable, that's why. Maybe twenty, thirty stormers in all the Isles, if that many. Takes real talent, real skill, you know—working the wind, the waves, the storms. Worth their weight in gold, enough so's some'd risk breaking the rules to get hands on one. That's why the Council banned 'em from Surpakat entirely, to cut that trouble off before it started."

"Why's Nalan here at all, then?" Sundra asked.

Another snort. "That captain of his, Khandereo, he's a rebel, hey? Doesn't work for a raja, goes his own way, likes to flaunt his independence. Guess even so far as bringing his weather mage right up to the edge of the city. Not stupid enough to go any further, though."

Ruhi was digesting this new information along with the rich meal. "So if Nalan's the only one around here, and he's not talking, that means if we want to speak to others—"

"You'll need to go find 'em," Padmini agreed, rising again. "Most of the rajas keep theirs holed up in strongholds when they aren't at sea."

"Like Jasleen herself did with this missing Makiya," Sundra pointed out. "At Dveep Kile, wherever that is."

"A week's travel northeast," the worldly tavern owner answered. "Maybe a little less with a fast ship and fair winds." She shrugged. "Not as far as Khajaana, the Raja Falguni's stronghold, but near enough."

"We'll need to go there too, speak to the people who might've seen him last, see his rooms, all that," Ruhi said, ticking off each point on the fingers of her left hand.

"Which means talking to Kosala about putting to sea," Sundra noted, standing as well. "Lovely." He fished out a daniq, but Padmini waved him off when he offered her the small coin.

"Keep it," she told him. "Nice to have company when I eat, for a change."

She had all the other diners, of course, but Ruhi understood. It wasn't the same when they were your paying customers.

Sundra bowed, taking her hand and kissing the back of it. "Many thanks, dear lady," he told her in his grandest manner, and though she pushed him away, Ruhi saw the older woman's cheeks darken slightly. Apparently her brother's charms worked even on the irascible old tavern owner!

Ruhi added her own thanks, along with, "We'll let you know what happens." Then they were off, back toward home, but now with a goal.

The question was, how were they going to achieve it?

Chapter Eight

SUNDRA

The closer they got to home, the slower Sundra walked. By the time they'd reached the house's front porch, he was barely moving.

"Come on," Ruhi urged, resting a hand on his shoulder. "We need to talk to her about it."

"I know," he replied with a heavy sigh. "But does it have to be now? And do we both have to tell her?" There was no question about who they both meant.

"Yes, and yes," she insisted, leading the way up the stone steps and onto the porch.

Despite it being mid-day, with the sun high and bright overhead, it was cool and shadowed there beneath the tiled roof, and Sundra shivered.

Though perhaps that was just his dread at informing their employer that they would need to leave here somehow, and travel to a distant island, on this wild goose chase of theirs.

Entering the house, he numbly followed Ruhi down the hall and to the raja's private study. The door was closed, but he picked up sounds from within and stopped his friend from knocking just as her hand was about to strike the carved wooden surface.

She opened her mouth, no doubt to tell him off for his apparent cowardice, and he shushed her quickly.

"She has company," he explained in a whisper.

That stopped her protests, and he watched her tilt her head, clearly straining to listen. Now that neither of them was moving, he could make out two other voices, both male and both high-pitched, though whether naturally or from heightened emotion he couldn't tell.

"... surely you agree," one was saying. "It makes the most sense, after all."

"Absolutely," the second chimed in, his forced cheer evident even muffled by the door. "A perfect solution where everyone wins."

"I fail to see how." That was Kosala herself, her words sharp and clear as a glass knife. "*You* would certainly win by such a proposition. But as for myself, I fail to see any profit in this arrangement."

"Begging your pardon, but of course there is!" That was the second stranger. "All you need to do is..." They must have been moving about, perhaps pacing while speaking, because their voices trailed off now, only the faintest murmur still reaching Sundra's ears. *Kolossoi's teeth!*

He turned away in disgust, Ruhi backing up a pace to match him as he leaned against the opposite wall—and he was glad he had when the door suddenly flew open from within.

The man standing there was short and round, with a handsome dark mustache frosting at the tips and a fine pagri of a deep, dark blue. Sundra knew clothes and these were clearly of the highest quality—yet slightly out of fashion, at least compared to what he had seen before his untimely departure from the mainland.

Just behind the stranger was a second man, slightly taller and slightly slimmer, his own mustache smaller and offset by a neat, pointed beard, his pagri an almost iridescent green that matched the fine embroidery of his sherwani. Clearly these were both men of substance, though judging by their arms and bellies and by the lack of chapping to their skin they were not pirates. Merchants, most likely. Moderately successful ones, too.

Neither of them had opened the door, however. That honor belonged to its owner, who now stood half behind it, using the barrier to shield her from their unwanted proposal, whatever that might be.

"Shris," Kosala stated now, granting that single honorific such a note of finality as to almost make her next statement unnecessary. "I believe this conversation is at an end. Thank you for thinking of me, and I wish you a good day and good fortune."

Both stared at her a moment, mouths hanging open. Clearly they were more used to fellow merchants, who might be inclined to haggle and debate and negotiate. Sundra knew the type well. He'd seen his father face such an onslaught of words and compliments and nonsense many times before, and despised such a dance almost as much as the older Aruvar—just as Kosala clearly did. In flirtation and dalliance, weaving words into pretty poetry was fine, even desired. But in business or politics? Far better plain speaking, direct and to the point!

After a moment, the men seemed to realize that they were not going to get anywhere with this. Collecting themselves and their bruised dignity, they both bowed to their host, nodded frostily at Sundra and Ruhi, muttered some pleasant parting words of their own, and then exited the room, allowing Sanga—who had just approached—to escort them out.

"Good timing," Kosala said by way of greeting, retreating to her desk and beckoning them to follow. "If you hadn't been there to witness, those two might still be here entreating me. Or they might be laying on the floor, bleeding out from various wounds."

Sundra desperately wanted to ask what they'd been after but knew it wasn't his place, and while Kosala had proven in many ways a very accommodating employer, even a lenient one, he decided it was best not to push his luck. Especially when they already had something significant to ask.

"Now," the pirate lord continued, linking her gloved hands before her and tapping her lower lip with both index fingers. "What news?"

Sundra glanced helplessly at Ruhi, who sighed but took the lead. She was supposed to be the elder brother, after all!

"Not much," she admitted. "We spoke to Nalan, the thalakurios from the *Kalinga*, but he didn't have much to offer. We think…" She paused, clearly no more comfortable with this than he was, and finally Sundra took pity on her.

"We need to go to Dveep Kile," he stated bluntly. "That's where Makiya was last seen, so if there're going to be any clues to his whereabouts, that's where they'll be."

"We also need to speak with any other thalakurioi we can," Ruhi added. "We understand none can set foot here in Surpakat, and even Nalan's being at dock is a rarity. If the Parishad really thinks whatever happened to Jasleen's mage wasn't an isolated incident, the more of his fellows we can find and question, the better."

She fell silent after that, and Sundra held his breath, watching their employer. Kosala was by no means the biggest person he'd faced since they'd arrived here, but she might well be the scariest. It was her calm that did it. She was always collected, always careful, always precise. Nothing done in haste or in anger. He could only imagine that in a proper battle—he'd only ever seen her fight once, in a jail cell, armed with nothing but a stool—she'd be utterly lethal, waiting for her chance and then striking quickly.

He hoped she wasn't inclined to turn such deadly aim on them, with swords or with words.

"Very well," she said finally, and Sundra nearly toppled, his whole body sagging with relief. "It's high time I check on things back at Enkar Bindu anyway. We'll put in a stop there first. Sanga!" That last was a shout toward the open doorway, which her tall second filled an instant later. "Send word to the *Shikra*. We leave at first light tomorrow."

He nodded, disappearing again, and Kosala regarded her two lingering workers with a half smile. "Is there a problem?"

"Not at all," Sundra answered quickly. "It's just—I didn't realize—we didn't think—"

"You couldn't very well go without me, could you?" the raja pointed out, which was fair enough. The magic of their indenture agreement kept them bound within a certain distance of that document, which Kosala kept somewhere safe in the house.

They had roamed most of Surpakat without difficulty but knew that attempting to go any farther—like out onto the open sea beyond the city's natural harbor—would cause their bracelets to grow heavier and heavier, until the magical weight dragged them under like an anchor, to drown deep beneath the waves.

"No, of course not," Ruhi agreed. "Thank you."

She turned, and Sundra didn't need any further prompting to pivot and depart at her heels. He did pause at the door, however, glancing back with his hand on it. Their employer gestured for him to shut it, as he'd suspected she might, and he did so carefully, easing the door back into its frame before vacating the hall quickly, lest she think of some other reason to make him stay.

Dealing with Kosala often felt like petting a prickly cat—it might allow such attention for a while, only to turn on you without warning, and you always counted yourself lucky if you escaped the encounter with nothing worse than a scratch.

CHAPTER NINE

RUHI

Ruhi hadn't waited for her so-called younger brother to catch up to her, but had instead headed for the kitchen, which was already in an uproar. Madhav was still preparing the evening meal but Laila was grabbing things off shelves, both ready-to-eat foods like bread and preserves and also cooking supplies like meal and dried meat. One glance at the madness and Ruhi backed away, making for the quiet of the inner courtyard instead.

Several of the other servants were milling about, and the wide, open-air room was abuzz with conversation. Hearing a peal of laughter, Ruhi searched out its origin, unsurprised to find that it had emanated from Meera—or that she was laughing at something Sundra had just said.

Joining them, Ruhi smiled at the young housekeeper, who returned the expression. She liked Meera, who was quiet and practical and kind. What she wasn't as thrilled by was the look the other woman turned toward Sundra. Eyes wide and sparkling, lips slightly parted, cheeks rosy—no, that was definitely a bad sign.

Unless she missed her guess, Meera was smitten with her

so-called brother. And Sundra, Ruhi had learned very quickly, was an absolute flirt. He wasn't a bad person, not by any stretch, but he'd been born to wealth and privilege, with good looks and charm on top of that, and tended to treat other people—particularly young women—as playthings, or at least amusements. That might be fine when the lady in question was one you only met once in passing, but living in the same house, working together, sleeping under the same roof?

That could be a disaster.

"Meera is going with us," Sundra explained, and that startled Ruhi a little. What reason could Kosala have for bringing her housekeeper along—rather than leaving her here at the house to take care of it in her absence?

"I'm as puzzled as you are," Meera admitted with a little laugh. "The raja doesn't exactly explain her thoughts or plans. But Sanga said she wanted me on the boat with the rest of you, and of course I'm not going to say no."

She shrugged. "I've only been on a boat twice before—once to head to Enkar Bindu when Kosala first hired me, and then to come here with her and help run the household."

"She mentioned Enkar Bindu," Ruhi remembered. "Is it hers?"

The other woman frowned. "Not exactly, no." She laughed. "How do I put this?" Her eyes darted around the room, and she lowered her voice a little, for their ears alone. "Kosala isn't exactly... she doesn't like to be overly burdened with accountability."

"That's one way of putting it," Sundra agreed, eliciting a giggle from her and an eyeroll from Ruhi. It hadn't even been that funny! "She does like being in control, though."

Meera nodded. "She does. So with Enkar Bindu... it's a durga, and a good one, very solid, very secure. Not like here, though. Surpakat is much bigger. The biggest place in the Isles."

"Too big, you ask me," another voice intruded. A deeper one. Sanga had somehow joined their little circle without any of them noticing, and Ruhi shifted to give him more space, forcibly resisting a sudden urge to check her beard and hair.

"You can't exactly defend the place, not really," the lean pirate continued. "The older half you could, that's why the wall is there. But once it grew past the Pirate Line, forget about it."

"Right." Meera lowered her eyes. "They wanted to know about Enkar Bindu," she explained, suddenly shy—or embarrassed, Ruhi realized, that she might be accused of gossiping or giving away secrets.

But Sanga didn't reprimand her. "Makes sense," he said instead. "Since that's where we're headed."

He shrugged. "It's a durga, like she said, but it's not Kosala's. Not because she couldn't take it, but because she didn't want it. Too much trouble, ruling a stronghold. Too much time spent in one place, to maintain it. She's contributed to its growth, though. Donated to its defenses. The governor, he listens to her, asks her advice, that sort of thing."

Sundra nodded. "So all of the influence and none of the responsibility? Smart."

Of course he would think so, was Ruhi's first thought, but then she corrected herself. After all, he was right. Back home she'd helped her father, practically run the family warehouse for him, but he'd been the ultimate boss, which meant she could always defer to him when a question was too tough—or when it was one she didn't want to answer. That had been a blessing. So yes, having sway but not having to oversee everything? Kosala was no fool to prefer such an arrangement.

Which, she realized, also probably explained some of those other entries in the account books. Kosala had invested in various outside ventures, it seemed. Giving her access, influence, and evidently some profit, without her having to control everything. And probably being able to disavow any knowledge or involvement if anything ever went wrong.

"She has a house there, of course," Meera was adding about Enkar Bindu. "That's probably why she wants me along, in case it needs straightening out."

Sanga gave her a strange look but didn't say anything, and

Ruhi wondered what that was all about. Not that she'd find out if he didn't want her to. The man was a closed book most of the time, keeping his thoughts and emotions to himself. A lot like their mutual boss.

Now, however, he straightened, patting both Sundra and her on their backs. "Best gather whatever you want to bring along," he advised. "And get some rest. We'll be heading for the docks before first light. Kosala likes to raise sail with the dawn." He offered Meera a smile and then was gone, no doubt seeing to some other aspect of their intended departure.

In his absence, Meera shook herself. "I'd better get back to it, too," she said. "Lots to prepare before we go." She graced Ruhi with a small smile—and Sundra with a much bigger one—before heading for the kitchen and the storerooms.

"Don't you dare break her heart," Ruhi warned her "brother" once they were alone, or at least not near anyone else.

"What?" Sundra frowned at her. "What're you talking about? We're just friends."

"Friends my braided beard hairs!" she shot back. "She's completely besotted with you, and you know it!"

"Is she?" He grinned, destroying any attempt at ignorance. "Well, maybe I did detect a little partiality. But so what? I can't help it if I'm charming."

"See how charming you are when I dunk you in a rain barrel!" She glared, glad she was a little taller so she could peer down at him. "I mean it, Sundra. She's a nice girl, and we're all in the same household together. You want to be friendly, that's fine, but don't lead her on."

"I'm not," he promised, and managed to look affronted. "Seriously. She *is* a nice girl, and I wouldn't do that to her."

"Good." She still wasn't completely convinced but figured she should at least try to trust him. After all, he'd had her back up till now. "Last thing we need in this place is some romantic entanglement."

His grin returned, widened into a smirk. "Good advice," he

agreed. "Maybe you should follow it yourself."

"What're you talking about?"

This time her glare had no effect on him. If anything, it made him even more smug. "Oh, I don't know," he practically sang. "Maybe I should ask Sanga about it?"

"What?" She swatted him on the arm, trying to ignore the way her cheeks had heated. "Don't be ridiculous!"

Sundra just laughed. "What's so ridiculous about it?" he persisted. "He's tall, you're tall. He's handsome, you're... handsome. He's bossy, you're bossy. It's a match made in the heavens."

"Shut up!" she warned, which only made him laugh harder. "Quiet! People are looking."

She made to hit him again, and Sundra ran, leading her around the room and down the hall toward their shared room, giggling the entire way. Ruhi was less amused. What in the world was he thinking? She didn't like Sanga like that. It was preposterous.

Utterly preposterous.

Chapter Ten

SUNDRA

The next morning, they headed for the docks. It was just the five of them going, which Sundra supposed made sense. After all, Kosala would presumably keep most of her ship's crew on the ship itself, or close to it. They wouldn't be much help managing a house and, unlike a few of the other rajas, she didn't bother surrounding herself with thugs everywhere she went. Sanga was her first mate, obviously, and he and Ruhi had to go, plus she was bringing Meera for some reason, but everyone else was staying here.

Which was surprisingly unsettling. He hadn't even realized how much he'd grown used to some of their fellow workers. Especially Naaz.

"Make sure to walk her and Svarn regularly," he'd told the girl last night over dinner. "Kaala too, but watch that right foreleg, and stop at once if she starts favoring it. Don't let her fool you, though—if she pretends it's bothering her even before you start, tug her a few times and she'll stop."

"I will," Naaz had promised, though he suspected that last part was a lie. She was good with the horses and followed instructions, but she was too tenderhearted to yank on the reins. Kaala knew it, too, and took ready advantage of that fact.

Chaaya and Svarn were milder and better behaved, as a general rule, though the latter's endless curiosity sometimes led to trouble. They'd still all be a bit spoiled by the time he returned, but it couldn't be helped. Still, Sundra felt a pang at the thought of leaving the horses—and his stablehand-turned-assistant-and-friend—behind.

It was still dark out when they left the house, though the sky was beginning to lighten right along the horizon. That, and the torches jutting from iron brackets along the Pirate Line, provided more than enough light to see as they followed that path east, toward the water.

It was also quiet, with even the heaviest partiers having long since collapsed or toddled off to bed and only a few enterprising souls up and starting to prep for the morning's business.

Eventually the road turned north, and they followed that before switching to a different, narrower lane. That route took them past a sturdy, stone building with a bright-blue roof and a set of heavy doors done in the same color, and Sundra repressed a shudder. He did not have the fondest memory of the Indentures Hall where they'd received these enchanted shackles of theirs.

Still, they left that place behind soon enough and continued on, the scent of the sea growing stronger as they began to see water through the gaps between buildings. At last, the houses and shops fell away, and the road now ran along the island's edge, with wooden docks jutting out to their right.

"Dock three," Sanga informed them, and they started in that direction.

Despite the early hour, there were plenty of men and women about, hefting heavy bundles and casks along the docks or in and out of the big warehouses squatting directly across the road.

Sundra glanced at a knot of such workers, but his attention was quickly captured by a man working on his own along the dock they were quickly approaching.

It was a man he recognized, especially since they had renewed their acquaintance just the other day.

Druv looked up as they neared, then turned away. He had a big bundle of cloth held against his chest, both thick arms wrapped around it, and backed up, nearly trampling Sundra in the process. They both stumbled, trying to avoid either fall or collision, and as they did the former cook leaned in closer.

"Run," he whispered.

"What?" Sundra stared at the man, who grimaced, muttering curses as he regained his footing. He swung the bundle around, almost smacking Sundra in the face with it, and shifted his grip, the tightly wrapped fabric groaning from its mistreatment. The sound nearly drowned out his voice.

"Run!" Druv warned again, a little louder this time, and a good deal more insistent. "Now!" His eyes darted past Sundra, toward that same cluster of sailors, and then he was tromping away, making for a warehouse farther along, his burden lending even more weight to his steps.

Sundra frowned, studying the men in question. There were a dozen or so, and they seemed to be fussing over a barrel. Drink, perhaps? There was no way it was heavy enough to require all of them to carry it.

Then one of the men turned, and Sundra caught the glint of metal in the first rays of dawn as something was hauled up from the barrel's open top. A sword.

"Ambush!" he shouted, hand going to his belt and grabbing air. Of course his talwar wasn't there; he wasn't allowed a weapon.

His head whipped around, and he saw Sanga draw his sword. Kosala pulled hers from her sash, scabbard and all—and then tossed the entire bundle at Sundra. Startled, he reared back but recovered in time to fumble for and finally catch the weapon. He yanked the blade free and turned just in time to intercept the first attacker.

The man facing him was Sundra's height, a bit broader but with slightly shorter arms. That difference quickly proved fatal. Sundra beat the man's blade aside and thrust, the tip of his borrowed sword cleanly piercing his opponent's chest. The man's furious screams cut off with a gargle, and he dropped lifeless at Sundra's feet.

The next was already swinging for his head.

For a moment, Sundra didn't think. He didn't ponder. He just fought. Fortunately, he had been well trained, and had a natural aptitude for the blade besides. He parried the next thrust, riposting and putting his blade through the other man's eye, then spun to block a new challenger's attack. That one lasted a few moves longer. Sundra ended their bout by slashing the man's throat, stepping back to keep the blood from spraying his face and chest. His sleeve might have a few droplets, but he could live with that.

After the third man fell, Sundra found himself with a lull. He took advantage of the small gap in foes to peek around, checking to see how the others fared.

Sanga was holding his own. So was Kosala, who fought with a long dagger in her off hand and an unfamiliar blade in her right. No doubt taken from one of the men already dead at her feet.

Ruhi did not have a blade, which was probably for the best; she had no skill at the sword. She stood off to one side, evidently transfixed by the violence piling up at their feet, with Meera beside her. At least Ruhi made it look like she was merely protecting their friend, rather than cowering away from danger herself.

Another moment, and it was over. Whoever was behind this, they'd sent a decent number of men and women, all of whom had clearly seen combat before. But they'd never faced Kosala or Sanga or Sundra himself, all of whom Sundra judged to be excellent with a blade. And the advantage to being outnumbered was that you didn't have to be as careful with your targets—even a wild lunge could strike true if you were surrounded on all sides.

"Everyone all right?" Kosala asked, wiping her face with a cloth tugged from one of the dead men's pockets. She cleaned the sword she held as well, then offered that to Sundra, holding out her other hand at the same time.

Sundra knew what she wanted. He cleaned her blade, sheathed

it, and hooked his thumb through the guard, reversing the sword so he could offer it back to her hilt first. They swapped weapons, and Sundra tried not to feel disappointed. It had been a fine sword, slim and well-balanced. He'd enjoyed wielding it, even if only briefly, and greatly appreciated the loan, especially since that was the only thing that had kept him alive.

As he accepted the confiscated blade, Sundra had a sudden vision, his Gift showing him where his new weapon had been at dawn—which, since the sun had not yet fully risen, meant morning of the day before. Unfortunately, all he saw was a large room, richly appointed if not well maintained, and several other men around. Whoever these men had been, they had not been sailors—that room was nothing like a dockside tavern. No, they had been sent here specifically to stop Kosala and her little group. The question was, why?

Sanga confirmed that he was unscathed, as was Sundra, and they'd kept anyone from even getting close to Ruhi or Meera.

"Shall we?" Kosala asked, and Sanga took the lead as they continued along the waterfront.

"What was that all about?" Ruhi whispered, catching up to Sundra as they walked.

"No idea," he whispered back.

One thing was certain, though—that hadn't been a random attack. Nor a crime of opportunity. Not with what he'd seen from the sword. Whoever had targeted them had known exactly where they would be and when, and had come at them with a large, organized group. There had been no request for coins and jewelry, either, so this wasn't a botched robbery.

These thugs had been out for one thing, and one thing only: blood. The question was, whose? And for what purpose?

"I don't think they were after me or Meera," Ruhi continued. "None of them were really trying all that hard to get through to us."

Sundra turned that over in his head. No, she was right. There was a certain attitude when you were trying to fight past someone as opposed to just fighting them, and these thugs had all been the latter. Which meant they'd been after him, Sanga, or Kosala, or any combination of them. "I don't think they were after me, either," he admitted after a second. "More of them were focused on Kosala, it felt like."

"So they were trying to kill her, and we were just in their way," Ruhi stated. "But why? This can't have anything still to do with Udayin or Vihaan's murders, right?"

Udayin's death hadn't upset many, to be brutally honest—the young raja had been a horrible person, a bully and a sadist who delighted in torturing his servants.

But even though he'd only met the man briefly, Sundra had liked Vihaan. The other young raja had been kind and thoughtful, if a bit on the dramatic side. People could easily still be angry about his death. Of course, Kosala had been publicly cleared of any involvement, so no one should be coming after her for revenge over Vihaan. But what did that leave?

Sundra thought about asking, but their employer was walking briskly down the docks, staying close behind Sanga. Was that fear making her move so quickly, even beyond her usual no-nonsense pace? Or was it anger? A bit of both?

CHAPTER ELEVEN

RUHI

S undra whistled as they approached the two-masted ship that was clearly their destination, seeing as how it was the only one secured to the dock they'd just turned onto.

"Very nice!" Ruhi's apparent brother proclaimed. "A kotia. I should've guessed."

Ruhi must have looked as puzzled as she felt, because her friend glanced her way before explaining, "It's of a size with a baglah like the *Aden Star*, but slimmer and a good deal faster. See how there's an additional lateen sail on the forward mast? A kotia can maneuver a good deal better than either of those and outrun them both too. Rigged right, you'd only need maybe eight, nine sailors to handle it, but you can fit more in case of a fight." He nodded approvingly. "If I were a pirate, it's exactly what I'd pick for my ship."

"So glad you approve," Kosala commented dryly, and Sundra flushed a little, then laughed.

"You know a lot about boats," was their employer's next remark, and despite its casual tone, Ruhi tensed. How was it the raja always seemed on the verge of seeing through their shared disguise?

Sundra didn't appear to notice. "Oh, I've spent a lot of time on the water," he agreed offhandedly. "One of my favorite places to be, honestly." Ruhi coughed, and he caught on. "Not poor Rawal, though," he added quickly. "He gets terribly seasick." Which was true, or at least had been on her one and only water voyage thus far, though that had passed after the first few days. Thanks in large part to Sundra's ministrations.

Their employer frowned. "Can't have that," she stated, and headed for the gangplank. "Fortunately, we have something to help. In the meantime, welcome to the *Shikra*." The name meant "hunter," which Ruhi judged apt, and she noticed that the front of the ship ended in a carved bird head, a sharp-beaked raptor like its namesake.

Sundra had been right, she saw once they'd all boarded and the gangplank was being pulled up. The *Shikra* was as long as she remembered the *Aden Star* being, but not as wide. It was clearly well-maintained, the wooden deck planks gleaming and sanded smooth, the sails taut, ropes tucked neatly away for use.

A handful of sailors had already been aboard, and now one of them, a grizzled older woman with graying braids beneath a wide, shallow straw hat, approached.

"Ready to cast off, Captain," the woman declared, her voice deep and gruff.

"Thank you, Uma," Kosala replied, then lifted her voice. "Heave anchor, raise sail, and away!"

The crew cheered and sprang into action, leaving Ruhi, Sundra, and Meera standing mid-deck, afraid to move as people rushed past, both on foot and swinging by on ropes to reach one of the masts or the net riggings that hung from them. Well, Ruhi was afraid, and Meera looked the same. Sundra was tensed, but his eyes were wide and he was grinning, like he wanted nothing more than to join in.

Sanga, who'd left them when they'd boarded and now rejoined, noticed. "Check the aft sail is properly furled," he told Sundra, who nodded, shucked his boots, and was off like a shot.

"Guess he really does like being on the water," the tall pirate remarked, even as he proffered something to Ruhi. "Here, put this on."

It was a narrow, metal bracelet, cuff style, with a flared middle. She took the item, sliding it onto her bare wrist—and was surprised when Sanga took her hand in his, turning her arm and then adjusting the bracelet so the middle was over her pulse instead, its bulging center pressing down gently there. His hand was big and strong, his fingers calloused, and she felt warm. No doubt from the first rays of the sun that were just starting to break across them.

"Old sailors' remedy," he explained, releasing her after a moment. "Pressure point on your pulse, helps prevent nausea."

"Thank you." She smiled, and he did too, though only for a moment.

"No problem." Clearing his throat, Sanga turned and started barking orders at various crewmembers, even though it looked like everyone already knew what they were doing.

"He likes you," Meera said softly, sidling over so only Ruhi would hear. "I didn't know he was inclined that way."

It took Ruhi a second to realize what the young housekeeper meant. Then it struck her, and she felt like an idiot. Of course! She was presenting as a man. She knew some men were attracted to other men, just as some women were interested in other women—she'd seen a few like that back at her father's warehouse and had heard stories from the workers there as well. It just hadn't occurred to her that of course Sanga only knew her as Rawal. And he was interested? She wasn't entirely sure how she felt about that.

Right now, however, she just laughed it off with a quick shake of her head. "No, he's just being kind," she insisted, and Meera shrugged but didn't press the point as the ship's sails unfurled and suddenly the craft leapt into motion, pulling away from the docks and picking up speed as the sails caught the morning breeze.

Ruhi braced herself along one railing, prepared to feel as queasy and awful as she had the last time she'd sailed—and was surprised and pleased to discover that she felt fine. The remedy worked!

Relieved, she lifted her head, closed her eyes, and just enjoyed the feel of the wind on her face. Strange through the beard, but otherwise cool and pleasant, the chill of the air was offset by the sun's warmth. The salt tang was strong, of course, but balanced by the scents of wood and oil and hemp, and the breeze kept anything from being too overpowering. She was starting to see why Sundra enjoyed this so much.

❦ ❦ ❦

There was nothing for Ruhi or Meera specifically to do onboard, and neither of them were sailors by trade, but they both offered to pitch in where they could, in part so they would not seem a burden—or like they thought they were too good for the work—and in part to prevent boredom. It turned out one could only stare out at the rushing water for so long before wishing to do something more useful.

Meera was quickly tasked to help Onkar, the pirate in charge of cooking aboard the *Shikra*, whose own lean frame belied his skill. Ruhi would have been happy to assist there as well, and clearly the pirates did not care as much about such things being traditionally women's work, but Sanga set her a different task instead.

"We keep the ropes coiled when not in use," the rangy sailor explained, and if he was ill at ease around her, Ruhi couldn't tell. "Not the most exciting job, but a necessary one."

"I don't mind," she assured him. "Anything to help and keep busy."

He nodded. "If you notice any frays or tears, let someone know. Might be we can just patch that with wax, but if it's bad we'll need to replace it."

He wandered away after that, leaving Ruhi to her task, which was fine. Coiling rope was simple enough, and it did give her something to do and a way to help. It also left the pirates free to attend to anything that needed real expertise.

Sundra, of course, had settled right in with the crew, who were every bit as tough and crude as you'd expect from pirates, but either were less bloodthirsty and murderous than anticipated or simply kept that tucked away when among their own. Regardless, by the time the first day had passed, Sundra was laughing and joking like he was one of them, and to see him swing past or scale riggings or heave sails, he might as well have been. Ruhi didn't begrudge him that. He was her friend, after all, even if not really her brother, and it was good to see him happy.

Nor was he the only one. On their second day, as the dawn rose, Meera, who'd emerged from belowdecks and was leaning on the railing near the ship's prow—Sundra had told Ruhi that's what the front was called—gasped in delight. "Look!" she exclaimed.

Ruhi and Sundra, who were both up as well, followed the house-keeper's waving arm and saw, up ahead, a large patch of green and brown against the blue water. Land, and rapidly approaching.

"Another island?" Ruhi asked. "We can't be at Enkar Bindu already!" Sanga had mentioned that it would take several days to reach that durga.

"We're not." But, if anything, Meera sounded even more excited at that fact. "It's Bahut Saare!"

Ah. The plantation whose previous overseer, Bhadra Khatri, had murdered two rajas and framed another—and Sundra and Ruhi—for the crimes. But of course Meera wasn't focused on that. She'd grown up here, after all, and had lived her whole life here before being hired by Kosala.

"We'll pass near enough for you to see it, at least the tops of the buildings," the young housekeeper explained, leaning forward to see better. "I wish I could show it to you properly."

Ruhi suspected that wistful comment was aimed more at her brother and managed not to sigh. If anything, Sundra's display of nautical prowess had only impressed Meera further. He'd even taken to wearing just a vest above his shalwar, same as many of the pirates—including Sanga—which only showed off his lean phy-sique better.

Speaking of Sanga, the tall pirate was nearby, consulting with

Uma who had the wheel, and heard the remark. "You'll get that chance," he informed them all. "We're putting in there."

"We are?" Ruhi turned to study him, but as usual Kosala's first mate was inscrutable. Still, she'd have thought they'd be in a hurry to get to Dveep Kile. Why stop off along the way if they didn't have to?

That was Kosala's call, though. And she could only assume the pirate lord had her reasons.

CHAPTER TWELVE

SUNDRA

Uma steered the ship along the island's coast just as dusk struck, and since he'd currently been relieved of other duties Sundra joined Meera and Ruhi at the prow. The former reached out and grabbed him by the hand when he approached, her smile dazzling, and he tried not to wince. Yes, his "brother" had evidently been right, the girl had a bit of a crush on him. Not that he didn't like her, of course, but he'd have to find a way to let her down easy. He wasn't looking for anything like that right now—life in the Isles was complicated enough as it was.

Right now, though, he could see that much of her excitement was at going home again after so long away.

"There's the entrance to the canal!" she announced, pointing.

It took Sundra a minute to spot it, but finally he saw where a heavy, iron gate had been erected across a gap in the rocks. He judged the space sufficient for a baglah, which meant the leaner *Shikra* would be able to pass through easily—provided the gates were open.

Even as he thought this, he heard a horn sound from somewhere deeper back on the island. An answering blast came from beside the gate, and dark figures appeared on either side, clambering out onto the thick gate to meet in the middle. They heard a clank, audible even over the flapping of sails as the *Shikra* slowed, and then the two halves swung inward, the men and women still perched on them. Clever. The rush of the water forced the gate open once it was unlatched—but opening it from the far side would be next to impossible, as you'd have to climb over the top and would be an easy target for the guards if you did.

The *Shikra* slid cleanly through the widening gap and passed into the canal. It was already too dark to make out much, the sun dropping quickly and shadows rushing in, but Meera pointed out landmarks anyway.

"Those are all fields, to the right," she explained, gesturing. "Rice, wheat, barley, maize, tobacco, and cotton. To the left, that's the farmyard, where we raise sheep, goats, cows, and pigs. The orchards and garden are past that, in front of the main house."

Ruhi was nodding. "So this place is largely self-sufficient, then?" she asked. "You produce everything you need right here?"

Her father was a merchant, Sundra remembered. Of course she'd be interested in stuff like that. He only knew where his food and clothes came from because his father had insisted he be aware of the time and effort others put into providing those.

"It is," Meera agreed. "We keep back what we need for ourselves and sell the rest, mostly for things like spices or specific foods we don't have the space or climate to grow ourselves and stuff like silk or muslin for clothes. But almost all of those are luxuries we could manage without, if we had to."

The ship was nearing a wide dock that ran clean across the canal, preventing further travel. To the left, Sundra noticed that the waterway curved back around but narrowed considerably, far too much for them to pass through. Good for something like a badan, though. That made sense—the workers here no doubt used flat-bottomed boats like that to ferry crops to this dock, where a larger boat could be loaded up for delivery to Surpakat or some other market.

Several people stood waiting on the dock, and one of them stepped forward to catch the rope Sanga tossed over, fastening it tight to one of the heavy mooring posts. The gangplank was quickly lowered, and Kosala led the way down. Sanga gestured for Meera, Ruhi, and Sundra to go as well, and brought up the rear. Sundra almost declined—he always slept better on the water—but curiosity, as well as the desire to keep his employer happy, propelled him along.

One of the people waiting to receive them was a stout older woman with graying hair in a bun and a very businesslike sari, ghagra, and dupatta. Her lined face creased into a smile, however, when she spotted Meera, and she held out her arms, the younger woman ignoring decorum to rush into them.

"Arivai!" Meera exclaimed happily from the embrace. "You're in charge now?"

"For the time being, yes," the gray-haired woman agreed. "After that, we'll see. Now let me look at you."

Gently but firmly she disengaged and held Meera at arm's length, inspecting the young housekeeper with a keen eye. "You look well," she judged after a moment, releasing her grip. "Are you happy where you are?" She said that without glancing at her other visitors, as if she'd forgotten they were there, though Sundra noticed her back was very straight and her chin up.

"I am, yes," Meera confirmed. "I'm treated well, the people are good, and the work is engaging."

She stepped back, pivoting on her heel to make room for Kosala. "This is my employer, the Raja Kosala. And these are Sanga, Sundra, and Rawal, who all work for her too."

Arivai bowed to Kosala as the pirate captain approached. "Raja, I bid you welcome to Bahut Saare," she intoned formally, her voice strong and clear. "And, on behalf of all here, know that we regret the hardships you faced at the hand of our previous owner. No one else here was aware of his plans or had any part in them."

Kosala paused a few paces from the overseer, looking as imperious as ever. After a tense moment, however, she nodded. "Thank you," she stated, her own voice ringing out. "I believe you, and hold no one presently here responsible for Bhadra Khatri's actions. I have no animosity toward this place or its residents."

Arivai and her attendants visibly relaxed. "We have prepared rooms for all of you," she said, "and would be honored to have you stay with us as our guests." Her eyes flickered to Meera. "Though, if you would prefer, your old room is still as you left it."

Meera turned to Kosala, who let a brief smile touch her lips. "Go ahead," the raja allowed, and the housekeeper was off like a shot, offering only a parting grin to Sundra before racing across the dock and down onto the darkened lane beyond.

"We were very sorry to see her go," Arivai admitted as the rest of them followed at a calmer pace. "But I am glad for her sake. She is too bright, too full of energy and spirit, to stay here all her life."

Kosala nodded. "She is a valued member of my household," she agreed. "And I count myself very lucky to have her."

That admission clearly warmed the other woman's attitude, and she was far friendlier as she pointed out things along their way. Not that they could see much, now that night had fallen fully, but Sundra got the impression of a very large, very organized settlement.

Beside him, Ruhi was nodding. "It's very well laid out, from the sound of it," she commented quietly to him and Sanga.

The three of them were walking just behind the overseer and the raja, with one worker out in front holding up a lantern and the other two trailing behind them.

"I'm still not sure why we're here, though," Ruhi said.

Sundra didn't know either, but Sanga grunted. "No?" the rangy first mate replied. "Think about it. Why was Shivaji so keen to see you two?"

"Because he wants Udayin's ships and money," Sundra answered at once. "And figures we—or Kosala—will have a say in who gets them."

Sanga nodded. "But Udayin and Vihaan aren't the only ones whose property is now up for grabs," he pointed out, keeping his voice low.

"Ah!" Ruhi straightened as if she'd been slapped. "Of course!

With Bhadra Khatri dead, this plantation is free for the taking!" She glanced behind her, embarrassed, but if the locals following them heard, they didn't react.

"It is," their companion agreed more quietly. "And, as not only a raja but the person he was aiming to kill or frame, Kosala has the strongest claim on it." He grinned, his teeth a flash of white in the evening gloom. "And who wants to buy a place they've never seen?"

"So, since we were heading this way anyway, she figured she'd stop and inspect it," Sundra summed up. "Makes sense."

And she'd brought Meera along to show goodwill—and have someone who could confirm how well she treated those in her employ. Of course, that also meant that he and Ruhi didn't need to be here, but that was fine. He was happy to play the visitor and relax a little.

Their path ultimately led them around to a large, handsome house in the Nalukettu style, very similar to Kosala's own with its long, covered porch; slanted, wood-shingled roof; and sturdy, varnished wooden columns.

"This is the main house," Arivai told them as they approached, someone already opening the front door for them so that a welcoming light spilled out from within. "I have a late dinner ready, if you're hungry, and each of you has your own room."

That was a luxury, and Sundra noticed Ruhi slumping a little in relief beside him. Which made sense. She shared a room with him back at Kosala's, but he knew her secret and helped guard it, plus he would never dream of imposing upon her or breaching her privacy. But quarters on the *Shikra* were tight, and "Rawal" had had no choice but to take a hammock with the rest of the crew. Sundra could only imagine how much of a strain that had been. At least Ruhi would be able to sleep securely and without worry tonight!

Kosala inclined her head, the stately but appreciative guest, and Sundra tried filing away her behavior for later. In some ways, his employer reminded him a great deal of his father—tough but fair, outwardly stiff but always aware of the staff and their own needs and wants, gracious, if somewhat formal to any who deserved it, and searingly cold but polite to those who did not.

Of course, his father was not a bloodthirsty pirate, but he'd always told Sundra that a leader had to be able to act swiftly when needed, and sometimes that included making hard decisions and even taking lives. Just never without a real need, such as for the protection of those who deserved it.

Inside, the house had the same rustic feel as its exterior, its walls whitewashed and its floors clean but rough tile, its columns stained and worn smooth from use. The central courtyard was wide, lit by lanterns hung from the edges of the roof, and a long table there had been set with dishes. Bench seats hung beneath the overhangs, and after collecting plates of food, Sundra and the others adjourned to those to eat.

Afterward they were shown to their rooms. His was small but clean, and it was late enough that he washed up and collapsed on the bed there straightaway. It took a little time to get used to the lack of motion once again, even after only one night at sea, but eventually he drifted off.

CHAPTER THIRTEEN

RUHI

R uhi woke the next morning feeling better rested and more at ease than she had in weeks. Though she hated to admit it even to herself, sharing a room with a man, even one as kind and understanding as Sundra could sometimes be, had been wearing on her. It was stressful to be on guard all the time, even in the privacy of your own room. She always had to be careful not to hop out of bed too quickly, not to stretch too vigorously—she knew he would do his best to turn away, to pretend he'd seen nothing, but her disguise and their brotherly bond was like a gossamer sheet, so thin as to be barely there, and easily torn by the slightest misstep. And once torn, impossible to fully mend.

The *Shikra* had been even worse. There were only two cabins, one of which was obviously Kosala's. Uma had the other, and there was a second bunk in there, which they'd naturally given to Meera. But that meant Ruhi had been in among the crew. Sundra had been able to convince the others that his prone-to-seasickness brother should take the spot against the bulkhead, at least, and had claimed the one next to her, so she had some shelter from unwanted attention, but she had still been on edge every night, and slept poorly as a result.

So she'd been thrilled when she'd been shown to this tidy little room with only the one bed and had been able to close the door and shut the entire world out for a while. She'd left the beard on—it was too much trouble to remove it, especially without the oils and ointments Padmini had gifted her for that purpose—but Ruhi had shed the amulet that had formed another part of her disguise. Then she had daringly loosened the stanapatta she wore beneath her kurta, removing the cotton band so she could breathe fully. She flopped back on the bed and just laid there for a while before rising long enough to wash up and use the chamber pot. After that she'd quickly fallen asleep.

Now, rising to a knock at the door, for an instant Ruhi forgot where she was. It was not her father's apartments above the warehouse, and her face felt scratchy, her bedclothes unfamiliar, yet she was warm and cozy, and the sun starting to creep in through the window was still shy and gentle. Only when the knock came again, followed by a "Sir?" did she remember.

"Yes?" she called out, careful to pitch her voice low. Another thing she had to constantly remember.

"There's food set out, and tea, and if you set out your clothes we'll wash them for you," the woman or girl outside offered. "There are clean ones on the shelf above the door."

"Thank you. That's very kind, but I believe I am good," Ruhi replied, hopping out of bed and shaking off the last of her sleep with a vigorous shudder. "I'll be along directly."

She didn't trust that any proffered clothes would be as well fitted to her, which meant it might not hide her true shape as much. Fortunately, she'd washed her own garments before they'd set out from Surpakat.

Splashing some water on her face—and checking hair and beard in the mirror—Ruhi wrapped herself again in her stanapatta and shrugged back into her shalwar and sadri, slipping the amulet back over her head so the dark red crescent at its center lay in the modest hollow between her constrained breasts. With a sigh, she straightened, once more donning the role of Rawal Chera, before tugging the door open and venturing out into the hall.

The sounds of laughter drew her forward, and Ruhi followed them to the courtyard she'd seen the night before and then through that to a wide, cheery kitchen beyond. Here, at a rough-hewn table nestled in one corner, was Meera, along with a young pair whose features were similar enough Ruhi knew they had to be brother and sister.

"Ah! Here's one now!" the sister exclaimed, round face stretched into a warm, welcoming smile. "Good morning, sir! Now, which brother are you, hm? Meera's been telling us about you both." She giggled, and Meera shushed her with a quick elbow to the side while the brother rolled his eyes.

"Rawal, the elder brother," Ruhi replied, taking their invitation and joining them at the table after nodding hello to the older woman tending the stoves along one wall. "And you?"

"I'm Kavya," the girl answered. "And this talkative chap is my brother Kabir."

He smiled and raised a hand in greeting.

"We all grew up together," Meera explained cheerfully, beaming at her two companions. "Kavya's my closest friend. And Kabir's not so bad either."

He laughed and tossed a roll at her, which led to a minor skirmish involving pastries and fruits, and though she did her best to avoid getting hit, Ruhi couldn't help smiling at the obvious affection between them all.

She glanced up at the older woman, who was watching as well—just in time to see her grasp the handle of a pan and lift it off the stove. Without a glove or any sort of protective cloth and not the tiniest wince of pain.

The cook saw her looking and grinned before shoving the same hand directly into the flames themselves! Ruhi gasped, but after a second the woman pulled her hand back and held it up, showing that it was completely undamaged. Then she winked at

Ruhi before getting back to her work.

"Don't let Aaina upset you," Meera whispered. "It's her Gift, she can't be burned."

"She's been tricking people with that since way before us," Kabir agreed, and Ruhi felt a little better.

They were chatting and eating—with Kavya doing most of the talking—when the other girl fell strangely silent, her eyes fixed on a point somewhere behind Ruhi. The way she started giggling then, and Meera blushing, told Ruhi exactly what she'd see next.

Sure enough, a second later a slim shadow appeared at her side.

"Morning, all!" Sundra declared, hipchecking Ruhi over on the bench so he could sit as well. "I'm Sundra. You must be the twins, Kavya and Kabir."

He helped himself to a mug of fresh milk and a roti he then slathered with mango preserves. "Meera said how excited she was to see you both again."

It was very smooth, and Ruhi could see his easy manner, good looks, and charm had already won Kavya over. *Great, another one,* she thought, suppressing her groan. At least Kabir shared a look with her over the others' heads, raising an eyebrow, but he seemed more amused than anything else. Which was probably for the best.

"Arivai's going to give Kosala and Sanga a tour of the whole plantation," Meera told them. "I think you two're invited, if you want."

Beside her, Kavya wrinkled her nose, then laughed. "Or, instead of traipsing through a whole bunch of rice and corn and wheat, you can spend the day with us."

"That does sound more enjoyable," Sundra agreed, snatching a slice of fresh mango from a plate and popping it into his mouth. "What were you three planning to do?"

"Just catch up," Meera answered.

Kabir snorted. "Well enough for you two," he said, waving at Meera and his sister. "But I've got to check on the herd, at least. We've had some wandering off recently, almost halfway to Suraksha."

"Kabir's a shepherd," Meera explained. "He's got a Gift too—with animals." Her friend ducked his head at the praise, but Ruhi was curious about something else in what he'd said.

"Safety?" she asked, catching the way he'd said it like a title—or a location. "Is that a place?"

"It's a durga," Meera confirmed. "At the southernmost tip of the island."

Taking a piece of roti and setting it on the table between them, she poured a dollop of honey onto the flat bread, tracing out a rough shape something like a thick boot.

"We're here, in Bahut Saare," she said, setting a grape at the farthest right edge, up near the top. "Suraksha is here." That was a second grape, at the bottom right, the heel. "And Phasal Kaatana is here." This was a third grape at the toes, the farthest left tip.

"Another stronghold?" Sundra asked, studying the improvised map.

"A plantation, like ours but a good deal smaller," Kavya corrected. "They're decent neighbors. We trade with them a bit."

Ruhi was trying to make sense of all this. "Is it common to have more than one settlement on a single island?"

"Why not?" Meera replied. "There's plenty of room—we don't see each other unless we want to. But if we do want, it's only a few hours' walk." She shrugged. "It's why the island itself has a name, Harit Maarg, in case there's ever anything going on that affects the whole place, like a big storm. I don't think anyone outside here even knows that, though."

Ruhi heard what Meera was saying, but she was busy wondering about those two other locations, specifically their ownership, and clearly her so-called brother was as well.

"Who controls those two, then?" he asked. "Who owns them?"

The siblings shrugged. "No idea," Kavya said. "There's a woman, Maravi, I usually see taking charge at Suraksha, and a man, Himmat, who's always bossing everyone around at Phasal Kaatana, but couldn't say if they were owners or just the ones tasked with supplies and such."

The older woman at the stove let out a chuckle, startling Ruhi, who'd forgotten she was there. "Those two ain't in charge of nothing!" she exclaimed, her high, reedy voice at odds with her stocky frame.

"Oh, what do you know, Aaina?" Kavya retorted, tossing a grape at the cook, who deftly snatched the fruit from the air and popped in in her mouth.

"More than you, chit!" she replied around the small morsel. "I met Suraksha's real owner once! A few years back, when they had that bout of fever over there. We were bringing soup and curry and fresh bread over, like a good neighbor should, and there was a gentleman there."

She smiled at the recollection, pausing in her stirring of the pot before her. "Young and handsome, he was, though too thin by half. And his clothes! Oh, they were gorgeous! All of a color, a rich blue, trimmed with gold thread. Gloves and sash to match. Only his sword didn't. It was scabbarded in black with silver."

She returned to her present and her audience. "He thanked us kindly for our generosity, lovely manners, and gave us each a daniq. I've still got mine, kept it for good luck."

Ruhi had felt a chill upon hearing this gracious neighbor described. "Did you catch his name?" she asked now.

The cook shook her head. "No, but no question he was the lord of the manor. Maravi was all bows and scrapes."

Sundra glanced Ruhi's way. "It has to be," he said softly. "Who else?"

"But all the way out here?" she countered. "How likely is that?"

Kavya leaned forward, interrupting. "What are you two whispering about?"

At Sundra's nod, Ruhi explained. "That man, we think we know who it was. Vihaan Dhar." When the twins still looked blank, she added, "One of the rajas. Or he was. He died."

Kavya started to say something, eyes wide, but a swift swat of her brother's hand silenced her for a moment.

Instead Kabir asked with a frown, "And this dead raja, you think he lived out here?"

Sundra was toying with a handful of dried apricots. "He could have. Vihaan was smart. And careful. If he'd owned a place here, he might not've wanted anyone to know."

"You sound like you knew him," Kavya remarked, her tone half mocking and half curious.

Her brother glared at her but didn't try quieting her again. Ruhi suspected that was always a losing venture.

"I did, a little," Sundra responded, though his voice and face were carefully blank.

Ruhi knew what he was leaving out—that he'd watched the young raja die—and saw from her sudden somberness that Meera remembered as well.

Ruhi spoke up, to cut off that depressing thought. "We should go see for ourselves." The others all turned to look at her. "You said it wasn't far, and I want to take advantage of not being cooped up on a ship."

She rose to her feet and started shoving Sundra to make him move so she could slip out of the bench. "I'm going to go."

Sundra stood as well, giving her room. "Me too." He grinned, though it seemed forced to her. "Nice day for a walk and all that."

"Let's do it!" Kavya declared, hopping up. "Come on, it'll be fun. We can bring a lunch!" And she turned imploring eyes on the old cook, who snorted again.

"Oh, I'll feed ya, if it means getting ya out of my hair for the day," the old woman complained, but Ruhi could see she didn't mean it.

"We'd best let Kosala know," she pointed out while they waited for the provisions to be assembled. "Just in case." She also had no idea if such a trek would stay within acceptable range for their bracelets, and that was something she wasn't about to take for granted.

The raja was in the courtyard, breaking her own fast with Arivai and Sanga and a few others, and tilted her head at the news—Ruhi hadn't meant to reveal it right then and there, especially among outsiders, but as was often the case the raja's sharp questions brought everything out.

"Interesting," she commented. "Yes, that would be like Vihaan to own a place and no one knew it. Let me know what you find."

"We will," Ruhi promised, nodding to them all as she backed away.

Sanga caught up to her before she'd gone far. "Here," he said, offering her a pair of small, carved bone discs. "These will extend the range enough for you to get there safely."

Ruhi nodded and accepted the chits, tucking them into her pouch for safekeeping before resuming her retreat.

Sundra had chosen to wait in the kitchen with the others and must have seen the answer on her face, because he relaxed at once.

"Excellent!" he declared, clapping his hands together. "We're off on an adventure!"

Ruhi just hoped it was quieter and less dangerous than some of the other ones they'd had lately.

Chapter Fourteen

SUNDRA

Sundra paused, both to catch his breath and to take in the view. "All right," he declared, lifting a hand to shade his eyes from the rising sun. "That is impressive."

Ahead and below them, past where the hill they'd just climbed fell away before yielding to a stretch of sand, was a small town. From up here Sundra could easily make out the neat grid of streets, the sturdy docks jutting from its curving front into the water of the small bay before it—and the sturdy stone wall surrounding it all. A wall not dissimilar to the one that still ran behind Surpakat, and right down its middle as well. This wall was far more prominent, and looked well-maintained.

Sundra considered the placement of the town, bringing to bear some of the military history and tactical thinking his father had insisted he be given. From up here you might be able to get off a decent shot at someone guarding the back of the walled settlement, but you'd have to have excellent aim, strong arms, and favorable winds. Crossing the sand between hill and town would be a death trap, and coming from the water would leave you wide open as well. It was a highly defensible position, and someone had thought to take proper advantage of that fact.

"Suraksha," Kabir pointed out unnecessarily. "Come on, there's a path down."

The young man was a pleasant companion, Sundra had discovered—quiet but not mute, amusing but not ridiculous, easygoing but not meek.

His sister was pleasant as well, but in very different ways, being far more boisterous and far more assertive. Not to mention talking almost nonstop. She wasn't mean or obnoxious about it, though, so he found he could deal. He'd certainly been forced to put up with far worse, in his former life.

They took the winding path down to the sand and then across that to the stronghold, where a guard up on the walls trumpeted hello in response to Kabir and Kavya's waves. By the time they'd reached the wall itself, a small gate had opened and a handful of men and women emerged. All of them were dressed practically, and all but the woman in front wore helmets and mail shirts similar to those of Pillai and her guards, if not as fine.

"You I know," the woman stated, nodding at Kabir. "We've seen you with your flock. And you I've seen." This to Meera and Kavya. "Who are your friends, and what do you want?"

The question wasn't so much rude as direct, which Sundra appreciated. He'd had more than his fill of verbal subtleties and careful diplomacies over the years.

"I'm Sundra Chera," he replied in kind, stepping forward. "This is my brother Rawal. We work for the Raja Kosala. Are you Maravi?"

"I am." Maravi was neither tall nor short, fat nor thin, and her square face was lined and blunt, her hair just beginning to show gray, but her tired gait belied her well-preserved appearance.

"What do you and your employer want from us?" Her guards had shifted slightly, not attacking or even sneering but waiting in case they were needed.

Ruhi edged forward, and Sundra could see from her face that she was prepared for another long, drawn-out conversation like a pair of starved mice circling a bag of grain, both watching for even the slightest opening but too afraid to create one.

Well, he'd never been much of a mouse, and he suspected this Maravi wasn't either.

"We're here about Vihaan Dhar," he announced easily across the short gap between them.

The woman didn't respond at first, but her eyes had narrowed and her bearing straightened. "I don't know who that is," she said finally, but everyone already knew she was lying. Especially since her guards were far less practiced at concealing their own surprise, dismay, and even grief.

Sundra played his best card. "I'm sorry," he told her, allowing his very real sorrow to creep into his voice. "I don't know if you've been told already, but Raja Dhar is dead."

Before him, Maravi stumbled as if struck, one of the guards reaching out to support her if needed. "I know," she answered after a moment, brushing aside the helping hand. "We heard."

"Then you might also know that the man who killed him and another raja was caught by a pair of brothers," Sundra went on. "That would be myself and Rawal here. At your service." He dipped into a bow.

Beside him, Ruhi did the same, with considerably less practice or grace. But to offset any inadequacies there, his so-called brother came up with and held out a rolled-up paper. *Oh, well played!*

"These are our credentials from the Parishad," Ruhi explained, offering the paper to the older woman, who took it gingerly, like it might bite. Maravi unrolled and read the simple proclamation before returning it, along with a grudging nod. "So Vihaan Dhar did own this place?" Ruhi asked, tucking the document back away in her vest.

"He did," the woman admitted after another, shorter pause. "He wouldn't have wanted us to say so out loud to strangers, but I don't suppose that matters much anymore." Her earlier defiance had vanished, leaving her looking older and far more vulnerable.

Sundra felt bad about adding to her woes. "We didn't mean to upset you," he insisted, moving closer, though at a cautious pace because of her ever-vigilant guards. "And we didn't even know about this place until we came to Bahut Saare." He glanced past her, at the tall, sturdy wall beyond. "It's a handsome-looking place, though. At least from here."

That brought a small, proud smile to Maravi's thin lips. "Thank you. Our lord's grandsire was a good man and a clever one. He laid out the streets and had the wall built, then the houses and shops within. We work metal and leather and cloth and wood, trading those wares with our sister site, Phasal Kaatana, in exchange for produce and dairy and meat. There's no real coin to be had from it, but we don't starve, and we don't have to worry about making outside trades."

Ruhi was nodding. "That's smart," she agreed, and Sundra thought so as well.

Between the stronghold here and the plantation there, they were basically self-sufficient—which allowed Vihaan, and evidently his ancestors before him, to keep both places private and secure.

"We didn't mean to intrude. We were visiting Bahut Saare and heard about your town and wanted to see it for ourselves."

The town overseer snorted. "With that, you hardly need worry," she pointed out, gesturing at Ruhi, or more precisely the paper she carried. "You speak for the Parishad. Who would dare deny you?"

Off to the side, Sundra saw Kavya making soft, strangled noises, her face red, and inwardly he sighed, already imagining the thousands of questions the curious, talkative girl would pelt him with as soon they were away from here. But the reminder did at least make him think about the reason for that paper. "You don't happen to have any thalakurioi here, do you?"

He was honestly surprised when Maravi nodded. "Aye," she responded. "One. Puvanti. She served on some of the raja's ships, but many years ago now. Why?"

"Might we speak with her?" That was Ruhi, being polite.

And of course, having already acknowledged their authority, there was little the other woman could do besides acquiesce and turn to lead them all inside. Meera followed with her childhood friends but wisely kept back, giving Sundra and Ruhi space to accomplish their assigned task.

Past the walls, Suraksha proved just as neat and tidy as it had seemed from the hill. Walking down the wide, straight main street, Sundra could already see it ended in a small, square courtyard before a modest two-story building he had no doubt was the town's main hall.

He nodded to himself. Yes, if the child had been anything like the sire and grandsire he could see Vihaan's family's influence here—the young man had been the type to appreciate order, care, and quiet pride in one's own property and accomplishments. Everything about the town felt like that, without the showy but tasteful adornments the raja had used to disguise his very real talents. That last, Sundra suspected, had been all Vihaan, rather than an inherited trait.

Maravi stopped just shy of the courtyard, at a small but neat house. Rapping on the door, the overseer called out, "Puvanti! You've visitors!"

After a moment's noise from within, the door opened. The woman inside appeared a bit older than Maravi, shorter and thicker with braids of steel gray starting to fade to white, but her dark eyes were still clear—and around the shoulders and over the head she wore a durpatta of swirled blue-gray like a storm cloud.

"Yes?" Her voice was gruff, though the tone was mild.

"Hello," Sundra offered. "I'm Sundra Chera. This is my brother Rawal. The Parishad has tasked us with investigating the disappearance of some of your fellow mages, including one named Makiya. Do you know anything about that?"

The aging weather mage peered at him. "Hm? Makiya? Aye, I know him. Missing? Oh, that's not good."

She shook her head, braids whipping about, and reached up to smooth them back. As she did, Sundra noticed a faint white line around her wrist. A scar? Had she been indentured like them?

"No, it's not," Ruhi agreed. "So you didn't know anything about it?"

"Not Makiya, no," Puvanti answered. She looked distracted, a little disoriented, or maybe just sad. "I'd heard, though—a few others are missing too. Strange." She frowned down at her own calloused, square-fingered hands.

Maravi had prudently backed up a bit, herding Meera and the twins and her own guards with her, giving Sundra and Ruhi space to talk with the weather mage in at least some semblance of privacy.

Sundra took advantage of that now, picking up the subject. "What can you tell us about any of those?"

At first the woman just shook her head. Then she mumbled a single word, or a name.

"Who's Yilai?" Sundra asked, having just caught it. "One of your friends that's gone missing?" He thought he'd heard the name before. Perhaps at the Council meeting?

But Puvanti sighed. "Not missing," she corrected. "Dead. Sank with the ship." He couldn't tell if her frown was from sorrow, confusion, or something else.

"Whose ship?" Ruhi pursued, but gently, putting a hand on the old woman's shoulder.

"Ehsaan," came the answer. "Yilai worked for the Raja Ehsaan. The whole ship went down. A month ago or more."

Still that frown twisted her features, and it made Sundra wonder. Was that normal, for a stormer to drown at sea? He'd have thought they'd be immune to such dangers, given their particular magic.

"Any others?" Ruhi asked.

"Tara," Puvanti replied after some thought. "And Ojas. Both missing." Her frown deepened into a scowl. "No trace, and not off a ship, either. Just gone."

She glanced up, catching Sundra's eye. "Find them." It was a heartfelt plea, and he dipped his head at the intense emotion behind it.

"We will," he promised. Her fierce expression eased, and after a moment she withdrew, retreating back into her house and shutting her door once more between them. Evidently the interview was over.

Ruhi had already turned to Maravi. "Thank you," she was saying to the overseer. "Are there any other weather mages here or at Phasal Kaatana?"

The older woman shook her head. "No, only Puvanti. Her health had deteriorated years ago—life on a ship is for the young and the hearty—and so the old raja, Vihaan's father, allowed her to settle here instead. She goes out with the fishermen most days and helps guide fish into the nets and toward the lines."

She studied the pair of them. "Was there anything else?"

Sundra consulted Ruhi with a look, and she took only a moment to respond. "No, I don't think so. Thank you."

Maravi bowed. "Of course. If you are headed to Phasal Kaatana, I can send someone to show you the way."

It was actually Meera who stepped forward to answer that question for the group. "We should head back," she pointed out. "In case Kosala is looking for us." The trek here had taken a little longer than expected, since they hadn't been rushing at all, and it would be nearing nightfall when they returned, so Sundra knew she was right. Besides, best not to be traipsing around in unfamiliar terrain after dark.

Accordingly, they let Maravi and her sentries guide them back out of the town and then headed back toward Bahut Saare.

"Did we learn anything new?" Sundra said softly to Ruhi once they were safely away.

"Not much, no," his supposed brother replied just as quietly. "Though now we have a few more names. And it sounds like this Yilai might have been the first disappearance. If a sunken ship even qualifies."

"Right." Sundra wasn't sure about that, either. It was hardly the same as disappearing without a trace. Still, it was probably worth adding to their list of things to find out more about.

For now, he just wanted to find out more about supper, and about how much longer they were staying. His bed had been fine, but he already missed sleeping aboard the *Shikra*.

* * *

"Sundra."

He glanced up at Ruhi, seeing the worry on her face. "What's up?"

"It's too quiet," she answered. "And we're all alone out here."

He'd been woolgathering, he had to admit—the walk back to Bahut Saare had been just as relaxed as the trek to Suraksha, and they'd just topped a small rise and spotted the neat rows of trees that he'd seen along the plantation's outer edge when they'd left that morning.

Meera and her childhood friends had run on ahead, no doubt excited to be back home and sad that this meant the end of the day's excursion and their visit together. It was just him and his so-called brother now.

"Relax," he told her, resisting the urge to pat her on the shoulder. "We're almost back, and it's still light out. Everything's fine."

She nodded, but he could see he hadn't convinced her. And her doubts proved contagious, making him tense as they strolled down the hill and entered the orchard, walking side by side down a long, broad, tree-lined swathe of grass.

The next second a masked man stepped from the shadows and swung something at Sundra's head.

If he'd been as distracted as earlier, the heavy blow would have caved in his skull. As it was, already jumpy thanks to Ruhi, Sundra jerked away, feeling his hair stir in the wake of the swing.

Instinct took over. Though his hand went to his waist and came up empty, Sundra still stepped in, moving within the stranger's reach so he couldn't make a second attempt.

One hand shot out, trapping the other man's wrist and arresting the club at the end of the swing. The other fist smashed his assailant's nose, making the man reel back in pain. As the fellow staggered, Sundra stripped the club from his suddenly limp grasp. He twirled it, getting the feel of the sturdy length of wood. An axe handle, he judged. No head, but still an effective weapon.

Which was a good thing, seeing as several more masked strangers had just emerged to surround them. And all of them were armed as well.

"What do you want?" Ruhi demanded, putting her back to Sundra's so they couldn't be struck from behind. Smart thinking, at least. Of course, without a weapon there wasn't much else she could do, and Sundra already knew she wasn't much of a fighter.

Good thing he was.

"Murderer!" one of the strangers, a stocky woman, hissed. Her dark durpatta was wrapped across her nose and mouth to conceal her features, but it was easy enough to tell her gender.

"What are you talking about?" Sundra shot back. "We haven't killed anyone! That was all a lie!"

"You killed Shri Bhadra!" another insisted, charging in to bring his club down on Sundra's head. Sundra blocked the blow easily enough, angling his own weapon to slide the attack down and away. Then he twisted, knocking the man's weapon clear and leaving him a wide opening. He took it, hammering a quick strike to the forehead. The man stepped back, then dropped onto his backside, stunned.

"We didn't kill anyone!" Ruhi insisted. "Bhadra Khatri did! He murdered two rajas, Udayin and Vihaan!"

It was true, of course, that the Parishad had executed the former plantation owner for that, but they'd had nothing to do with that. Still, they were responsible for exposing the truth, which Sundra supposed could make some view them as responsible.

Like this lot, apparently. "Lies!" another one shouted, leaping forward and swinging at Ruhi. She yelped, and Sundra looped his free arm with hers and spun them both around. His own weapon arced up to deflect the blow before flicking back to tap the woman on the temple. She slumped, and that was another out of the fight.

Too bad there were still several more. And the remaining attackers had evidently learned from their fellows' failure—they were circling, holding back, waiting for their moment.

"Grab one of the clubs," Sundra hissed over his shoulder.

"Just swing it around any time they get near!" That would be a definite help. He couldn't defend them both *and* take out this lot before someone landed a lucky blow. Not with nowhere for them to stand safely.

But there was a place, of course. Many of them.

"Grab it and make for that tree!" he told her, gesturing toward a particularly large tree off to the right.

The minute she bent to retrieve the fallen axe handle, Sundra roared and made a charge of his own, swinging as he ran forward. As he'd hoped, the sudden reversal confused his attackers. They froze for a moment, unsure how to deal with prey that fought back. He'd taken out another one before they recovered. By then Ruhi had reached their target. Sundra spun around and sprinted after her, ducking a few belated attacks.

A minute later, breathing heavily, he was beside her, with the tree's thick trunk at their backs. That was better! Now these strangers could only come from the front and the sides. And, with Ruhi swinging her club to and fro, they'd all aim for him first.

But were they really strangers? He was sure he'd seen a few of them earlier, on their way out. And that one at the back, the tall, slim one—he seemed even more familiar.

Sundra couldn't worry about that right now, though. Not when two of them had finally come up with the idea of both attacking at once.

His salvation was that none of these people seemed trained to fight. They were clearly residents of Bahut Saare and presumably farmers, cooks, craftsmen, and so on. Fit, perhaps, but that didn't prepare you for trying to kill someone.

Sundra, on the other hand, was a Kunwar, son of a Sirdar. He'd been raised in all the gentlemanly arts.

And one that he'd particularly excelled at was dueling.

Now he shifted his grip on the axe handle, holding it as if it were merely a long, heavy, blunt sword. No tip, no cutting edge, but a hard jab with it still hurt. Particularly in sensitive spots like the throat where his next lunge took the attacker on the right.

The man gasped and tumbled away, dropping his own weapon as he clutched at his throat, wheezing for air. That left the woman on the left. Sundra neatly disarmed her before rapping her on the side of the head. Her fall elicited a cry from the tall man who'd hung back, and both his voice and the name it called sent a shock through Sundra:

"Kavya!"

Kabir—because Sundra knew him now—rushed forward, but not to attack. Instead Meera's old friend dropped his club and grabbed his sister instead. He wrapped his arms around her middle and lugged her to her feet and back into the trees, where they were soon lost from view. Only one attacker remained, and he fled once he realized he was now the one outnumbered.

"Well, that was exciting," Sundra huffed, lowering his weapon and leaning upon it as he caught his breath. "You all right?"

Ruhi nodded. "Yes. Thank you. That was… you were…"

Despite everything, he grinned. "Yes, I am rather good, aren't I?"

Lifting the club and tucking it under one arm, he shook out his arms and hands. Their attackers might have been unskilled but several of them had been strong, and the impacts from their strikes had been jarring. His arms felt weak, and his hands were cramping.

"I just hope they don't come back."

"Sundra." Ruhi set a hand on his arm. "That was Kavya and Kabir."

He sighed. "I know. And now we know why they ran off earlier—and how this lot knew to wait for us here." He shook his head. "Damn it, I liked them!"

His friend nodded, but she wasn't done. "What about Meera?" she asked next. "They ran off with her."

Now he straightened to stare at her. "Oh, come on! You don't really think she was involved, do you? We know her!" He waved at their downed foes. "This crowd, they knew Bhadra Khatri, and probably heard a garbled version of what happened, so of course they'd take his side. But Meera, she was there! She saw the whole thing. And her father…" Meera's father, Dalpat Laghari, had been involved in the plot to kill the rajas. Admittedly, that was because Bhadra had convinced him Meera would be in danger otherwise, but still.

Ruhi was shaking her head. "No, of course not. I like her too. But, I don't know, it's awfully convenient, isn't it?"

She broke off as they heard fresh footsteps approaching in a hurry. Sundra wearily raised his club again, but the figure that burst from the trees was the very woman they'd just been discussing, and she skidded to a halt, unarmed, out of breath, and visibly alarmed at the sight of them amidst all those bodies.

"Are you hurt?" Meera asked between gasps. "Kabir... he said someone attacked you all... I'm sorry... I went to see Arzoo, they told me she wasn't doing well, she was my old teacher." She shook her head. "I shouldn't have left you."

Sundra exchanged a look with Ruhi but couldn't tell what she was thinking as she replied, "We're fine. They seemed to think Bhadra Khatri was innocent and we set him up instead."

"What?" Now the young housekeeper looked outraged as well as appalled. "That's insane!" She frowned. "I'm so sorry. I was your guide, and I left you. Even with Kavya and Kabir here, that wasn't right."

"So you saw the twins?" Sundra asked carefully, propping himself up on his club again.

She nodded. "Kabir said one of them hit Kavya too, but they think she'll recover."

She nudged one of the downed locals, who groaned, and she sighed. "I know him. I know them all." Her eyes were bright with tears as she repeated, "I'm sorry."

"It's not your fault." And Sundra meant it. He didn't think she'd had anything to do with this. Her friends, on the other hand...

"I'm glad Kavya will be all right," Ruhi said, and shook her head when he stared at her. "We were all very lucky." She straightened. "But perhaps we'd best get back now, to prevent any other incidents."

"Yes, of course." Meera led the way, staying close, but Sundra was still able to lean in to whisper to his brother.

"What are you doing?" he asked. "You're going to let them get away with it?"

Ruhi shrugged. "What does it help to expose them?" she replied, too soft for Meera to hear. "They're her oldest friends, remember? And we'll be gone soon enough."

Sundra didn't necessarily agree—the twins had not only participated in the attack, they'd clearly helped plan it—but at the same time, he saw her point. Why cause Meera more pain? Her father had already been exiled, and her mother was long since gone. As Ruhi'd said, they'd be away from here and all this, and then what would it matter?

He kept a tight grip on the axe handle, however, until they were safely back at the main house, with Sanga and the other pirates close by. He'd never thought he'd be happy to be surrounded by such scoundrels.

But he still used the club to wedge his door shut that night. Just in case.

CHAPTER FIFTEEN

RUHI

Two days later, the *Shikra* sailed into the harbor at Enkar Bindu. Ruhi watched from the ship's railing beside Sundra, Meera, and Sanga.

"What an... interesting... place," Ruhi commented, and the others all laughed at her tone.

She hadn't meant it meanly, but the durga before them was certainly a far cry from the orderly rows of Suraksha. Indeed, what she could see so far reminded her far more of Surpakat, at least the older, upper portion—narrow, twisting streets, jumbled-together buildings, and a general air of chaotic activity and barely restrained violence.

Part of that most likely came from the dozen or so ships lined up along the docks. Most of those bore Kosala's pennant, a pair of crossed swords beneath a fierce-looking bird. On the *Shikra*, the bird was closer, only its head and beak showing, while on these others it was the entire raptor, down to the talons. As they sailed past, each of those ships gave out a vigorous cheer. Kosala herself, standing at the prow, acknowledged each shout with a dignified wave, every bit the regal monarch accepting the adulation of her people.

The ships without that symbol fell into one of two types. A few were older, slightly battered-looking vessels, clearly hard-used but still seaworthy. The rest were bigger, newer, prettier—and largely unmanned.

"Those are recent captures," Sanga confirmed when Ruhi gestured at one. "The others are traders."

They put in at the dock, in a prime location right by the shore, and once the gangplank had been lowered, Kosala stepped onto it but paused there, turning back to face her ship's crew.

"Two days' liberty!" she declared, and the cheers were louder and more energetic than those from the other ships had been.

Ruhi supposed that made sense. This was their home port as much as Surpakat, if not more, and from what Sanga and Meera had said previously, if they were safe anywhere it was here, so why not let the sailors relax a bit?

She and Sundra followed Sanga and Meera and trailed behind the raja, of course. They wound their way through the dockyard, out onto an only slightly wider street, and then made straight ahead, toward what could only be the town square. A pair of large, handsome buildings faced off across it, both of them standing out from their surroundings by virtue of size and grandeur, but Ruhi wasn't the least surprised when they turned toward the one on the right, which was built in the same style as Kosala's house in Surpakat.

It seemed the pirate lord had a type.

The doors were flung open before they'd reached the porch, and several men and women poured out onto the shaded veranda. One of them, a big, broad-shouldered woman with strong features and a vividly colored durpatta stepped forward from the rest, beaming.

"Welcome home, Raja!" she called out, her voice as imposing as the rest of her but as warm as her smile. "You've been away too long!"

"Exactly what I said," Kosala agreed, hopping up onto the porch and, much to Ruhi's surprise, embracing the bigger woman.

"How are you, Lakkoli? How is everything here?"

"Fine, fine," was the answer. "Nothing of any note."

When their employer tilted her head slightly, Lakkoli sighed. "All right, I had to let Zahra go, the girl stole again, and Sabina and Vinay are fighting, which is causing some tension, and Sumer broke his leg cleaning the gutters. But that's all." At Kosala's nod, she chuckled. "I don't know why I bother trying to keep anything from you."

"Me either," the raja agreed. "This is Rawal and Sundra," she explained, gesturing at them. "They work for me now as well. Find them a room while we're here—they're brothers, so they can share."

Ruhi masked any hint of a sigh at that. She'd known the luxury of her own room at Bahut Saare had been an anomaly, but it had certainly been nice while it lasted!

"Of course," the other woman—clearly Kosala's housekeeper here—agreed at once. "Welcome!" That was directed to them, and Ruhi smiled in reply. "Come in, all of you, and we'll get you something to eat. A proper meal!"

Kosala had already turned toward one of the young men waiting nearby. "Farhan, let the governor know I'm back for a day or two and would like to speak with him when he has a moment."

The lad nodded and took off at once, charging down off the porch and across the courtyard, aimed straight at that other big building. So Kosala lived directly across from the governor? Interesting. Clearly, Sanga had not been joking about her having some serious pull here.

Meera was hugging Lakkoli and already telling her about their visit to Bahut Saare. Leaving there had been rough on the younger housekeeper, though of course she'd understood and had been happy to get to see her old friends again, even if just for a day. They'd also been careful not to linger too long after the attack, which Arivai had promised them she would deal with appropriately.

The house's interior was much like Kosala's other one as well, enough so that Ruhi found it comforting.

Beside her, Sanga must have guessed at least some of her thoughts, and laughed. "Yes, once she finds something she likes, she tends to stick with it," he said. "Nothing wrong with that."

"Nothing at all," she agreed. "As long as it doesn't mean she's closed off to trying new things. Which I don't think she is."

"Is she really going to go speak with the governor?" Sundra asked from the other side.

Kosala had gone on ahead and disappeared into her study, which was in the exact same place here as in Surpakat.

"More like the governor will stop by to pay his respects," the tall pirate answered with a grin. "Maha Ayarpa owes a lot of his position to Kosala, and he knows it. She doesn't meddle much, but she will want to hear about any general news and any plans he has for the town overall."

"Are all of the ships in dock hers?" Ruhi asked. She was thinking about their mission. Could any of those have thalakurioi on them?

But Sanga was nodding. "Every so often, another raja's ship will put in here, especially if it's damaged and this is the nearest port. Or we'll get one like the *Kalinga* that's unaffiliated. But in general, yes, they're all Kosala's. Most won't venture into another's stronghold without a good reason." He raised an eyebrow in mute question.

"I was hoping we might find another thalakurios to talk to while we're here," she explained.

He frowned, though that vanished an instant later as they reached the inner courtyard—and saw the fine lunch already being set out by some of the household staff. "We don't have any in port," he said. "Kosala doesn't believe in using them—she considers their control over weather too unpredictable, and doesn't like the idea of having to rely so heavily on any one person. But some of our captains might've served with them in the past. I can ask."

Ruhi smiled at him, and he returned the expression for a second, then looked oddly troubled.

"That would be excellent. Thank you," she said. Then, to hide her own flustered thoughts, she focused on the meal, and on meeting the many people Meera introduced her and Sundra to.

❈ ❈ ❈

That afternoon, Ruhi was speaking with Lakkoli, going over the house's books and explaining what she'd done to improve the bookkeeping at Surpakat, when Sanga returned.

"I hear this one's spared you from the numbers," the big housekeeper told him with a laugh.

She'd proven to be outspoken and friendly, and Ruhi had liked her right off. So had Sundra, though he'd been a little dismayed to find that his charms didn't fully work on her—she'd referred to him as a "handsome pup" and patted him on the head instead.

Sanga's own smile now was rueful. "Aye, and I'm eternally grateful," he agreed, dipping his head toward Ruhi. "Rawal's far better at it than I ever was."

His next comment was to her. "I found one. Did you and Sundra want to meet him?"

"Yes, thank you." Ruhi bowed to Lakkoli. "Nice chatting with you." Then she hurried off to find her "brother."

Sundra was, as expected, surrounded by the young women of the household, and regaling them with how he and Ruhi had exposed Bhadra Khatri's plot and freed Kosala. He looked less than thrilled at leaving his adoring audience, but rose and followed Ruhi anyway.

"They'll still be here when you return," she pointed out as they joined Sanga on the porch.

"I know, but some of the immediate excitement will have faded," her friend said with a small sigh. Then he brightened. "Still, that just gives me the fun of building it back up again."

"You're incorrigible."

He just laughed, of course, and they walked the rest of the way back to the docks in a companionable silence. This time they turned toward a slightly smaller boat the next dock over, where a heavyset man with a ruddy face and a thick, curling beard waited. His broad chest was bare beneath his vest, as with many of the pirates, and covered in old scars, white against his tanned skin, and he wore a bright red sash and a matching pagri.

"This is Parth," Sanga introduced, and the man sketched a bow. "He captains the *Baaz.*"

"Sanga says you are asking about stormers," the man boomed. "I've used them before. Helpful enough, when they wish to be. But hard to control. Think they're better than us nonmagical types. Don't take orders well. Act like they're doing you a favor, just being on your ship."

That fits with Nalan's attitude back in Surpakat, Ruhi thought.

"Have you heard anything about any of them going missing, or any other trouble?" she asked.

Parth shook his head. "No, and I wouldn't expect to, even if there was any." He stroked his thick beard. "They're closemouthed, especially about their own. Don't talk about stormer stuff except to other stormers. If you don't have that cloth, forget about it; they won't tell you nothing."

Which also matched. Unfortunately.

"When was the last time you saw one?" Sundra asked, joining the conversation.

The captain frowned, thinking. "A few months back," he recalled at last. "Out on the open waters. Didn't see them myself, to be fair, but no doubt one was on that ship—there was a storm, big one, and we were doing our best to weather it, when this other dhangi goes sailing on past, pretty as you please. And the storm's literally parting around it like a set of curtains, blue skies and calm waters along its path, a nice brisk wind at its back. Meanwhile, we're struggling to furl sail and bail water afore we capsize, sink, or both!"

He shook his head. "Could've extended that calm to us, if they'd wanted. No prey at hand, no reason not to help a fellow pirate. Didn't bother. Then they were gone again, and the storm closed back in behind them." He scowled at the recollection. "Like I said, only help if they feel like it."

"Thank you," Sundra told the man, and Ruhi nodded.

Not that they'd learned anything new, really, she thought as they headed back. But at least it was confirmation, and a slightly clearer picture of how the weather mages viewed themselves and their place in this odd pirate society among the islands. That might prove useful, though she admitted she had no idea how at present.

CHAPTER SIXTEEN

SUNDRA

They'd been back out to sea two days when Sundra emerged from belowdecks to find everyone tense beneath a slate-gray sky.

"Storm?" he asked Uma, who was over by the tiller.

Normally he'd have been up here at dawn, like the rest of the crew, but he'd stayed down below until he was sure Ruhi was up and moving. Thus far there hadn't been any issues with their sleeping arrangements, or anyone figuring out Ruhi's secret, but he still made a point of not leaving her alone down there. They were bunking with pirates, after all, and despite Kosala's clear control over her crew, well, he knew only too well what men could be like.

Now, however, he was more concerned with that sky and the scent in the air and the fact that the waves were stronger and higher and faster than they'd been the night before.

"Aye," the woman answered, scowling up at the leaden, gray heavens. "We're already a notch farther north than we should be, veered this way during the night in the hopes of skirting it, but no such luck. We're in for a ride, and that's certain."

Sanga had been speaking to some of the other crew and now

joined them. "I'd say an hour before we're in it fully," he gauged, also studying the heavy clouds massing ahead.

"You'll want to either be below or tied to a railing," he warned Ruhi, who'd just clambered up onto the deck, and there was nothing joking about his manner.

"How is that even a choice?" she protested, clearly unsure why anyone would opt for the latter. Sundra knew that, if left to it, she'd pick the apparent safety of being down in the main cabin and quickly moved to dissuade her.

"Go for the railing," he advised. "Once we're in the storm, everything's going to be tossing and turning, and I doubt that trinket can handle it." He gestured at the bracelet she still wore, which thus far had done an admirable job of keeping away the nausea. "But down below, you won't have any light or fresh air, and that'll only make you feel worse. Up here, at least you'll have space, and you can breathe. And if you're sick"—he shrugged—"there's gonna be water and wind everywhere anyway. No one'll notice." He grinned as he said that, but hoped she could also see the sympathy in his eyes.

"I suppose..." Ruhi considered, but finally nodded. "I'll stay up here."

Sanga quickly led her over to the left side and produced a thick rope, which he tied first to the railing there before handing her the rest.

"Loop it around at least twice, then make sure it's secure," he warned. "And don't feel bad. Meera's going to be offered the same choice, and the rest of us'll have rope too, just with a lot more play to it so we can still reach things."

Meera had just joined them, and came to the same decision Ruhi had about being up here.

"Guess we're in for a show," the young housekeeper said as Sanga helped her, but her face was pale and her smile weak. "Sorry—we had some rain on my trip to Surpakat, but nothing like this."

No, Sundra would imagine not. Already the air was thick and cool and so filled with moisture, there were droplets clinging to his face and hair. That made him think of something else, and he disappeared back below, returning a minute later wearing a heavy storm coat and carrying two more.

"Put these on, then retie the ropes over them," he advised, handing one garment to Ruhi and the other to Meera.

The buff-colored sherwani were made of waxed canvas, stiff and heavy and largely waterproof. They had thick leather belts stitched directly into the coat, and hoods that could be cinched tight, leaving only the face exposed, along with hands and feet.

"Thank you," Ruhi told him, doing as instructed.

He could see the relief on her face—the garment would not only protect her from the elements, but keep her secret safe in a way drenched clothing would not. He winked at her before wandering off to help with the sails.

Sanga's estimate proved optimistic. It was only perhaps ten minutes later that Sundra felt the wind pick up, tugging at his hood and the cuffs and hem of his coat.

"Get ready!" he heard someone shout, and since he hadn't yet tied on a rope, he gripped the nearest rigging tight, weaving his fingers through the mesh.

Then the storm was upon them.

The heavens opened up first, sheets of water sluicing down on their heads, the sheer weight of it staggering him. Even with the storm coat, water seeped in. Good thing he was barefoot like the crew, or his boots would have been like leaden weights.

The impact knocked one of his hands loose from the rigging. Sundra quickly grabbed back on, just before the rising wind hurled more water in his face. The gale lifted him off his feet, and only his renewed grip kept him from being tossed overboard and out to sea. He heard a scream as the same happened to Meera, but the rope around her waist held, keeping her safe. Ruhi yelped but otherwise gave no cry, likewise secured.

"Furl the sails!" Uma shouted, her words barely audible over the roar of the storm, and Sundra hastened to help.

They'd already been bringing down and tying up the sails, but the storm had moved much faster than expected. The remaining sails were now fluttering and straining and tugging in the wind. They had to be stowed before they could tear free or snap the mast. Either would be a disaster, especially out here on the open water.

Working with some of the crew, Sundra got the main sail tied off. Their hands kept slipping on the water-slick ropes, and their feet were sliding on the deck. They almost lost a man to a sudden gust, but Sanga latched onto him before he could disappear; he gripped the man's ankle and managed to haul him back onboard. After that they all wrapped ropes around their waists, though everything was now too wet to tie properly. The whole world smelled of wet rope and damp wood and salt water.

With this much wind, and the waves so tumultuous, their slim, light kotia was getting tossed about. They tipped side to side, nearly spilling out into the water at the end of each arc, and were slammed by waves when they swung close on that side.

"We need to get out of this!" Uma shouted, and Sundra looked up.

There was no end in sight, the whole of their view being heavy, almost black clouds. Most strong storms also moved fast, passing by quickly, but this one looked to be far bigger, and that was a problem. The *Shikra* was a sturdy craft, but wood could only endure so long against something this fierce.

"Raise the aft sail!" Kosala ordered. Sundra had only vaguely noticed the raja stationing herself over at the tiller. "We need to make for shore!"

"How?" Onkar asked, and it was a mark of their employer's nature that she allowed such questions to her commands. "We'll just be battered against the rocks!"

At least, here on the ocean, they weren't liable to hit anything. Getting in close to a cliff was far more dangerous. Few survived a contest between wind and rock.

But Kosala had an answer for that, in a single word shouted against the storm: "Riyaasat!"

Ah. Sundra remembered the map he'd seen of their intended

voyage. Riyaasat had been marked on the southern edge of a large island just west of their path, perhaps a third of the way from Enkar Bindu to Dveep Kile. If they were near it, the town could provide adequate shelter. Being docked was by far the safest option in such a powerful storm, but even sitting within a harbor would provide some shelter.

Everyone else nodded as well, and Sundra moved back to help raise the rear sail. They couldn't risk the mainsail, but this smaller one wouldn't get battered as heavily. He just hoped it could get them to shelter before being torn apart.

The second the sail went up, the wind tore at it, nearly slamming Sanga in the face with one of the spars. The tall sailor leaped back, the wind carrying him almost over the aft rail before he caught himself. Everyone else prudently moved to the side rails, letting the sail fill while watching it for any sign of trouble.

Sundra heard a ripping noise and pointed toward the middle. "We've got a tear!"

There was nothing they could do about it, of course, not without bringing the sail back down. But it was a bad sign, especially since that meant the wind was slicing through there instead of belling out the sail further. Still, the rest of it was holding, and the *Shikra* began to force its way through the waves, its carved prow battering against the water.

Meera screamed again, and Sundra spun about. One of the main sail's riggings had ripped free, the heavy knot at its end whipping through the air. Onkar was in its path, and Sundra threw himself at the pirate. He knocked them both to the deck just before that thick rope end would have connected. Then he leaped to his feet and helped Sanga catch the rope. They wound it tight round the rear mast. Hopefully that would keep it from getting loose again.

"Thanks," Onkar told him, standing as well and clapping Sundra on the shoulder. "I owe you one."

"Remember that next time I ask for seconds on dhal," Sundra replied, and they shared a quick laugh before returning to their efforts.

No more ropes snapped, and although the sail's tear did widen and lengthen until it was running nearly the full height, their momentum was now enough to carry the *Shikra* along, albeit at a limping pace.

Soon, however, one of the others shouted, "Land ho!" and pointed ahead, where a dark shape was rising across the water.

Sundra hurried to the prow, giving Meera and Ruhi reassuring nods on his way. Both of them were still by the railing, clinging white-knuckled to the wood there, and both seemed fine, if shaken. Not that he could blame them.

Reaching the front, he peered into the swirling rain, squinting against the wind. Much of the shape was the same, but after a second, he spotted a lighter spot to the right.

"Harbor slightly starboard!" he shouted over his shoulder and felt the ship turn immediately after.

The new angle put them less at odds with the wind, and the pressure eased even as their speed increased now that the gale wasn't trying to force them back.

As they approached, he could make out more details. It was definitely a harbor, with a single, long wharf at the far end. Beyond that Sundra could just make out the faint outline of buildings.

They sailed in, no one trying to block their path, and he continued to call out directions. Kosala was still at the tiller, he assumed, and the pirate lord deftly steered them into the mouth of the harbor, then ordered them to drop anchor. The torn sail was furled, and the entire crew now hunkered in place along the hull, ducking beneath their storm coats as best they could as the storm continued to slam icy cold water down onto them.

At least they were safe from it now. Of course, whether Riyaasat itself was safe remained to be seen.

CHAPTER SEVENTEEN

RUHI

I t felt like hours before the storm finally began to slacken, though Ruhi couldn't be sure. The entire time within the storm felt almost dreamlike, untethered to reality. What she did know was that she was frozen and drenched and her knees hurt, as well as her head, and she was generally miserable. She could only assume the rest of them felt exactly the same.

"Ahoy, the ship!" The shout startled her, and she jerked, cracking her elbow against the railing.

The resulting jolt of pain traveled all the way up to her shoulder and neck, and for an instant Ruhi saw and heard and felt nothing else. When her vision cleared, she realized that the voice had come from someone on one of the nearby wharves. Rising up from her crouch, she peered down through the balustrades.

They had anchored only a boat length from one of the outermost wharves, it seemed. A large man stood there, hands upon his hips, water streaming down from his bright-yellow pagri, over his broad, deeply tanned face, and out along his stiff beard until it dripped off the pointed tip. His open vest was of leather, dyed an orange as vivid as the yellow above, though his equally leather

AARON ROSENBERG

churidar appeared to be an unadorned black. Thick leather bracers covered much of his powerful forearms, and a tegha was thrust through the sash at his waist—and, unlike Ruhi, he looked like he could wield the heavy blade one-handed.

"The governor demands to know who has dared enter his harbor unannounced and uninvited!" the massive fellow shouted, his deep voice carrying easily despite the continuing wind and rain. "We have no desire for visitors at this time, so if your business is not pressing, you had best be off!"

He looked prepared to wade out and shove the *Shikra* back into open water with nothing more than his own enormous hands, and Ruhi's heart sank at the thought of being forced back out into that storm again, even if the worst had passed them by.

Meera made a sound beside her, somewhere between a gasp and a sob, clearly feeling the same way. But Kosala merely sniffed from where she likewise sat beneath her storm coat.

"Don't worry," the raja assured them, keeping her voice too low for their unfriendly greeter to hear. "Watch."

Ruhi started to ask what they were watching for, but then she heard footsteps approaching along the wharf. Peering down, she saw a pair striding toward the big fellow in the yellow turban, a man and a woman perhaps her own father's age, perhaps a little less. The man carried a large parasol to shield them from the storm, though the wind kept tugging it in his hands.

"That's quite enough of that, Bipin!" the man called out, and Ruhi saw the big man glance down at his feet as if ashamed. "That's no way to treat a ship in need!"

The pair stopped beside the colossus, and Ruhi could see that they were both well-dressed, and other than his talwar, neither looked to be armed.

"Hello, up there!" the gentleman continued. "Do you seek shelter from the storm?"

Kosala rose to her feet, tossing her heavy coat aside and ignoring the rain now pelting her. "You know perfectly well we do, Nayak Banerjee," she declared, her tone as ringing as ever. Then she dipped her head slightly toward the woman. "Tarabai."

Tarabai Banerjee? Ruhi squinted, blinking away raindrops, and saw that her employer was correct. The woman was none other than Kosala's fellow raja. Whose husband, Ruhi now recalled, was the governor of their stronghold. How convenient.

"Why, Kosala, is that you?" the same Tarabai was now calling up. "How strange to see you here, of all places! What can we do for you?" She grinned, looking younger than she had before, more lively—and more dangerous. "Whatever it is, I'm sure we can work something out."

That produced a scowl in response. "Would you charge for suc-cor?" Kosala demanded, crossing her arms over her chest. "The law of the sea is quite clear on that matter."

"Of course, of course," the other woman replied. "Which is why you'll notice we did not have our jal dvaar in place. But now you're here, safe and sound, the rules of civility have been satisfied. Anything else is open to negotiation."

Kosala made to resume her seat on the deck, and her peer actu-ally pouted. "Oh, come now!" Tarabai stated, stomping her foot as if she were going to throw a tantrum. "I'm just playing with you! Come on, pull up to the dock and let's get all of you in out of the cold!"

Sanga was watching Kosala for his cue, as they all were. When she finally nodded, he leaped up and began shouting orders. They quickly unfurled the damaged aft sail, using it to maneuver the short distance to the dock before tying it down again. Uma tossed the mooring rope across, and the big man—Bipin—caught it easily and secured it to a post, then grabbed the gangplank Sanga thrust at him and tugged that into place, anchoring it with one enormous foot.

Kosala was first off the ship, showing no sign of fear, as always, and motioning the rest to follow. Ruhi had no objection, even if standing and moving meant the gale-driven water found every gap in her coat and soaked her further. At least there was the prospect of someplace warm and dry at the end of their trek.

Fortunately, they didn't have far to go. Tarabai and her husband led the rest of them away from the wharf, up two blocks to a large house set at an angle from the rest, its back nestled against the city's thick outer wall. The house was big and squared, with ornate columns, arches, and balconies across the front, but Ruhi only had eyes for the wide doors servants were holding open and the warmth and light emanating from within.

There was an open courtyard ahead, as with most homes, but the raja led them to one side, under the columns ringing the space and into a large, pleasant room. More staff waited there, young men and women, each carrying large, thick towels and equally thick, hooded robes.

"Through there," Tarabai directed, pointing to a row of curtains along the far wall. "Strip off your wet clothes, dry off, don a robe, and then we'll hang everything up to dry."

Ruhi was relieved to see that each curtain led to a small alcove, perhaps a meditation space or small storeroom. She was alone in hers and wasted no time in peeling her sodden clothing from her body, keeping only the stanapatta and of course her amulet—and the Parishad's somewhat damp writ, which she laid out for now to dry.

She scrubbed herself dry with the towel she'd been handed, enjoying the vigorous motion and the heat it produced. Then she wrapped herself in the large robe, belting it tight at the waist and raising the hood over her still-damp hair. Ah, so much better!

Tucking the writ into the robe before returning to the larger room beyond, she found the others similarly dry and attired, and Tarabai waiting to lead them out to a different chamber, where hot tea and equally hot curries and rice and roti were being set out.

"Come, eat, warm your insides along with your outsides," the raja told them all, and since Kosala consented to do so, the rest quickly followed.

Once they'd eaten, Tarabai turned to a short, slim man with a sweeping mustache and long, pointed beard. "Pagavan will see you to your rooms," she explained. "We can speak more in the morning." And she departed, leaving them in the man's capable hands.

Ruhi found it interesting that the governor himself had vanished as soon as they'd entered the house. It was clear who the real power at home was.

Right now, however, she didn't care much. After eating a little food and downing a large mug of hot, sweet tea, she let herself be led to a small but private room, where she quickly fell asleep.

Ruhi felt far better the next morning, and, looking out through the ornamental grille of her room's narrow window at the bright blue sky, she almost wondered if it had all been an awful dream. The robe she'd been given, which she'd fallen asleep in, suggested otherwise, as did the pile of neatly laundered clothes she discovered folded just outside her door. Putting her own clothes back on, however threadbare they were becoming, helped stave off any anxieties about their current situation, and she was in good spirits as she exited into the long hall beyond.

A young girl appeared almost immediately. "This way, shri," she called cheerfully, and after a second Ruhi realized the girl meant her.

Laughing at her own foolishness, she followed, back to the room they'd dined in the night before. There was more food there now, including fresh fruit, and more tea. Several of the crew, including Sanga and Meera, had gotten there before her and were already wolfing down their breakfasts, but Kosala and Sundra were nowhere to be seen.

Just as she was about to sit down, the man from last night entered. "Ah, there you are, shri," he said, stepping up beside Ruhi. "The raja has asked that you join her." He'd already turned away, clearly assuming she would follow, and really there wasn't anything to do but obey.

The man led her down a smaller hall and to a pair of doors

opening onto a private terrace. Tarabai Banerjee sat at a handsomely carved table there, along with Kosala and Sundra. The latter's face showed his relief at her arrival, and Ruhi quickly took the empty seat beside him, farthest from their hostess.

"Good morning," the raja told her, and Ruhi nodded back.

"Good morning, Raja. And thank you for your hospitality."

Tarabai waved that off. "Of course, of course. As Kosala rightly pointed out, the laws of civility and the sea require no less. Still, you're welcome."

She smiled, but there was something sharp about it, almost predatory. "I'm glad fate washed you up here, actually," the woman continued. "I'd hoped to speak to you three at some point, and this gives us the perfect opportunity."

Kosala held up a hand. "I know what you're going to say, Tarabai," she stated. "Or rather, what you're going to ask."

Ruhi was starting to suspect as well, and her guess was confirmed when their hostess sighed. "Can you blame me?" Tarabai said, her face and manner shouting distress. "Of course I'm going to ask! Did you see how many ships I have in harbor here? Five! And do you know how much of my fleet that is? A full third! A single bad storm and I won't even meet the requisite number to retain my title."

She reached out, gripping her fellow raja's hand. "Kosala, please! I'm not asking for anything unreasonable here, but you know as well as I do that Koliya would like nothing more than to kick me out and install one of his puppets in my place."

Their employer's face twisted. "Koliya doesn't control the Parishad," she said, carefully extracting her hand from Tarabai's grip. "And even if you were to stop being a raja, you would still have Riyaasat."

"My husband would, you mean," her fellow pirate lord corrected, though that claim rang hollow, given what Ruhi had seen so far. "I'm not asking for the money, or the lands," Tarabai continued. "Just the ships. Not even all of them! Just some. Enough so I wouldn't have to worry every time I send a few boats out in a storm."

Kosala considered a moment. "That's not entirely unreasonable," she conceded.

Tarabai's eyes narrowed slightly, her seeming panic vanishing as if it had been whisked away. "Perhaps," she said as she poured cups of steaming hot chai for each of them, "while you consider it, I might entertain some of your staff. These two, for instance. Or Sanga, I'm sure he wouldn't mind a brief respite from his responsibilities."

Although the offer was made in a light, casual tone, Ruhi didn't miss the implied threat. Nor, by the way she stiffened, did Kosala.

"That's very generous of you," her employer replied, accepting the delicate teacup and raising it to her lips, the steam rising up over her face like a filmy curtain but doing nothing to mask the hard gleam of her eyes. "But I prefer to keep my people with me, and it is far easier for them to accomplish the Parishad's task if they are. I'm sure you understand."

"Of course, of course." Her fellow raja nodded. "Much easier to protect them that way." She brightened as if struck by something. "You know, if you have concerns, I could always loan you a few of my men. Bipin, for example. He could keep all of you safe until the next meeting."

Move and countermove, Ruhi thought, and she noticed that Sundra was watching the political maneuvering closely as well. Which made sense, as he'd been raised to it. To her, it was like observing some strange, shadowy game. Fortunately, it was a competition Kosala was clearly very good at.

"I appreciate the offer," she replied. "But I couldn't ask you to weaken your own defenses that way. Besides which, we still have a long ways to travel, and the seas can be dangerous. I would hate to see anything happen to someone that means so much to you."

That was well played, and their employer followed immediately with a raised hand. "You know me well enough to know that trying to pressure me will only make me more resistant, not less," she pointed out bluntly. "But I have already agreed to consider your request, and you also know I am a woman of my word."

Though it was far from a promise of any particular outcome, their hostess beamed like she'd just been handed an ironclad contract.

"I do indeed!" She clapped her hands together, acting positively giddy, and sipped at her own tea before changing the subject, any previous tension cast aside—for now. "Is there anything else I can do for you while you're here as my guests?"

Kosala caught Ruhi's eye, arching her brow and giving her a slight nod. *Ah, of course.*

"There is one thing, actually," Ruhi said carefully, wincing as she received the full weight of their hostess's gaze. "Do you have any thalakurioi in your service here?"

"Oh, I do, yes." The raja smiled. "Tevi. She lives on the other side of the wharf, by the pond we have there."

Lifting a small bell from the table, she shook it, and the sweet chime had echoed only once before the same slim man appeared.

"Pagavan, our guests need to speak with Tevi," she explained. "Would you take them to her, please, and tell her I said to answer all their questions?" It was stated as a request, but there was little doubt it would be obeyed as the command it really was.

"Of course, Raja," the man agreed at once, bowing deeply. "If you'll follow me."

Ruhi rose, as did Sundra—though not without him grabbing a jam-filled pastry on his way. They both bowed, then followed the man back into the house and through it to the street beyond.

The dark and the rain had kept her from seeing much the night before, but Ruhi studied the town now as they walked. It was fairly tidy, though not as orderly as Suraksha had been, and a bit larger than that stronghold.

The people walking about were a mix between pirates and craftsmen and merchants, the latter two far outnumbering the former. Everyone nodded politely as they approached, but then their eyes darted past and they all paled a bit.

Looking back over her shoulder, Ruhi immediately saw the reason why—the enormous man from the night before, Bipin, was stomping along perhaps thirty paces behind them. And as they continued to walk, it became increasingly clear he wasn't simply heading in the same direction.

Evidently she and her brother rated not only a guide but a minder.

The pond Tarabai had mentioned proved to be a natural one, filling an irregularly shaped, sharp-edged basin in the rock right near the durga's eastern wall. No, not near it, she saw as they approached—the wall actually bisected the water, cutting clear across it before turning to angle back up. At the turn stood a guard tower, and above that were a few smaller, more scattered houses, the uneven terrain not lending itself to gridded streets. They headed toward one of those homes, a solid little stone building with oddly small windows covered in ornamental grillwork, and Pagavan knocked upon the heavy wooden door.

After a moment, he knocked again. Then, abandoning any pretense, he waved Bipin forward to join them. The big man raised a massive fist and pounded, the whole door shaking from the impact.

Still nothing.

"She is not scheduled to take ship for another week," Pagavan muttered.

Extracting a large iron key from his pouch, he inserted it into the door's keyhole and twisted, but to the man's visible surprise the door didn't budge. Retrieving the key and stepping back, he gestured to his much larger companion, and Bipin's next blow was from his enormous shoulders rather than his fist. One slam, two, a sharp crack, and the door flew open, revealing a small, simply furnished home beyond.

A small, simply furnished, shadow-filled but otherwise empty home.

"That's probably not a good sign," Sundra whispered to her as they stood back, letting the two locals search the house.

When both of them emerged, shaking their heads, he nodded. "No, definitely not good."

It wasn't, Ruhi agreed privately. They were already on the trail of several missing weather mages.

Now it appeared they had one more to add to the list.

Chapter Eighteen

SUNDRA

Sundra was relieved when they finally cast off from Riyaasat the next day. Tarabai Banerjee had been nothing but gracious throughout, but he had met people exactly like her before, all smiles and pleasantries on the surface, utterly cutthroat beneath.

The few times he'd seen her before, she had always seemed mild, even meek, but clearly that was because she'd felt her position among the rajas to be precarious, given her much smaller fleet. Here, she was in her element, and the true Tarabai had emerged— confident, almost arrogant, and absolutely in control of everyone and everything around her.

Sanga had confirmed his assessment, once they were back on the *Shikra*.

"Tarabai's a shark," the tall pirate confided, careful not to let his voice carry past their railing to where that same raja stood watching from the wharf. "Puts on a 'don't hurt me!' act when she's in Surpakat, but here? These are her waters, and you don't swim here without her permission—or you get eaten alive."

That had been all too apparent when they'd gone looking for

that storm mage. Sundra hadn't missed the fact that the windows had been barred, however prettily, and the door was heavy and fitted with a very solid lock—one the town's overseer had a key to. It might have been a house, but it was also a prison. Evidently Jasleen Lal was not the only one to consider the weather mages too valuable to let roam free.

Yes, Sundra was glad to be gone. And impressed that Kosala had been able to win them all free with only the vaguest of promises to examine her peer's request.

The rest of the crew evidently felt likewise, and the mood was high as they sailed from the harbor and back into open water. The *Shikra* had fared better than he'd hoped from that big storm, the only significant damage being the torn aft sail, and that had already been replaced.

One of the crewmen had sore ribs where he'd been struck by a rope line, and another bore several large bruises from an encounter with a wind-tossed barrel, but on the whole they had survived surprisingly unscathed. Now they were out of the lioness's den, and back on their way to Dveep Kile.

Meera approached him the next day while he was coiling a rope from the rear sail, which wasn't currently in use. Sundra had barely seen the young housekeeper since the storm, and even now she looked hesitant, never meeting his eyes.

"I'm sorry," she blurted out after a moment's shifting and swaying.

"For?" he asked, finishing the coil and stowing it in a woven basket at the mast's base before rising to his feet and taking a step toward her. He didn't approach further, though. He knew a skittish horse when he saw one.

"Back at Bahut Saare," she continued, studying her hands and biting her lip. "I ran off and left you and Rawal behind. I shouldn't have done that. And then you got attacked and I wasn't there to help."

Sundra studied her face. "Not much you could've done," he pointed out. "Not unless you've got a sword or two hidden up your sleeve."

She scowled and finally glanced his way. "Still. I was the one showing you around. I should've made sure you got back safely, not just left it to Kavya and Kabir."

Just as before, he didn't see anything there to indicate that she'd been involved in the ambush, or even knew about it, or her friends' participation in such. So he said the only thing he could, under the circumstances:

"It's fine, Meera. It wasn't your fault." And he believed that.

The relief spread over her face like the break of dawn, blindingly bright. "Really?"

Sundra couldn't help smiling back. "Really."

When she turned and moved away, it was with her natural gait, and a quick, shy glance back. That was far better.

❖ ❖ ❖

Later that day, Sundra saw Uma conferring with Kosala by the tiller. "What gives?" he asked, making his way over there.

Uma frowned, but their mutual employer answered succinctly, "Storm." And she pointed to their right, where he saw a nasty patch of purplish-gray on the horizon. "Going around."

That made sense, and certainly the woman knew her craft. Sundra's frown was more for the ugly weather itself, as he considered it.

"It's not the one we just survived, is it?"

He had no desire to encounter that monstrosity again! At the same time, would there be another storm so close to the first, and so soon after it? He didn't know the currents or weather patterns here among the islands.

But Uma shook her head. "Different one, this time. That one's already moved on." That was a relief, at least.

"There is one good thing about the change of course," Kosala added, drawing Sundra's attention. The pirate captain offered a small smile, barely more than a quirk of the lips, hand steady on the rudder. "Normally we would run straight to Dveep Kile, but with this weather forcing us to port—well, that means we're going to veer significantly closer to Ooncha Need than originally planned."

Her gaze was on the horizon, though it flicked to Sundra as she delivered this news. "Thought we might stop off there."

When she saw that he didn't understand, the raja added, "Ooncha Need belongs to Ehsaan."

Ah. And her fellow raja had lost a thalakurios, as well. Perhaps from that very port. Sundra nodded.

"Makes sense. Thank you."

It felt strange saying that, since he was still indentured to her, and since she was part of the council that had ordered him and Ruhi onto this investigation in the first place. Still, he'd been raised to have excellent manners, and the way the pirate lord arched a single brow and dipped her head showed she understood completely.

Ruhi was at her now-customary spot near the prow, not far from Meera. Both of them were busy braiding rope, a frequent task at sea and one they'd both offered to do—a way of helping that let them sit still rather than venturing out onto the riggings or up the masts, or forcing them back into the closed-off spaces belowdecks. She smiled when she saw him, as did Meera.

"We're stopping at Ehsaan's durga, Ooncha Need," he explained.

His supposed brother nodded. "Excellent. Even if that one mage, Yilai, wasn't based there, we're bound to find someone who knew him."

Of course she'd grasped the reason for the stop at once. Sundra had already resigned himself to the fact that his friend was most likely smarter than he was. Good thing "Rawal" wasn't as pretty, or as good with the sword, or he might've started feeling truly inadequate!

✦ ✦ ✦

They were able to skirt the storm without too much trouble, experiencing some wind and rain, but nothing tumultuous, and two days later they put in at Ooncha Need. The stronghold was long but shallow, Sundra saw as they approached, with stonework along the front to shore up that edge and keep the streets level and solid. There weren't any outer walls, which he thought odd at first, until he noticed that all the buildings there along the shoreline were made of stone as well, and that a second row of buildings behind those were the same material, and staggered from them. Smart—taken together, those two rows presented a secure front without the need for a separate fortification.

There was a second defensive feature here, though Sundra didn't realize that until the *Shikra* veered left. Then he noticed that there weren't any wharves or docks along that stonework. Instead, there was a thin strip of brown and gray at its base. Of course! Ehsaan had built his stronghold back from the water, close enough that you could probably fish off it but far enough away that a boat wouldn't quite be able to dock there. Instead they had to navigate a narrow river to the left, pulling into a small harbor there at the durga's lower corner. That meant no ship could approach unobserved, and it would be simple to cut off access by putting a chain across the river's mouth. Well, Padmini had mentioned once that Ehsaan was clever, as had Chetan. This confirmed it.

The harbormaster was waiting when they finally reached the dock, and nodded when Sanga called out, "The *Shikra*, the Raja Kosala commanding!"

"The Raja Ehsaan is not currently in residence," she shouted back. "But you are welcome!"

She met them as they came down off the gangplank, a wiry woman with graying hair and sharp features but calm gray eyes. "How may we serve you, Raja?" she asked Kosala, bowing. "Ehsaan has standing orders to extend every possible courtesy to his fellows, provided it does not violate his own privacy or the safety of his people."

Kosala nodded back. "Nor would I wish to cause any harm

to him or his," she replied. "We are here at his own request, as well as our fellow rajas." And she gestured for Ruhi to present her document, which the harbormaster perused, and to take over the conversation.

Sundra moved closer to provide support and participate if need be.

"We've been charged with looking into the missing thalakurioi," Ruhi explained. "We understand one of them was from here. Yilai?"

The harbormaster's mouth twisted. "Aye, that one." She spat to the side. "Good riddance, you ask me. He was a malcontent, always whingeing about his treatment here, how he deserved more money, more respect, more freedom. Valued for his skills but disliked for himself." She sighed. "The loss of the ship, that came hard—lot of good men and women on there, including my second son, Aditha. But him? Not so much."

Sundra cleared his throat. "I'm surprised a ship could go down, though, with one of the weather mages aboard," he said. "That seems… odd."

The woman shrugged. "They're a difficult lot, stormers. And some're stronger than others." She frowned. "Though Yilai was potent enough, and no mistake. Half of why he felt so entitled. Still, they're just normal folks, underneath all that magic. You catch one sleeping, they'll go down, same as anyone else."

That almost sounded like a confession, and Sundra glanced at Ruhi, who was watching the woman closely as well. Kosala, however, shook her head.

"Is there anything else you can tell us, about him or about stormers in general?" Ruhi continued.

"About him? No, other than being glad he's gone," the harbormaster said. She shook her head. "The other two who disappeared after him, not so much. And those weren't shipbound at the time, just up and vanished, one one night, and the other a few nights later. All within a week of Yilai."

The glare she gave them was direct, daring them to contradict her as she added, "The raja liked having them in his employ, said they were a valuable tool and one he'd be a fool not to use. I don't agree, myself. More trouble than they were worth, the lot of them, even though the other two were a lot more biddable." She sniffed. "Give me honest rope and sail, water and wind, and hard work any day."

"Would we be able to see where they stayed, those three mages?" Sundra asked. Maybe there would be some indication of what had happened.

The harbormaster shrugged. "Don't see why not. All three lived together, anyways. Two blocks back and two over, blue-green door."

They thanked her and left, following her instructions to a small, neat stone dwelling with a door reasonably close to the weather mages' signature color. Unlike the mage's dwelling at Riyaasat, this one had large, open windows. It also wasn't locked, and Sundra and Ruhi stepped inside, Kosala and Sanga following.

The front room was clearly communal, with comfortable benches and cushions and a low table for meals. It was messy but not filthy, and with a twinge of guilt Sundra recognized some-one who was used to having others clean up after them. Nothing looked particularly out of place, however.

"Not big on housekeeping," Ruhi commented, wrinkling her nose as they passed through to a narrow hall with two doors on either side. Three of those proved to be bedrooms, small but still light and airy and equally untidy, while the final door was a washroom.

"All men, I'm guessing," she stated after seeing the latter. "A woman would've been appalled at the state of things." She started and quickly added, "That's what our mother would've said, at least."

Sundra tried not to roll his eyes, but he suspected she was right. This struck him as the home of three confirmed bachelors. Still— "One of these is messier than the others," he pointed out. And it was true, the second bedroom was far more disordered, the sheets and pillows knocked onto the floor. While hardly neat, the other two at least looked more sedate, and more like the usual casual disinterest in cleaning up.

Unfortunately, they had no way of knowing whose room was which, and the harbormaster hadn't mentioned names for the other two missing mages, so they couldn't tell if that difference had any significance. Certainly they didn't find any notes saying, "If I'm gone, blame X" or anything else that useful.

"Did we learn anything?" Sanga asked as they headed back to the ship.

"Only that Yilai wasn't well-liked and wasn't happy here," Ruhi replied. She was walking beside the rangy pirate, and Sundra wondered if she'd even noticed how often she did that. "And that he wasn't the only one here, nor the only one who's gone missing. If his death even counts as such."

Sundra wasn't sure about that either, but figured every little piece of the puzzle helped. And knowing about the other two who'd disappeared from here certainly counted as another piece. He just wished they knew what shape this puzzle was supposed to take, rather than trying to assemble it blind.

CHAPTER NINETEEN

RUHI

The next day passed uneventfully at sea, and Ruhi had to admit that she was becoming used to life aboard the *Shikra*. Kosala's crew, clearly handpicked, were all competent sailors and, though rough, crude, and boisterous, not particularly villainous. She'd known just such men and women at her father's warehouse, hard workers and reliable ones, and basically decent folk, if ill-mannered. Ruhi had also met and dealt with far worse, unfortunately, and so was particularly relieved that her employer clearly knew how to weed out such people, the violent and ill-tempered and just generally cruel. She had no doubt these pirates were capable fighters, but they evidently reserved any such activity for combat, and even the squabbles amongst themselves were short-lived and of the type often experienced when you lived at close quarters for extended periods.

She would never be fully comfortable sharing those quarters, of course, and had already endured some mild ribbing from a few of the men for her retiring nature and insistence upon privacy when changing, bathing, or relieving herself. But it was nothing she couldn't handle, and the fact that she could escape to open deck and feel the sun and wind forestalled any sense of being trapped. Having three women on board also made things a bit easier, since the male crewmembers were more accustomed to giving personal space than she suspected might have been the case otherwise.

Still, she felt a prickle of excitement on the second morning when one of the pirates called down from the rigging, "Land ho!" Especially since this should be Dveep Kile, their intended destination.

As they sailed closer, Ruhi saw that the island ahead was not very large, bigger than the one that held Enkar Bindu but far smaller than those that housed Ooncha Need, Riyaasat, Bahut Saare, or Surpakat itself. She also noticed two settlements, one at either end. They were making for the northern location, which was up against the shore and boasted high, strong walls, as opposed to the southern spot, which appeared to stand higher and deeper in.

"That's Dveep Kile," Sanga told her as he passed. "The other is Khet Parivar, Jasleen Lal's khet. Can't reach it from the sea at all, only from a river within the island."

Ah. Ruhi considered that. So the Lals had both a stronghold and a plantation on the same island, and outsiders couldn't get to the latter except through the former? Clever. It must have been difficult finding an island with the right geography to accommodate such a pairing, which explained why they were this far from Surpakat. But probably worth it for security and self-sufficiency.

Approaching the durga's harbor, Ruhi was surprised and slightly alarmed to see a heavy chain slung across the opening, dangling from thick stone towers on either side. Men stood watch from both but made no move to lower the chain and let them pass.

Kosala signaled, and the crew furled sails, letting the *Shikra* slow and finally drift to a stop with its carved prow tapping the thick, barnacle-encrusted chain.

"I am the Raja Kosala!" she called out, her voice carrying easily over the mild breeze. "Lower the jal dvaar and let me pass!"

One of the men on the leftmost tower shook his head. "None shall pass without the raja's permission," he replied, his own voice deep and strong.

"*I* am a raja, and I demand entrance!" Kosala snapped back. "I am here by order of the Parishad itself!"

But the guard stood fast. "We await word from the raja," was all he answered as Ruhi saw another man burst from the tower below and disappear at a run into the stronghold at large.

They waited, the waves causing them to bump against the chain, Kosala growing visibly angrier with each moment that passed. Finally the runner reappeared, leading someone else toward the tower. Once they'd climbed it and emerged onto the guard balcony, Ruhi saw it was a woman, small and slight, with fierce features and a thick plait of dark hair. Even from here, her resemblance to Jasleen Lal was uncanny.

"Go away," the woman stated without preamble. "Whoever you are, you're not welcome here."

"Antara," Kosala called back, standing straight and proud at the prow. "It is Kosala. I'm here at your mother's behest, and that of the Parishad as a whole. Lower the chain and let us moor. Please." That last was grudgingly added, for all the good it seemed to do.

"My mother?" Antara Lal laughed, the bitterness in that sound all too clear. "She's an old fool, doddering away her last years in that town of hers. She's left the real work to me and my sisters, and I rule here, not her. Now go away."

Kosala seemed on the verge of losing her temper—a rare sight, and not one Ruhi could imagine helping the situation any—so Ruhi stepped up and cleared her throat, drawing both women's attention.

"Raja Lal," she started, bowing deeply, for she'd gathered this was who the guard had meant before. "My name is Rawal Chera. My brother Sundra and I have been charged by the Parishad to look into the disappearance of your thalakurios, Makiya. Might we be permitted to dock and come ashore to speak with you and your people about the matter?"

Antara considered only a moment before finally nodding. "You and your brother may dock," she declared, before directing a nasty grin at Kosala. "The rest of you will wait there beyond the chain. Unless you care to try your luck against all my guards?"

Ruhi's employer opened her mouth but then shut it with an audible click of her jaw. "We will wait here," she stated finally with all the stiff dignity of an affronted regal.

Turning away, she waved for the crew to lower one of the *Shikra*'s two rampini, and Ruhi hastened to climb into the narrow, mastless boat, as did Sundra. Together they clung to the built-in benches as the small vessel was lowered over the side and began bobbing about on the water. Ruhi felt her stomach burble in protest despite the bracelet on her wrist, but ignored that as best she could, focusing on the land she saw over her brother's shoulder, beyond the chain.

"Just do what I do," Sundra whispered, taking up a pair of teak oars from the bottom of the boat and sliding them into brass oarlocks on either side. Ruhi copied him and then began hauling on the oars when he did, making sure to push when he pulled so that they rowed together rather than canceling each other out. The little rampini fit beneath the sea chain where it rose by the tower, and they merely ducked their heads to glide past and into the harbor.

Ruhi's arms and shoulders were on fire by the time they reached the shore, and her palms burned as well where the wood had left them raw. Sundra, curse him, didn't seem any the worse for wear as he hopped out onto the wooden dock and offered her a hand up, though at least he didn't rub it in. Antara Lal had already descended and stood waiting, several vicious-looking pirates massed behind her.

"Put these on," the pirate queen ordered, and one of the men handed each of them a rough burlap sack. "Over your heads."

"Why—?" Sundra started to ask, but that same pirate stepped forward and punched him in the stomach, doubling him over. He coughed, gasping for air, and straightened, a retort already on his lips, but Ruhi grabbed his arm.

"Don't," she urged, tugging her own sack over her head.

She could only assume her so-called brother had done the same, because she didn't hear any more sounds of violence. A second later, someone shoved her forward and said, "Start walking."

Without being able to see where she was going, the walk felt endless. Ruhi stumbled more than once, eliciting laughs from her captors, though rough hands did haul her upright before she could actually sprawl on the ground. She supposed that was something.

After a time, her legs and sides aching and her head throbbing, Ruhi was pulled to a stop. Then the bag was yanked free, and she blinked, breathing clean air once more. They were standing before a solid two-story building, and she immediately thought "jail" when she saw its thick walls and barred windows. It reminded her of the stormers' home back in Riyaasat, and she remembered Koliya's comment about how Jasleen Lal treated her weather mages—and the older raja's own mention of her daughter not letting them slip away so easily.

"He lived here," Antara stated now, stepping into view on their left. "Along with the twins Utaya and Utama. Makiya disappeared almost a month ago, now. No idea how or where." She scowled, which Ruhi thought was most likely her default expression, judging from the lines on her face. "I run a tight ship, no deserters."

Was that because they didn't want to desert, or because you didn't give them the option, Ruhi thought but knew better than to say. Especially since she was sure it was the latter.

She reached for the door, which Ruhi thought looked oddly loose in its frame, but Sundra stopped her.

"You keep them locked up?" he asked Jasleen's daughter instead.

She glared even as she nodded, but he hadn't been asking just to protest such treatment—instead, he nudged the door, which immediately slid inward a few inches. It was open!

"Did you say those twins were still here?" was his next question.

Ruhi wanted to laugh at the way their unpleasant hostess responded. Antara's jaw dropped, her eyes shocked wide, but only for an instant before she purpled with rage.

"They were here this morning! Get to the docks and find them!" she snapped, and her men took off, racing back through the streets and leaving her alone with the two of them.

"What are they good at?" Sundra asked, and it took a second for the raja to register his presence or his question. "They're weather mages, but what in particular are the twins good at?" he restated.

"Wind," she answered distractedly. "They're strongest with wind. Why?"

"Because you sent your men to the docks," Ruhi put in, catching on. "But that's the obvious way out. If the twins just got free and are looking to escape, and they control wind, they're not heading that way."

And she and Sundra both turned south and east, toward the plantation they could clearly see from here—and the tall cliff it sat upon. A cliff that a mage might use strong winds to carry him from, much like a leaf drifting out to sea.

After a single, startled glance, Antara took off running, and Ruhi and Sundra immediately followed her. Dveep Kile proved to be a small stronghold, fortunately, and though its streets were narrow and twisty, the woman clearly knew her way around, and never paused or hesitated. It was perhaps only ten minutes later that they burst onto a second, smaller set of docks, this one at the city's back and facing onto a narrow, swift river. Several flat-bottomed boats sat there, some still evidently loaded with supplies from the plantation—and a man was just raising the sail on a small boat by the far end.

A broad-shouldered man wearing a pagri of a particular blue-green.

"Stop him!" Antara bellowed, causing every worker along the dock to look up, then follow her gesture. The mage saw it as well, and laughed.

Sundra sped by Antara, paused to scoop up something from an open barrel, and ran right out to the water's edge.

"You'll never get me now!" the mage shouted back, waving his hand and causing the sail to suddenly billow out, the little boat leaping forward. "Stormer solidarity!"

Ruhi watched her friend stop, toss what looked like a wood apple in his hand once, then rear back and fling it as hard as he could.

It was a good, solid throw, but likely to fall short nonetheless. Until the raja beside them pointed her own hand at the airborne fruit, which suddenly soared straight away as if shot from a bow. Apparently, she and Sundra weren't the only ones here with Gifts.

The small brown globe flew through the air—and connected solidly with the fleeing mage's head, striking his left temple with a resounding thud. The man staggered, fell against his boat's mast, and then toppled to his knees as the wind died away, the sail slackening and the boat slowing to a stop.

"Always hated those things," Sundra remarked, dusting off his hands as he turned back to rejoin her and Antara. "Good for throwing, though. Hurt like hells when they hit, too." He nodded at the raja, who nodded back, both tacitly acknowledging that working together had been the cause of their success.

Several dockworkers had already taken his place by the water, using long, hooked poles to catch the boat's stern and drag it back to shore. The mage was then pulled from his escape craft and hauled up in front of Antara.

"What do you think you're doing, Utama?" she demanded, getting in the still-dazed man's face. "And where's Utaya? For that matter, where's Makiya? What is going on here?"

He'd regained enough focus and composure to glare back at her. "I'm not talking," he insisted, clamping his mouth shut.

Antara grabbed him by the arm, then stared at the limb, hoisting it up in front of her face. "Where's your bracelet?" she shouted. "How did you get out of it?"

The mage laughed in her face, yanking his arm free. "Gone for good," he answered with a smirk. "Just like Makiya and my sister."

"We'll see about that." Some of her men had caught up to them, and Antara waved for them to drag the mage away before looking over at Sundra and Ruhi.

"Thank you," she grumbled. "He'd be long gone if you hadn't noticed and taken him out."

"Glad we could help," Ruhi responded, though inwardly she wasn't so sure. Still, if it put the other woman in a more cooperative mood, she meant to take advantage of that. "Can you tell us anything about Utama and his sister, or Makiya? Were there any signs of trouble before this?"

The raja's mouth twisted. "Complaints, you mean? All the time. Especially Makiya. Constantly griping about how he was treated." She sniffed. "But that's how it always is. People don't want to do the work, and they want a lot more credit and money and freedom than they deserve."

"So he complained a lot, and then he disappeared," Sundra reiterated, with a significant glance at Ruhi. Yes, she'd noticed too that this didn't quite match what Jasleen had said. Then again, she wasn't the one living here with the mages. "And you don't know how? Or where either he or Utama's sister are now?"

Antara shook her head. "He was just gone one day. Supposed to set sail and never showed, wasn't there when my men went to fetch him. As for Utaya, I've no idea. Until just now, I thought she and her brother were still at home where they belonged."

"And you knew they had to be, because they all wore bracelets." Sundra held up his wrist, revealing his own enchanted wristlet. "Like this one. So they were indentured?"

"Under contract," the raja corrected. Her scowl deepened. "And now they're in breach, the lot of them. Utama'll regret trying to cut and run on me, and if he knows where the others are, I'll get it out of him."

Ruhi repressed a shudder thinking how the fierce pirate intended to accomplish that. "If you do find anything out, could you let us know?" she managed instead. "We're heading back to Surpakat after this." At least she hoped so. Odd though it sounded, she was starting to miss the pirate town, which seemed almost warm and friendly after all this!

Antara nodded. "I will send word as soon as I have any," she promised, and held out her hand. First Ruhi then Sundra clasped it, both knowing better than to spurn such a gesture, and when the raja turned away, beckoning them to follow, she didn't bother with sacks. Apparently they'd earned at least that much trust.

"You're the two who caught Bhada Khatri and Nayak Laghari," she commented as they retraced their steps past the mage's home and toward the outer docks. She chuckled. "Bet they're all coming to you now, hat in hand, huh?"

Sundra nodded. "There have been requests for our support," he answered carefully.

Antara laughed outright. "Nicely worded! Yes, I'm sure there have been. Pack of vultures, circling so they can swoop in and pick the carcasses clean."

Spinning about to walk backward a few steps, she pointed at them both. "Eyes sharp," she warned. "You're not just potential advocates, you're possible bargaining chips, and some'll try collecting you to cash in." That advice delivered, the pirate queen pivoted back around and led them to their boat without another word.

"That was... exciting," Sundra commented quietly once they were rowing back toward the chain and the *Shikra* beyond. "I almost feel sorry for those mages."

"Same here," Ruhi agreed, keeping her voice just as low. "But did you hear what Utama said? 'Solidarity.' These aren't isolated incidents at all. There's someone behind all this, someone with an agenda. And he's bought into it. Makes you wonder how many of the others did, too."

Her companion nodded. "Maybe that's why one bedroom was messier than the others, at Riyaasat?" he suggested. "Two planned to go, and the third decided last minute?"

"Could be."

But that begged the obvious question—went where, exactly?

And what was this really all about? Ruhi had the feeling they were getting closer to the answer. She just wasn't sure she'd like it once they found it—or that she'd be happy about handing it over to the Parishad, given how some of them had been treating the people involved.

Chapter Twenty

SUNDRA

Sundra was glad that they didn't have to stop anywhere else on the way back to Surpakat. Nor, except for swinging wide to starboard to go around another storm—a lot of those out in these waters—did they have to deviate much. Even the weather stayed pleasant for the six days it took to get back, with fair skies and light clouds and a good, clean breeze broken only by that one brush with rain and stiffer winds. Honestly, he could have stayed aboard the *Shikra* forever.

That wasn't to be, of course, and soon enough they were sailing between the islands holding Bahut Saare and Riyaasat, with the long, almost crescent-shaped island home of Surpakat dead in their sights. They headed straight for the harbor there, returning to the same dock they'd left almost three weeks ago, and Sundra felt a pang at the thought of being stuck on dry land again.

That pang turned to a twisting in his gut when he saw the big, powerfully built figure waiting for them, his black vest blending into the shadows even as his red turban blazed forth like a torch over his craggy features.

Shivaji.

"I knew you'd have to come back eventually," the big pirate shouted up at the boat as it pulled in, effortlessly catching the rope Sanga tossed him and tying the ship fast to one of the mooring posts there. "You can't avoid me forever."

"What do you want, Shivaji?" Sundra asked, leaning on the railing. But the burly pirate shook his head.

"Come down here and face me!" he insisted, and even though he knew he shouldn't, Sundra nodded, if only to quell the shouting. Some of the others had been readying the gangplank, and he headed for it now, stopping only when both Kosala and Ruhi got in his way.

"Let me talk to him," he asked the raja. "I won't do anything stupid, and I don't think even he's dumb enough to try anything against an entire ship's crew."

She considered a moment, then backed up a step, twisting to the side to let him by. His supposed brother was next, but Sundra just patted her on the shoulder.

"I've got this," he promised, and she too chose to believe him.

Sundra just hoped their faith wouldn't prove misplaced.

Striding down the gangplank, he had to pause after the first step onto dry land. It was always so strange, transitioning back to that after being at sea. The ground seemed so rigid, so unyielding, and his legs had long since gotten used to the sway of a deck above the waves, so he found himself automatically trying to compensate, which only made him stagger like a drunk. Shivaji, watching, smirked but didn't comment. Surely the big pirate had felt the same disorientation himself.

Finally feeling that he could stand straight again, Sundra faced the other man and was reminded once again what a brute he was. Sanga was just as tall, but lean, whereas Shivaji was powerful as an ape, with a broad chest, wide shoulders, and thick arms. He could probably pick Sundra up and hurl him across the dock with one hand, and those massive hands were already clenching into fists.

"All right, I'm here," Sundra told him, trying to forestall any violence. Out of the corner of his eye he saw Kosala's crew raising spears and bows, but the fact that they'd swiftly avenge his sudden death was small comfort. "So talk."

"You've gotta help me," Shivaji announced, but his mouth worked like he didn't know how to shape the word that emerged next: "Please."

Sundra stared at the other man. "That's it? You want my help? After everything you did to me?"

The hefty pirate had tormented him during his and Ruhi's time working for Udayin, mostly at their shared master's bidding but sometimes just for his own amusement. And that had only gotten worse after the cruel young raja had died in Sundra's arms— Shivaji had blamed him, and tried to kill him more than once. True, they'd more or less made their peace after convincing the pirate that someone else had killed his employer, but that didn't erase their past.

Shivaji must have realized any attempt at an apology would ring hollow and do no good, or he simply never considered such a gesture. Either way, he launched into a different tack. "You know I deserve Udayin's ships," he insisted now. "I was his lieutenant! His right hand! No one deserves those ships more than me!"

"And if the Parishad agrees, they'll award some or all of those vessels to you," Sundra replied in his most soothing, placating tone. Though, privately, he couldn't picture the big, bullying man as a raja. Or at least he'd really rather not.

And right now, that man wasn't so easily consoled. "Who knows what they think, or what they'll do?" he snarled back. "Probably just take all the ships for themselves. But that's not right! I served him best! Those ships belong to me!"

He took a step forward, raising a big fist, and Sundra hastily retreated, raising his own hands to defend himself, though he knew that wouldn't help much of the powerful pirate did attack. If only he had a sword! "That's not up to me!" he reminded quickly. "I'm indentured, remember? Not even a free man like you."

"But your word carries weight with them," Shivaji pointed out with surprising awareness. "Yours and your brother's." Turning, he peered up at Ruhi, who stood by the railing, watching. "If you tell them I should have those ships, they'll listen." He leaned in close. "You owe me."

In an instant, anger drove fear away, allowing to Sundra to straighten and glare at the other man. "I owe you? For what? Beating on me? Trying to kill me? Threatening me? And you think that entitles you to those ships somehow?"

But Shivaji shook his head. "I helped you catch the real killer," he reminded now. "Without me, you and your brother and your own precious raja would've been the next ones to die."

That was at least partially true, much as Sundra hated to admit it. After agreeing to a temporary truce, Shivaji had aided in their plan to expose Bhadra Khatri's deception and trick the plantation owner into confessing. Could they have pulled it off without the big pirate? Maybe. Maybe not. But as far as Sundra was concerned, that just made them even, if anything. Besides which, it wasn't like Shivaji hadn't wanted Khatri caught, himself.

"And without us, *your* precious raja would never have been avenged," he countered, and tensed as Shivaji swelled, face darkening with rage. "So I'd say we helped each other," Sundra added quickly.

The big pirate stared down at him a second, but finally nodded. "Fine. So help me now, and I'll help you in turn." He grinned, which was not a pleasant sight. "A dinar for you and your brother, once the ships are mine. That's another chunk out of your indenture."

Now that was an interesting proposition, and Sundra paused to consider it. He and Ruhi still owed perhaps two dinar each. If he could talk Shivaji into one apiece, that would halve their remaining debt!

A sharp cough caused him to glance up to where Kosala was watching intently, and once she had his eyes, she shook her head ever so slightly. Ah. There was probably something in the pirate's code that prevented them from accepting such an obvious bribe. Because of course nothing was ever that easy.

"You know that won't work," he told the brutish pirate, and

the way the man grimaced told Sundra he was right. Damn it.

"I don't care!" Shivaji bellowed, rearing up to his full height. "I want those ships!" His fists raised up, and Sundra braced himself for the oncoming blow.

Instead there was a faint whooshing sound, and droplets struck his face—strays from the entire bucketful of water that had just drenched Shivaji.

And it was Ruhi who held the now empty bucket.

"You've said your piece," she stated clearly, glaring down at the sopping wet pirate, his sodden turban starting to unravel and sink down over his ears and forehead. "We heard you. We'll consider it. Now leave before you get struck with something a whole lot worse than water."

Beside her, Sanga drew back on a powerful bow, the wicked tip of his arrow pointing right at Shivaji's heart. A well-stated argument, indeed!

Even Shivaji thought so, as the big pirate shook his head, sending water flying everywhere. "Fine," he snapped. "But I expect those ships. Otherwise, there'll be trouble." Turning, he stomped away, the threat somewhat offset by the squelching sound of his drenched boots on the wooden planks and the way he had to grapple his turban to keep it from falling into his eyes and blinding him.

Only once the big man had gone did Sundra slump against a mooring post, taking in a long, deep breath. That had been close.

Chapter Twenty-one

SUNDRA

Sundra woke to someone pounding on the door. The room was too dark to make out much more than vague shapes and Ruhi was still asleep in her bed, judging by the faint sounds of snoring, which also told him it was still early as he stumbled to his feet and staggered to the door. Tugging it open, he found himself staring at Sanga.

"Get dressed," the tall pirate told him, his tone making it clear this was neither joke nor idle request. "Your brother, too."

"Right." Shutting the door, Sundra quickly stepped over and shook Ruhi's shoulder. Fortunately, she startled awake but didn't cry out—that might have been difficult to explain. "Get dressed," he told her, backing away hastily. "Sanga's at the door. Something's up."

She nodded and sat up, clutching her blankets close, and Sundra spun about, marching to the basin and splashing water on his face and hair. Then he managed to pivot and feel his way back to his own bed with his eyes tightly shut, shrugging into his shirt entirely by touch and memory.

"All set," Ruhi muttered, and he blinked, relieved to see in the pre-dawn gloom that she was already out of bed and dressed—and rewarding him with a grateful smile.

A minute later, hastily but adequately attired, they stepped out into the darkened hall, finding Sanga leaning against the opposite wall, waiting. If he had likewise hastily awakened, his demeanor and attire gave no indication.

"Come," was all the pirate said before leading them to their mutual employer's office. He rapped once and pushed the door open without waiting for a reply, motioning the two of them to follow him in.

The lamps had been lit here, so they were easily able to see Kosala seated at her desk, a handsome piece of furniture that resembled a ship with its polished teak and dark iron. The raja, also properly attired despite the early hour, was glaring at a parchment laying before her, and Sundra hoped she never had cause to direct such ire toward him.

"You've been summoned," she declared, shoving the offending paper forward and off her desk, and Ruhi hurried to catch it. Sundra sidled over to read with her. He'd assumed it was from the Parishad, though that wouldn't explain their employer's rage. Instead, he saw that he was only partially right.

"The Raja Koliya?" he asked when he reached the end of the terse missive, and the name grandly scrawled there above a seal. "He wants to see us? Why?"

"To get an update on this whole stormer affair," Kosala replied drily. "It says so right there."

She scowled, shaking her head and causing her thick braid to dance behind her from one shoulder to the other. "Of course, you can't trust a thing that oaf says. Or writes."

Ruhi was still frowning at the paper, most likely weighing their options, but Sundra understood the reality far better. "We can't refuse," he told her, glancing at Kosala for confirmation. "He's a raja, and part of the Parishad, and we're working for them right now. That gives him the right to insist upon an update in person."

Their own raja nodded. "It does, and he knows it," she agreed.

"Just as he knows I can't accompany you, or send Sanga or anyone else with you, not without basically telling everyone I don't trust him. Which I don't. But saying that so blatantly would start a war between us." She sighed. "You'll have to go alone."

Sundra dipped his head. "Just tell us how to get there," he said, taking the page from Ruhi. They'd need to bring it with them, no doubt.

Standing off to one side, Sanga laughed. "Just head up and to the right, all the way to the far end. You can't miss it."

This time Ruhi's frown was for the rangy pirate. "That's where Chetan lives."

A raised brow was the only indication that Kosala wondered how she knew this. They'd told her about enlisting the rough raja's aid, of course, but perhaps hadn't mentioned accosting him at his own compound.

"Just below him," was all she said. "On the water's edge."

"Ah." Sundra vaguely remembered seeing a few equally large buildings only a few blocks from the weather-beaten raja's equally unembellished home. "Well, best not to keep him waiting, I suppose." And, tugging on Ruhi's sleeve, he backed out of the room.

"Be careful," Kosala called after them. "I doubt he'd hurt you directly—that would have me coming for him, and he knows it—but with that fool, one can never be sure."

"Less than reassuring, thanks," Sundra muttered as he and his so-called brother headed for the door.

The Raja Koliya's home was indeed near Chetan's, though just far enough that you couldn't see one from the other. It was right along the water, as Kosala had said, with a single, long dock jutting straight out behind it, two smaller expanses angling off the first. The front of the building was big and rough, just like its owner, with a squared shape, a flat roof, and thick, squared columns in front. There had been clear attempts to elevate the architecture at a later date, judging by the ornamental structure perched on the roof and the fanciful swirls and patterns decorating the otherwise white exterior, glints of gold catching the early morning sunlight. Everything about the place said strength, power, and a belated desire to look good.

That, Sundra thought, described Koliya himself to a T.

Several pirates lounged about on the front porch beneath a garish skull-and-crossbones banner, swigging from ceramic pots of beer and playing at dice. They all glanced up as Sundra and Ruhi reached them, but no one yelled for them to stop as they slid past and made for the tall set of garishly yellow double doors. A short, stout older man greeted them there.

"Rawal and Sundra Chera, here to see the raja," Sundra told the fellow and displaying the letter they'd received.

The man gave it only a cursory glance before nodding and stepping aside, tugging the left-side door back far enough for them to enter.

Inside, the building was just as grand, solid, and decaying as the exterior. Koliya evidently didn't put much stock in appearances when he wasn't worried about others seeing them. The shorter man led them down a wide but shadow-filled hall to a room in the back corner. He knocked.

"Come!" That was unmistakably the raja, and the servant pushed the door open, ushering the two of them inside.

Sundra heard the latch once it slid shut again behind them and tried to ignore both that and the beads of sweat dripping down his chest.

If Kosala's desk looked like it belonged on a ship, Koliya's practically *was* a ship, or at least a raft, being a massive slab of dark wood simply laid across two heavy barrels. The raja himself lounged behind the makeshift contraption on a pile of pillows that could easily serve as someone's bed, and possibly more than one.

"There you are!" the big pirate lord boomed, waving them over. After some struggle he managed to extricate himself and rise to his feet, and Sundra had to gulp. He'd forgotten just how big the burly raja was, even bigger than Shivaji, as tall as Sanga or taller but twice or even thrice as wide, and none of it fat. The man's arms were nearly as thick as Sundra's head!

Still, it never did any good to show how scared you were. Instead Sundra swept into a bow. "We are at your service, raja, as always."

"Good, good!" Koliya grinned down at them. "How goes the hunt? Find Jasleen's missing mage yet?"

"Not yet, no," Ruhi replied carefully. "We are still putting the pieces together."

The enormous raja nodded, stroking his full beard. "Betcha they're either dead or gone," he stated after a second's thought. "And good riddance."

Sundra frowned. "You don't care what happened?"

That earned him a massive snort. "Why should I?" the pirate lord replied. "Never had one of those stormers working for me. Never will. More trouble'n they're worth, am I right?"

"I thought they provided a tremendous advantage—" Ruhi began before he cut her off.

"They can, if you handle 'em just right," he agreed. "But get it wrong, they blow up in your face. Who needs that?"

He thumped his broad chest. "I rely on me and mine, nothing else: strong backs, strong arms, sharp blades, and full sails. No magic involved or needed."

He winked at them. "The other rajas, we may rule together but we're still rivals—one of them loses something that valuable, that only makes me stronger, so I'm not exactly complaining about it."

"Someone," Ruhi corrected primly, and the powerful man laughed again.

"Nah, I meant what I said. They ain't people, they're tools, weapons. Locked up tight, taken out to use, then tucked away again the minute they're done. And if someone else loses their sword, it's no skin off my back. Especially if I have to worry it'll maybe get raised against me some day."

"But you went along with the Council's request for us to

investigate," Sundra pointed out. "And you summoned us here to provide a report on our progress."

"Eh, there wasn't any reason to argue it," their host explained, waving a hand expansively. "And this way they all feel they owe me." He grinned, teeth showing through his beard. "As for the summons, sounded like a good excuse, eh? Even your precious boss couldn't say no to that."

He folded his arms over his chest, as if to emphasize both's size and strength. "Truth is, you've got something I want."

Sundra managed to swallow the groan before it could emerge. Inside, though, all he could think was, *And here we go.*

At least the big raja didn't play coy. "Udayin and Vihaan's properties," he told them. "I want them. And you're going to give them to me."

Sundra had figured it was something like that but hadn't known if it was the ships, the money, or the properties—or all three. At least Koliya wasn't completely greedy?

"You know we don't actually get to determine that, right?" Sundra asked.

He practically felt Ruhi's glare at his tone, but he was tired of playing the obedient servant. Besides which, he figured someone like Koliya appreciated a little backtalk. As long as it wasn't too much.

Sure enough, the pirate lord chuckled. "No, but *you* know your word matters with all this." He grinned again. "What do you care, anyway? It's not like it can go to you. Put in a good word for me with those, and I'll help you in return."

Then his smile turned nasty as his eyes narrowed. "Don't, and I'll make things hard for you. Real hard. And real ugly. You may think you're safe with Kosala, but outside her house, you're as good as mine. Understand?"

"Understood," Ruhi practically squeaked, and her evident fear seemed to please the raja as much as Sundra's own defiance.

He patted them both on the shoulders—adding a little squeeze just to remind them how powerful those hands were—and then waved them away.

"Go on, now. Run on home." And Koliya turned his back on them, ending the audience. And demonstrating just how little he worried that they could do anything to harm him in return.

He was right about that part, at least, and Ruhi quickly retreated. Sundra moved a bit more slowly, his own temper on the rise, but finally let his "brother" drag him away.

"You know there's nothing you can do, and if you anger him, he could snap," she whispered once they were safely out of the room and following the same servant back toward the exit. "We need to go, while we still can."

She had a point. Koliya was a bully, if a smarter one than expected, and Sundra had seen plenty of those, enough to know that, if enraged, the man wouldn't hesitate to lash out, rules or no rules. They were only protected as long as he kept his cool, no matter what Kosala had said. No point in pushing the matter and putting themselves in danger, especially when they had nothing to gain by it.

CHAPTER TWENTY-TWO

RUHI

Ruhi was on edge from the meeting. Having Koliya threaten them had driven home the fact that, in her current guise, a man like that wouldn't hesitate to attack and injure her. It was a circumstance she really hadn't considered when she'd set out from home.

She was worrying over the repercussions when six men suddenly emerged from behind a cart and charged straight at her and Sundra.

The sextet looked like any other pirates she'd seen. They were tanned and weathered from so much sun and sea air, with hard muscles from crewing a ship and hard eyes from preying on others. They wore vests and trousers, boots and either turbans or head-bands, and nothing else. But their weapons caught her eye. Because these men didn't have talwars or even teghas. Instead, they each hefted short, solid-looking wooden clubs. Which was still plenty, since neither she nor Sundra were armed.

"Look out!" she shouted. Sundra reacted instantly, shoving her away and himself back at the same time. The club aimed at his head whooshed through the space he'd just been. The one targeting her did the same.

Then Ruhi stumbled into the man who'd just tried to knock her out.

"Oof!" He fell back as well, grunting as her shoulder slammed into his chest. Then again when her elbow struck his stomach.

Remembering the self-defense lessons Ganath and a few of the others had impressed upon her, Ruhi followed through with a swift kick—right between her attacker's legs.

He doubled over, squealing, then fell to the ground, clutching his injured groin. The club dropped from his hand, clattering onto the cobblestones. Ruhi quickly scooped that up, just in time to block a strike from one of the others.

She caught a quick glimpse of Sundra sidestepping a blow and punching his assailant full in the nose. That was all she had time to notice before the pirate facing her lunged.

Ruhi had no weapons training—but she had grown up working the warehouse, which included wielding a broom. And, more than once, she'd had to use that implement to fend off workers, passing laborers, messengers, and even the occasional client, playfully or otherwise. This club was both shorter and thicker than a broom handle, but she found it easier to use than a sword. There was no worrying about cutting herself or having the blade turned the wrong way round.

The man attacking her was clearly stronger than she was, but she was taller. That meant she could swing at him and he couldn't reach her. At least, not right away. She wasn't sure how long she could keep this up.

Meanwhile, the other men were circling, biding their time. That wasn't good.

Sundra had defeated his first opponent as well, and armed himself with the man's club. He laid about with a flurry of swings and strikes, all of which showed he had been trained in such things. That was good, anyway. Ruhi put her back up against him, which also helped.

But at least one of the remaining pirates was as tall as she was and broader across the shoulders, with thick arms. He'd be able to reach her, and she doubted she could fend off many blows with that much strength behind them.

She got in a lucky hit, catching one of the other men under the chin and sending him toppling. When he righted himself, leaping back to his feet with a snarl, there was blood dripping down his front and murder in his eyes. He dropped his club and drew a long, curved dagger from his belt instead.

But the man next to him struck the blade from his hand. "None of that!" the second one warned. "We need 'em alive!"

"Not both of 'em!" the bleeding pirate snapped. But after retrieving both weapons he sheathed the dagger, raising the club instead. "Fine, but doesn't mean I can't make it hurt," he told Ruhi with a cruel smirk.

Her response was to kick him between the legs, hard as she could. When he dropped, she pounced and snatched that dagger, which she thrust toward Sundra.

"Try this!" she offered. He nodded his thanks, tossing the sheath aside to wield blade in one hand, club in the other.

For her part, Ruhi snagged the fallen man's club for herself. She used the crossed pair to block the big pirate's first downward swing. The blow's force still jolted her back, but she was able to shove his club away.

Whether she could continue doing so until Sundra could help, remained to be seen.

She heard footsteps behind her but couldn't glance away from her assailant. A second sound, however, mixed in with those.

It was the sound of something small and metallic striking the ground hard, over and over between steps.

Ruhi smiled. She knew that noise.

"Stop!" someone shouted from that direction. "Explain yourselves!"

The remaining pirates—they were down half their number—sneered and cursed, but didn't answer otherwise.

Nor did they let up their attacks.

Ruhi gasped as she took a blow to one arm, dropping one club as that side lost any strength. Behind her, she heard Sundra grunt in pain as well.

"Stop at once!" the voice was closer now. "By order of the Town Guard!"

Still the pirates attacked, and Ruhi did her best to block or dodge.

Then a long, gleaming spear arced down in front of her. It knocked a club aside before spinning back up and kicking the weapon free of its owner's grasp. At the same time, a man in sturdy armor and a conical, metal helm stepped in front of her, shielding her from additional attempts.

The guard's partner moved to join him. Together they brandished their long spears at the startled pirates.

"Leave at once or be charged with assaulting the guard," the one on the right warned.

The pirates glared at her, especially the big one—but after a few seconds they grumbled and turned away.

It was only after they'd gone that Ruhi realized two guards had stationed themselves by Sundra's side as well.

No wonder those thugs had run!

"You hurt?" Sundra asked her, locating the dagger's sheath and reuniting that with the blade before sliding the whole thing into his belt.

Ruhi shook her head. "You?"

"No, I'm fine." He rubbed the back of his neck, but more sheepishly than anything. "That was wild."

"What exactly happened?" That was from one of the guards, a solid woman with green eyes and hints of gray in her hair beneath the helmet.

"They attacked us," Sundra replied. "We'd just been speaking with the Raja Koliya. They were hiding here and jumped out once we'd passed." He frowned. "Mostly they were using clubs, though. So they weren't looking to kill us."

The four guards exchanged glances. "You work for Koliya?"

Sundra managed to laugh at that one. "Not exactly, no." He

nudged Ruhi, but not too hard. "Show them the paper."

Oh, right! Ruhi plucked the writ from her vest and unfolded it before sharing it with their rescuers. They read it through, and she saw their posture change, becoming straighter and stiffer as they cast sidelong glances at her and Sundra. Funny what a little note from the ruling class could do!

"We should report this to the captain," one of the other guards suggested as they returned the paper, and Ruhi didn't think she'd imagined the sudden smile that showed briefly on her so-called brother's face.

"You're absolutely right," he agreed quickly, even eagerly. "In fact, you should take us to Captain Pillai. We can tell her ourselves."

Again the shared glances, but finally the guards shrugged. "Fine."

Sundra caught Ruhi's eye and winked—and she rolled her eyes at him. This was his cunning plan, to go seek Pillai for help? Or just for any reason at all?

Still, it wasn't a bad idea to keep the guard commander updated on their progress. And on the threats they'd faced.

Maybe she could help them make sense of it all.

The guard headquarters, an imposing, turreted structure made of big, thick blocks of some orangish, local stone, was down past the Pirate Line, which meant traipsing all the way through the older half of the city and then continuing on beyond that.

At least they were safe now, Ruhi thought as they walked, literally surrounded by guards. No one would be stupid enough to attack them again with such an escort.

The massive, double doors were shut tight, but one of the guards rapped on it with her spear. A small panel slid open, and the guard within took one look and then opened that side so they could all enter. Their companions wasted no time in leading her and Sundra to a side door set in the outer wall and up a narrow flight of stairs just inside there. Ruhi remembered the route from a previous trip and so was unsurprised when they climbed three stories to the wall's top floor, then went down a narrow corridor to a door in the building's back corner.

Last time, they had snuck in here when the commander was absent. This time, one of the guards knocked, and Ruhi heard Pillai call, "Come in!" from inside.

Pillai's office hadn't changed. It was still a good-sized room, well lit, partially by the two narrow windows in the outer wall but more by the heavy iron chandelier suspended overhead. Shelves covered one whitewashed side wall and an enormous, wooden cabinet the other, while a plain, wooden desk sat square in the center. The leader of the town guard was seated behind that, but rose as they entered.

"This is a surprise," she said. "What happened?" That last was to the guards, who quickly explained about the conflict they'd interrupted.

Pillai listened, then dismissed her people, though not before assuring them they'd done the right thing.

"All right, what's really going on?" she asked Ruhi and Sundra once the guards had left. "Knowing you two, it wasn't just some random attack."

Sundra nodded, rubbing the back of his neck. "No, probably not," he agreed. "They had orders not to kill us, anyway." He shrugged. "Maybe it was a warning? Or a threat?"

"Great," Ruhi muttered. "Two of those in one day." When the guard captain glanced her way, eyebrow raised, she explained about their meeting with Koliya, and the threats he'd made.

"Don't worry about it," Pillai assured her. "He can't touch you. You're under Kosala's direct protection, and he doesn't have the authority to go against another raja. None of them do. It'd be different if he caught you out on the open water or something, but he can't really attack you while you're here. That's the whole point, that Surpakat is neutral territory."

A thought occurred to Ruhi, though. "What if it's not anymore?"

she asked. "What if he could make good on his threat—because he's got influence here now? The same way Kosala has in Enkar Bindu."

It only took her so-called brother an instant to catch on. "Oh!" he exclaimed. "Right! Power without responsibility! But how?"

Ruhi had just remembered something, though. "I think I know." And she recounted the scene from before they'd left, when she'd seen a woman ordering guards away from a ship.

"I'd wondered who she was," she recalled. "Because she clearly had some authority, but I didn't recognize her."

Pillai was scowling even more than usual. "That does sounds like Chennama. And yes, my men would've obeyed her. So would I, if she gave me a direct order. I wouldn't have a choice."

"And the banner." Ruhi scowled. "A skull and crossbones, with gold hoops on the skull and a dagger between its gold teeth. We just saw the same one—hanging over Koliya's front door." She'd been too distracted to make the connection at the time, but now it was unmistakable.

"That's it, then," Sundra insisted. He turned toward Pillai. "You thought she might be up to something or hiding something. Sounds like she is. Like the fact that she's working for someone else besides the governor. Someone like a certain big, loud-mouthed raja."

Pillai paced back and forth behind her desk, thinking. "So you're saying she works for him, and thus he's taken charge? Or at least has some extra pull and some say in how things go?" She frowned, smacking one hand into the other. "Maybe." Then she shook her head. "But even if that's true, it's not like I could prove it."

She nodded at Ruhi. "You say you saw her there on the docks, but all she has to do is deny it, then it's your word against hers. Or come up with some excuse for why he had a right to that ship and she was merely expediting a just claim. We'd need something more definitive. But I just captain the guard, that's it. I don't even know what she's been up to since taking office."

Sundra shifted from foot to foot like he was nervous or excited or both. "I might be able to help with that," he said after a second.

"But I need some money to do it."

The captain speared him with a sharp gaze. "Do I want to know?" But she was already digging in her belt pouch, and handed over a pair of daniq. "That do?"

"It should, and no, you probably don't," he replied, taking the small gold coins. "Back soon." Then he'd done an about-face and was heading for the door.

Pillai glanced her way as Sundra exited, but Ruhi shrugged.

"No idea either," she admitted.

Her brain had been turning over the question of proof as well, wishing she could offer more than a distant glimpse from that previous incident, trying to think of how they could come by anything new. Suddenly she flashed back to a time when she and her father had suspected one of their workers had been selling information about their goods and shipments to a rival—but hadn't known which one was to blame.

Ruhi grinned. "What if we could get that proof?" she asked. "What if we could see, once and for all, if Chennama's working for Koliya, or anybody, really?"

Pillai came around the desk, stopping right in front of Ruhi, arms crossed over her chest. "I'm all ears," the guard captain promised. "What've you got in mind?"

Ruhi smiled and rubbed her hands together. "First off, we're gonna need…"

CHAPTER TWENTY-THREE

SUNDRA

Sundra groaned. "Why'd I let you talk me into this, again?" he asked as he staggered down the hall and toward the front door, slinging his jhola bag—the one Meera had made, and had given him when they first arrived—over his shoulder. Only a few of the other residents were awake and stirring, and the sun had not yet crested the horizon.

"I didn't talk you into anything," Ruhi hissed over her shoulder as she led the way. "You agreed to this, remember?"

"I didn't agree to it this early! But fine." He scrubbed at his face with one hand, trying to shake off his fatigue and fuzzy-headedness. "Let's just get it over with."

They headed out through the nearly quiet house, only a few of the others being already awake, but when they reached the end of the little front path Sundra turned right instead of left.

"Um, you know we have to go north to get to the docks, right?" Ruhi asked, stopping where she was.

He turned, however, walking backwards so he could grin at her. "I know. We need to make a quick stop first. Come on."

Then, with a pivot on his heel, he faced front again, still moving.

Which he felt ought to be impressive, considering he'd been asleep only a few minutes ago.

Ruhi sighed but hurried to catch up, her longer legs letting her close the gap quickly. "Does this have anything to do with your idea the other day?" she asked.

He nodded. "It does. But it'll only work if we hurry." And he increased his pace, leading them through the Pirate Line and down to the lower, newer portion of the city.

Once they'd passed the Quiet Fire, he was sure Ruhi began to suspect their destination, especially when they also passed the guardhouse. She didn't ask, though, and Sundra didn't say anything. Let her wonder.

A few minutes later, they entered an impressive stretch of ornamental public gardens. Sundra didn't stop to admire the carefully planted flowers and neatly trimmed hedges, however. Instead he made straight for the faceted, red brick building at the garden's center, its golden dome already catching the first rays of the morning light.

The governor's office.

"What are we doing here?" Ruhi finally asked, trying to grab his arm, but he tugged free and kept moving—skirting the double doors that were the building's main entrance and instead going to a smaller, single door positioned within one of the white stone arches around the side. There he knocked quickly.

After a minute, they heard a click, and the door slid open a crack, just enough to see someone peering out at them from within.

"There you are!" It was a woman's voice, young and sweet if slightly annoyed.

A second later the speaker yanked the door open further and slipped through. She was around their age and very appealing, with a pretty, heart-shaped face beneath her plain dulpatta and lovely curves visible even through her simple ghagra and sari. She was also clutching a sheaf of papers to her impressive chest.

"I'm sorry, Tanvi," Sundra told her, bowing. "We got here as quickly as we could. Is that it?"

"Yes." She held out the papers, but didn't let go when Sundra reached out to take them. "Remember what you promised."

"Of course," he answered. Leaning in, he kissed her cheek, and she flushed, releasing the papers as a big smile spread across her face.

"Dinner it is," Sundra continued, straightening. "My next rest day, I'm all yours."

She giggled at that, and then, with a distracted nod to Ruhi, ducked back through the door, shutting it behind her after one last, lingering glance in Sundra's direction.

"Now we can go," Sundra stated triumphantly, sliding the papers into his bag.

"Who was that, exactly, and what are those papers?" Ruhi demanded, taking charge this time and heading away from the governor's offices, back up through the Pirate Line and then north and east, toward the docks, at as quick a pace as she dared.

Along the way Sundra thought he saw someone going the opposite direction wearing a gleaming helmet and carrying a long spear, but he didn't point them out, and they didn't pause to check.

"That was Tanvi," he answered instead, keeping up easily. "She's a scribe, works for the governor. She caught my eye when we were here dealing with all that other unpleasantness, and we've chatted a few times since."

That elicited a half-groan, half-chuckle from his "brother." "Leave it to you to notice a pretty girl while in the midst of trying to solve a murder," she muttered.

"What can I say? I'm good at multi-tasking. And the papers—" He grinned. "I'll save that for when we're all together."

"We" in this case meant the two of them and Pillai, because the guard captain was waiting right where they'd agreed, along one of the docks in front of the Parishad's meeting space. She was perched on a mooring post, but hopped down as they approached, looking as alert and ready for action as ever.

"I sent Dhavak with the message just a few minutes ago," she explained when they reached her. "Chennama should have heard it by now."

Ruhi nodded, leaning against another post. "I think I saw him pass us. So we wait."

"While we do, I'll read over some of this," Sundra announced, pulling the papers out and brandishing them like an odd trophy. "A copy of the agenda for the next Parishad meeting, or at least the governor's portion of it—and copies of any new legislation he's proposing there."

Pillai was normally hard to read, with her usual stoic nature and default stern expression, but now she gaped at him, her mouth hanging open.

"What? How did you even get that? You shouldn't have that!" She reached for it, but Sundra skipped back a step, holding the papers up out of reach.

"I told you you didn't want to know, and you don't," he reminded her gleefully. "Better that way. But if Chennama's really doing Koliya's bidding, I'm betting there'll be something in here that works in his favor."

"Even so—" Pillai started, but stopped as Ruhi, who'd been keeping an eye out across the bay, tapped her on the arm.

"Look." The guard commander turned to follow Ruhi's gaze, as did Sundra, and all three watched as someone hurried into a big, fortress-like house perched at the very edge of the city, right along the water.

Koliya's house. And the boy who'd just entered had been wearing the clothes of a clerical worker rather than a pirate.

"All right, she took the bait," Ruhi said with some satisfaction. This had been her plan, after all. "Now let's see if *he* does."

They didn't have to wait long. A small army of men and women came pouring out of the house almost immediately, heading for the single, long dock jutting out from the house—and particularly for a massive boat sitting anchored at the farther of the two sections extending off that main branch. A moment later, another man followed, this one much bigger than the others, his thick beard and bright turban visible even at this distance.

Koliya.

The raja headed for the same ship the others had, and a few minutes later they'd cast off their mooring ropes, raised their sails, and edged out of the harbor, onto the open sea. Within minutes, they were gone from sight.

"So," Pillai said, turning back to them now that the boat was gone. "Chennama gets word that there's trouble at Sharan, alerts Koliya, and he heads out at once."

Sharan was the pirate lord's stronghold, which Pillai had told them yesterday was little more than a bolt-hole in case he needed refuge and couldn't reach Surpakat. But clearly it was still too valuable an asset for him to risk losing.

"Which means she is reporting to him," Ruhi added. "We've got her!"

But the guard captain shook her head. "All we have is proof that the lieutenant governor warned one of the rajas about a problem with some of his own property. That doesn't mean she's working for him—she'll say she was just being a good neighbor, keeping the peace, and there's nothing to prove otherwise."

"Not from that, maybe," Sundra agreed, looking up from the papers he'd continued studying. "But this will." He held up one of the pages. "One of the new regulations being proposed. They want to rezone the northeast corner of Surpakat, bringing it more in line with the rest in terms of dock ownership and usage. Specifically, they want to restrict those with homes along the water from having more than two docks per residence."

Pillai shook her head. "So?" She glanced back across the water—they'd chosen this vantage specifically because they could see Koliya's house so easily from here. "He has only the one dock, it won't even affect him."

"No, it won't," Sundra confirmed. "But whose house is that next to his?"

He pointed to another large structure by the water, this one just a little to the left of Koliya's. It was not as big but had a cleaner, more refined look to it, with its whitewashed walls, red-tiled roof, and pair of window bays to either side of a handsome front porch.

Their companion caught her breath. "Ehsaan's," she answered after a second. "That's the Raja Ehsaan's house."

No one had to point out the obvious—in front of the quiet raja's home were no fewer than three docks, with two more to the side that were probably his as well.

"So this new ruling would mean he had to get rid of all but two of those," Sundra pointed out. "That'd hurt him a great deal, I'd imagine. And Koliya would be all the stronger for it." Exactly as the big pirate had said—anything that weakened his rivals helped him.

"He would, but there's nothing stopping Ehsaan from building his own docks out further and adding bends to them," Ruhi argued, though she didn't sound entirely sure about that.

Nor should she, since Koliya's position at the end gave him more leeway with docking his boats. And for all they knew there were preexisting restrictions about rebuilding docks—Koliya's were already that hooked shape, but Ehsaan might not be able to copy the idea with his own.

Plus, Sundra wasn't finished. "All right, what about this, then?" he asked, turning to another page. "This one's petitioning for the city to seize control of any unclaimed properties left behind by dead pirates, to be sold off by city officials at their discretion, the money to go into Surpakat's city funds for use in things like government salaries and public works."

He studied the bottom of that paper, frowning. "It says here that, in the matter of certain recently freed properties, there have already been inquiries, which should be allowed to count as first bids and grant the bidder first option to purchase."

He looked up. "Any guesses as to who that might be? Because it has his name right here."

Ruhi shook her head, and Sundra guessed from her expression that a tiny part of her couldn't help being impressed by the big raja's brazen actions. He certainly found himself admiring the pirate lord's boldness, at least a little.

"So the city would claim all of Udayin and Vihaan's property for itself, selling them off to the first bidder—and Koliya's already got bids in for them! Nothing blatant there," Ruhi said.

"Not at all," Sundra agreed, grinning. "But that was his mistake. Because now we've got him for sure." He offered Pillai the papers. "Here's your proof!"

But the guard captain held up her hand. "I can't take those," she warned. "They were obtained illegally."

Sundra stared at her, and so did Ruhi. "You're going to let something like scruples stop you from bringing them both down?"

That only made Pillai straighten more, thrusting out her chin. "That's right. Otherwise, I'm no better than they are."

"That's not—" Sundra started, unable to believe what he was hearing. "They're—and you're—do you know what I had to do to get these?" He waved the papers in her face. "And now you won't even use them?"

She only shook her head, and Sundra admired her more than ever, even as he hated the idea of Koliya getting away with this.

Though the two were not necessarily one and the same, he realized as his so-called brother spoke up.

"So you can't take the papers," Ruhi said slowly, clearly piecing things together in her head. "But at least now we know what they're up to. And that means we have a chance to stop it—even if it won't let us call them out for it, we can still scuttle their plans."

Pillai flashed a quick, grateful smile. "Now *that* I would very much like to do," she agreed. "As long as it's not illegal or dishonest, I'm in."

"Not at all," Ruhi promised her, evidently warming to her own idea. "We're just going to mention a few things to a few people. No need for you to be involved at all."

She stepped away from the post, brushing off her trousers as she did. "Come on, Sundra. We need to pay a friend a visit."

He grumbled a little, but didn't argue, and fell into step as they left the dock. "I can't believe it," he muttered as they headed north again. "After all that!"

Ruhi laughed. "Oh, you can't tell me you won't enjoy having dinner with that pretty scribe," she teased. "And I notice you didn't say anything about the money you got from Pillai, either. I thought that was to bribe her?"

"It was," Sundra admitted, chuckling himself as his bad mood dissipated. "But Tanvi was more interested in dinner, so I guess the money can go toward paying for that—and you're right, I don't mind that at all." He shoved the papers back into his bag. "So, where are we going now?"

Ruhi told him, and this time he did laugh. "Oh, that'll do it," he agreed. "Nice!"

They were both smiling as they passed Ehsaan's home and continued onward toward another house in the very topmost corner, just below the walls.

Sundra just hoped the man they sought was in—and that he was in a listening mood.

CHAPTER TWENTY-FOUR

RUHI

Ruhi sat back with a groan, reaching one hand behind her to rub her aching back. It was nearly noon, and she'd been nose-deep in accounts since dawn. Who'd have thought that being gone less than three weeks could result in so much paperwork?

Unfortunately, even though she'd begun to drill a few basic bookkeeping concepts into Sanga's head, the rest of Kosala's staff was either too dense or too stubborn to learn—and Sanga had been with her on the *Shikra*, leaving people like Madhav and Angad to make any necessary purchases around the place. And, it seemed, many unnecessary ones, as well. Three full bushels of apples? Ruhi knew Sundra used the fruits as both goads and rewards when training Kosala's horses, but the raja only had a handful of the great big beasts! How many apples could they eat?

Fortunately, she was slowly getting the accounts back in order. Another day or two and she should have everything tallied correctly again. Until the next trip, or until she could finally convince some of the other staff to follow her instructions.

A knock at the door drew her attention. "Yes?" she called out, and the door creaked open, revealing Ilan's big-eyed face.

"Pardon, shri, but there's a raja here to see you," the man said softly, glancing apprehensively behind him. "You and your brother both."

Ruhi frowned. Kosala was off somewhere, and Sanga with her, which meant there wasn't anyone in the house who'd dare bar a raja from entry.

But who'd come here looking for her and Sundra? She'd have heard stomping and shouting if it was Koliya, and besides, the big bully clearly liked making people come to him. Not to mention, he was halfway to his stronghold by now. Chetan would have sent a message asking to meet somewhere.

Regardless, it wasn't like she could refuse one of the pirate lords. Pushing her chair back from the big desk, Ruhi stood, groaning as her back and legs protested.

"Show them in, Ilan," she told him. "And then go get my brother, please."

Nodding quickly, her fellow servant pushed the door open and stepped aside. "This way, Raja," he said, bowing deeply as a slim, narrow-faced woman slid past him and into the office. It was Falguni.

"Thank you," she told Ilan, who hastily backed away down the hall, still bowing.

The sharp-eyed raja then turned her attention to Ruhi. "Shri Chera," she said, moving past her and claiming the newly vacant chair as her due. She'd only just seated herself when Sundra appeared in the doorway. "And Shri Chera," she added. "Excellent."

"My apologies, Raja," Sundra stated, bowing. "We were not expecting you, and I was working the horses."

Indeed, some strands of hay clung to his sleeves, though his wet, slicked back hair suggested he'd at least dunked his head in a trough before coming inside.

Falguni waved that away. "I understand Kosala is out at the moment," she said instead. "Please extend my apologies when she returns. I was not intending to intrude here without her knowledge and permission, but this couldn't wait."

She leaned forward, her eyes intense. "Another stormer has disappeared. One of mine. Farah."

She shook her head. "She was at Khajaana, my durga. I just got the message that she's gone, vanished, no sign of her anywhere." She scowled. "You need to find her!"

Sundra moved a little closer with small, careful steps. "Do you know if she ever expressed any unhappiness at being there?" he asked carefully, his voice calm and low. As if he were trying to soothe a skittish horse. Which wasn't inappropriate, given Falguni's bright but narrowed eyes, tooth-baring grimace, and clenched fists. Was she about to attack them?

But the raja merely shook her head. "No, nothing like that," she insisted. "She was happy where she was. I know it."

Ruhi carefully perched on the corner of the big desk, far enough from Falguni to not feel presumptuous. "Was she… under contract?" she asked, tapping her own indenture bracelet to make sure their visitor took her meaning.

She wasn't surprised when the raja nodded. "Of course. Do you have any idea how impossible it is to find an unclaimed stormer? I put her under contract the second I discovered her. Same with Shifa and Pranav. You find a mage available, you snap them up right then and there."

Ruhi could see that her "brother" was struggling to stay calm and quiet and agreeable. "What sort of precautions did you have against their leaving, besides the bracelet?" he asked with only the slightest wince. "Bars on the windows? Locks on the doors? Guards?" He stopped himself with a visible effort, and tensed when their unexpected guest nodded.

"All of those, yes," she agreed without hesitation. "But those were just precautions, like you said. I'd have done away with all that if it was just Farah there. But Shifa and Pranav, they were more difficult, and if I'd given Farah that freedom, I'd have had to do the same with the other two."

Biting her lip to keep from asking why it would be so bad to let everyone have their freedom, Ruhi instead said, "Do you know where they are now, Shifa and Pranav?"

"On two of my ships," Falguni replied at once. "At least, they were when they left home. I'll get word to both captains once they reach some other port."

She tapped her fingers against the chair's padded armrest. "You think the same could happen to them?"

"Maybe," Sundra admitted. "We don't know yet. You said they're more difficult. How?"

"Oh, always going on about how they should be making more and be treated better," their visitor said with a sniff and a smirk. "Not gonna happen. Not that I treat them badly, mind! They have everything they need."

"Except their freedom," Ruhi couldn't help muttering under her breath.

She was both shocked and mortified when Falguni turned, favoring her with a sharp laugh.

"You think so?" the raja asked. "You think if I gave them their freedom, they'd be happy?" She snorted, utterly unladylike and completely confident in her own skin, both things Ruhi admired despite everything. "Some people are never happy, no matter what."

"And Shifa and Pranav are like that?" Sundra repeated. "But Farah isn't?"

Falguni nodded. "Farah is a pleasure, always bright and cheerful, eager to get along with everyone. Never had a spot of trouble with her, like I said." She pounded a hand on the chair. "You need to get her back for me." It was not a request.

"We'll do our best," Ruhi promised, and their visitor nodded, rising to her feet.

"Keep me posted," Falguni instructed as she headed for the door.

Once she'd left, and the door had shut behind her, Sundra turned to Ruhi. "What in the Giants' names is going on here?" he asked, sinking into the chair their unexpected guest had just vacated. "If it was just the malcontents and the troublemakers, I'd totally understand—"

"Especially since it sounds like all the rajas treat their weather mages more or less the same," Ruhi interrupted, her own temper raised by the casual mention of such indignities.

"So why the one who wasn't complaining? Was it just an act until she could find a way to escape? And if so, where was she hoping to go?"

She pointed to the large map of the Areyat Isles mounted on the wall over the desk. "Do we think there are any safe havens out there? Places that might welcome a stray mage and protect her from outsiders?"

Sundra rubbed his chin. "That sounds pretty risky," he offered. "I mean, I'm guessing if one raja stole another's mage, there'd be war. Least, that's the impression I've had from everyone. They're like precious gems. Everybody hoarding what they've got."

"And hiding it away when not in use," she agreed, though she took no pleasure in it. How could she? "Honestly, the way they treat these mages is a disgrace."

Her brother nodded. "Sure, but who's gonna tell them to stop?"

That quieted them both for a moment. No one would dare take such a risk. Maybe the governor, if it were happening here in town, but this didn't concern Surpakat at all. And seen in that light, banning weather mages from here had probably been a wise move, after all.

"We're missing something here," Ruhi insisted, pacing back and forth before the desk. "I'm just not sure what yet. Or we have it and don't even realize."

"That's helpful," Sundra commented, shifting to prop his feet up on the desk. "Let me know when you figure out which thing we don't have—or have but don't know we have, or whatever." He leaned back, hands on his chest, and closed his eyes.

Ruhi shoved his feet off. "Wake up! This isn't naptime, we're trying to figure out what it all means."

But her so-called brother remained unswayed. "You figure it

out," he told her, not bothering to look. "I'm making use of your nice, comfortable chair and quiet, private office while I can."

Ruhi sighed but didn't argue. Instead she settled onto the corner of the desk again, tapping her fingers against her upper arms as she thought and thought. Weather mages going missing. Most of them unhappy with their jobs and with how they're treated. One disappears at sea, though that one might be dead—and possibly not from natural causes—and suddenly the rest all start vanishing too. Was it just the last straw, hearing how one of their own had been lost and no one seemed to care, so they'd all decided they were fed up and wouldn't stay any longer?

And that still brought her back to the biggest question, really—where had all the thalakurioi gone?

Solve that particular piece of the riddle and she had a feeling the rest would finally fall into place.

She just wasn't sure what the answer was yet, or how to go about getting it.

CHAPTER TWENTY-FIVE

SUNDRA

Eventually, Ruhi succeeded in waking and evicting him, and Sundra grumbled a bit about that as he headed back out toward the stables and his work. Giants' teeth, he was tired! Naaz had done her best while he was gone but, as he'd suspected would happen, she'd been too tenderhearted to push the horses the way they needed, and they'd gotten soft, lazy, and argumentative in just the short time he'd been away. He'd spent the past few days trying to restore discipline, and it was working—the horses responded to a firm hand, especially since they already liked him—but it was hard work. Sundra would have liked to just knock off for the rest of the day, but of course he couldn't do that. The horses were waiting.

Passing through the kitchen, he heard a commotion out back and quickened his pace. Was Kaala acting up again? That horse! It was lucky for her she was so pretty.

But as he stepped outside, Sundra saw that the black mare was not the cause of any disturbance—at least, not this time. Instead, that honor belonged to a pair of stallions who stood snorting and stamping and tossing their heads by the stableyard's rear fence.

Kaala, Svarn, and Chaaya had all wandered over to meet the new arrivals from their side of the enclosure. For his part Sundra didn't recognize the pair, though they were clearly expensive, but their riders were at least vaguely familiar.

"You! Boy!" the shorter, fatter one called, beckoning Sundra over. "We seek Rawal and Sundra Chera."

"And you've found at least one of them, shri," Sundra replied smoothly, dipping into a bow, though not a deep one. "What can I do for you?" Because, now that he'd heard the other man's voice and spotted his fine, carefully curled and waxed mustache, he recognized them.

These were the two merchants who'd risked trying to strike a deal with Kosala—and had stormed out, furious that the raja had not immediately acceded to all their wishes.

Now the man was suddenly all oily smiles. "Ah, of course you are!" he exclaimed, rubbing his hands together. "Viraja, do you see? It is one of the Chera brothers!"

"I do indeed," the second merchant agreed. "A stroke of luck for us." He leaned over the top of his saddle, crossed arms resting on the ornate family crest enameled there, and his horse nickered, fidgeting and taking a single sideways step but not reacting otherwise to the change in weight distributed upon its back.

Sundra was impressed. He knew he'd never be able to tolerate such high-handed treatment half as well.

"We have been speaking with your master, boy," the first merchant declared, a broad, false smile spreading over his face. "We've presented her with a business proposition, and she has found it agreeable. Still, it would be best for you to add your support as well." Reaching into the ornate shoulder bag he wore, the man extracted a paper and thrust it at Sundra. "It's a simple enough matter, though. Just sign this and we'll be on our way."

Sundra had to force himself not to goggle at the man. Exactly how stupid did they think he was? Plenty, apparently, if they thought they could make such claims, and in doing so, convince him to sign some unfamiliar document utterly unread. It was clear neither man remembered seeing him and Ruhi outside Kosala's office on their previous visit, either, or they would have realized he already knew the truth of how the raja had responded to their proposal. Of course, it was unlikely this sort ever bothered to learn a servant's face, anyway.

That, and his first question, gave Sundra a beautiful idea of how to handle this situation.

Letting his face go a bit slack, he focused his eyes on the paper. "What's that?" he asked, reaching up and taking it from the merchant. But after a second of studying the document—not its contents, just the piece itself—Sundra let his hand drop and the paper fall from it to the ground.

Right at Svarn's feet.

The big bay, ever curious, immediately bent his long neck to investigate—and clamped big, square teeth onto the paper's edge, scooping it up.

Before he proceeded to chew on it, quickly dragging the entire thing into his mouth.

"No!" the second man screamed, reaching out as if to grab for the document, but quickly pulled his hand back. Evidently he had enough sense not to try tugging something from a horse's mouth, if only just. "You idiot!"

Sundra glanced up at him, the sun's glare making it easy to squint and look confused. "Huh? What's wrong?"

"The paper, you fool!" the merchant continued. "Get it back!"

He did a quick turn, studying the ground at his feet. "What paper?" It was getting harder and harder not to laugh, especially as the man's face grew more and more purple.

"Ooh!" the rider finally exclaimed. "You—I could—gah!" And with that final explosion of sound, he wheeled his horse around, nudged it with his heels, and dashed away, back around the edge of the yard and off toward the street beyond.

The second man narrowed his eyes, glaring at Sundra, before finally shaking his head and taking off after his friend.

Only once they'd gone did Sundra let himself burst out

laughing. The sound startled Svarn, who lifted his head quickly, bits of the paper still dangling from his mouth.

"No, don't worry, you're not in trouble," Sundra assured the golden horse, patting him affectionately. "In fact, you were perfect."

The horse whinnied at the compliment, nibbling Sundra's hair affectionately now that his impromptu snack was finished before turning away to see what his stablemates were doing.

And, still chuckling, Sundra followed, determined to get back to work.

The pair of merchants might have been the only visitors that day, but theirs was not the only presence felt. A messenger dropped off a parcel shortly after lunch, evidently for Sundra and Ruhi, as they were summoned to receive it.

Kosala was still out, so it was Angad who handed the beautifully wrapped package to Sundra. "She said it's for you," the stablemaster explained.

Sundra could see that, since his name and Ruhi's false one were written on a card attached to the ribbons, but he'd already learned that his fellow worker couldn't read. There was no reason to point that out, however, so he just nodded and headed indoors with the item, seeking his "brother" so they could open it together.

"Who's it from?" Ruhi asked once Sundra had returned to her office and set the parcel on the desk before her, right on top of the heavy ledger she'd been writing in.

"No idea," he answered. "I guess there's only one way to find out."

He untied the ribbons and opened the package, carefully in case it was somehow dangerous. Inside was a handsome, wooden box with fine, bronze clasps. The box was not locked, and Sundra lifted the lid, revealing a pair of elegant, well-crafted daggers with glossy, black, wooden handles and silver tracery about the pommel and guard, those same materials and patterns matched on their sheaths. There was a card as well.

"'A token of my appreciation,'" Sundra read aloud. "It's signed 'the Raja Ehsaan.'"

"Clever," Ruhi admitted, taking one dagger and unsheathing it to admire the straight, sharp, almost mirror-bright blade. "He probably can't give us money outright, not if the thing with Shivaji at the docks is any indication, but these're worth a pretty penny."

"So it's a bribe, just a more subtle one," Sundra agreed, inspecting the other weapon. They were beautifully crafted, well-balanced and comfortable in the hand, and it was with some regret that he returned the weapon to its cask. "We'll have to give them to Kosala and see what she wants to do with them."

Ruhi nodded, returning the second dagger and closing the lid. "You're right. Taking them would mean we were accepting the bribe, and we can guess what he wants in return."

A large basket arrived at dusk, right as Kosala and Sanga returned, this one filled with fine fruits and jams. The note read "I thought you might enjoy these." And was signed "The Raja Tarabai." Kosala just shook her head and set the basket back out on the porch, its contents undisturbed. And, once they told her about Ehsaan's gift, that box was placed beside it.

"There'll be more," she warned, "and threats too, maybe. The closer it gets to when the Council makes its decision, the more they'll try pressuring you in their favor. Don't give in to any of it. It'll all pass, soon as everything's decided."

Which Sundra knew was absolutely the right response, and the same one his father would have advised.

That didn't keep him from gazing longingly at the box with the daggers, or at all that fruit just sitting there, begging to be eaten.

❦ ❦ ❦

Sundra woke suddenly from a sound sleep. It was still pitch dark in their room, only the faintest hints of stars and moon filtering in through the curtain, and Ruhi was nothing more than a motionless lump in her own bed against the far wall. So what had awakened him?

He lay still, eyes squeezed shut, straining to hear, but there was nothing.

And, after a second, he realized this was true.

He couldn't hear a thing.

Normally, there was the faint swish of the curtains in the night breeze, the soft flutter of Ruhi's breathing, the creak of the floor as the wooden planks shifted, the distant sound of birds and other small creatures in the trees.

Right now he couldn't hear any of that. He couldn't even hear his own breathing or when he tapped his thigh with his palm. It was as if he'd gone completely deaf.

Blinking, he allowed his eyes to adjust to the darkness—and, against the ever-so-slight glow from the window, he thought he saw an equally dark shape move.

But Ruhi was still sound asleep.

Sundra was sure he wasn't mistaken. Someone else was in the room with them. Someone who had either deafened him or masked all sound completely.

That didn't bode well.

Forcing himself to stay still, Sundra waited, his entire body tense. There was nothing for a moment, but then he saw that movement again, black against black, gliding closer. He could imagine details, edges to the outline, the hint of a shoulder here, an elbow there, the top of a head. Hands held out in front, something stretched between them.

Just before those hands came down upon his head or chest, Sundra threw himself up and forward.

He crashed into the stranger, bowling them over. They didn't make a sound as they fell backward and rolled quickly to their feet, hands loose at their sides, crouching down. Neither did Sundra as he turned less gracefully to face off against his dark-clad assailant.

At least this one wasn't carrying any weapons that he could see.

This time they leaped at each other, and the stranger's hands flashed out, striking Sundra in the chest and arm as he raised his own to protect face and throat. He swung in return, deliberately making the motion clumsy and slow, and his foe ducked the blow easily—only to get punched full in the face by Sundra's far-faster second attempt. He lashed out again, trying to leverage his temporarily strong position, and the stranger stumbled back, slamming into Sundra's bed hard enough for their legs to buckle for a second.

Sundra took advantage of that opening, bending to scoop up his chamber pot from under the bed and then rising to smash the heavy copper pot into the stranger's head.

The dark-clad figure dropped, this time in an ungainly sprawl. As their unconscious form struck the ground, sound returned with a dull thud. That startled Ruhi awake, and she sat up, groggily staring at Sundra.

"What?" she asked fuzzily. "You using that?" She gestured vaguely at the chamber pot he still held.

"After a fashion," he replied, returning it to its usual place.

Checking the ground revealed a long length of woven leather cord, evidently what the stranger had been approaching him with. To tie him up? If that was the case, Sundra was only too happy to put it to the same use against its original owner, tying the figure's hands and feet securely before dragging them out into the hall and going to wake Sanga.

He figured the tall pirate could handle it from here. For his part, Sundra planned on going back to bed.

CHAPTER TWENTY-SIX

RUHI

I don't recognize her, and she isn't talking, either because she can't or because she won't."

Kosala flipped the knife in her hand, the gleaming, metal blade flashing as it turned end over end, only for its handle to thunk solidly back into her palm, resting there a second before she tossed it again.

They were in her office, it was mid-morning, and the raja was explaining what she'd learned thus far from the mysterious assailant of the night before.

Which, evidently, was very little.

"So we don't know who she is, who she's working for, or what she was after," Sundra stated, scowling as he paced before their employer's desk.

His own Gift hadn't been much help either—he'd tried it on the leather cord last night but had only had glimpses of a small, simply furnished room that could have been anywhere. And of course now it was a new day, so he'd only be able to see as far back as this dawn, which wouldn't reveal anything.

Sanga, leaning against the closed door, chuckled. "Oh, we

know what she was after," he argued before pointing a long finger at Ruhi's so-called brother. "You."

"Me specifically?" Sundra asked. "Not both of us?"

But Sanga shook his head. "Just you. She had only the one cord, and I'm guessing her Gift has its limits, just like most. She was going to tie you up and drag you out of here, leaving Rawal to find nothing but an empty bed this morning."

Ruhi frowned. "But why?" she asked. "How would that help anyone any?" She could understand people maybe wanting them both dead—she wasn't the tiniest bit happy about it, but at least she understood it. But this? It made no sense to her.

Sundra had paused his steps, however, and was now rubbing at his chin as he thought. "I was the lure, in other words?" he said, and shuddered at Sanga's nod. "Great."

He glanced her way and must have noticed her confusion because he explained, "Whoever hired the woman wanted to use me as leverage. Take me, force you to do what they want. I'm guessing it was more people wanting us to say they should have Udayin's place, or Vihaan's ships, or whatever."

"Ah." Yes, that made sense. And Ruhi guessed they'd gone for Sundra because he was the younger brother, and so presumably both the weaker one and the more valued. Good thing the woman hadn't come for her instead. She'd probably be long gone by now.

That made her think of something else, however. "Does anyone actually know what Udayin and Vihaan left behind?" she asked. "If they'd made arrangements, that'd be one thing, but all this drama is because they didn't, right? So did the Parishad send anyone to inventory their house and goods and everything?"

Kosala sat back, using the tip of her knife to push up the brim of the broad black hat she wore today. "I'm not sure anyone did, no," she answered slowly. "Ships, yes—those were counted immediately. And properties, though I'm not sure how well, since I had no idea Vihaan owned Suraksha and Phasal Kaatana until you told me. But beyond that?" She shrugged. "After ships and land, everything else is secondary."

"Maybe, maybe not," Ruhi argued. "What if there's something in particular somebody's after? Something really valuable, at least to them? That might explain why so many crazy things keep happening."

The raja chuckled. "You think attempted kidnappings are crazy?" she asked, idly tossing the knife again. "You haven't lived here in the Isles very long. That's almost tame, for here."

Sanga coughed. "Still, Rawal's got a point," he said, his skin looking darker than usual in the shadows deeper within the room, where the morning light had not yet reached. "Might be good to do a quick check of their things, make sure there isn't anything that could go missing before the final verdict."

Their employer considered, then nodded. "Fine, go," she told Ruhi and Sundra, idly pointing the dagger their way. "But be back by midday. There's a Parishad meeting, and I'm bringing you with me." A brief, wolfish smile touched her lips. "I think you'll both be very interested in some of the items being discussed."

"Of course." Ruhi bowed, as did Sundra, and then the pair of them headed for the study door. And beyond.

Ruhi had thought it a little odd that Kosala had sent her and Sundra alone, without even Sanga along. What if someone tried to interfere with their task? Or simply didn't let them in? But when they reached Udayin's house, she saw why. The quartet of town guards straightened as she and her friend approached the big, gaudy front, with its ornate carvings and delicate balcony, and two of them crossed their spears in front of the massive double doors.

"No one's allowed in, by order of the Parishad," one of them declared, eyeing them cautiously. Ruhi thought she recognized him from previous encounters with Pillai.

"We're here *from* the Parishad," she stated, holding their writ so the guards could see it, especially the seals at the bottom. "Here to inspect the books on their behalf."

The one who'd spoken read over the paper before nodding and stepping aside. His fellow did the same, turning to let her and Sundra step up to the big doors and push one of them open, revealing the sequence of similar but successively smaller doors ahead.

They started forward, but Sundra paused on the threshold. "Where did they all go?" he asked, and the guards shuffled their feet. "All his staff, his servants, his crew—where'd they all go?"

"Servants went back to the Indentures Hall," one of the men finally admitted, not looking up from an avid contemplation of his own boots. "Crew, not sure. To the docks, most likely. Onto this ship or that." When he did finally meet Sundra's gaze, there was a hint of defiance there. "We weren't stationed here yet. Another squad cleared the place out. We're just rotating the watch now."

Ruhi nodded and grabbed her "brother's" arm, dragging him through the door. "Thank you," she called back over her shoulder. "Keep up the good work."

"What's your hurry?" Sundra demanded, pulling his arm free once they'd passed through the first gate and shut it behind them. "I didn't think you'd want to be back here any more than I do."

"I don't," she answered. "But I'd like to get this over with." She frowned. "Besides, the longer we were with the guards, the more likely one of them would realize our writ doesn't specifically say anything about being here. I figured we didn't want to give them that chance."

Her friend nodded, looking around them now. "Guess we know nobody's gonna bother us while we're here." He peered around the inner courtyard. "Weird seeing it so empty."

"Weird seeing it all," Ruhi replied with a shudder. They hadn't been in Udayin's employ very long, but that brief time ranked among the worst she'd ever experienced, before or since. The young raja had been not just a bully but a sadist, delighting in the pain and suffering of others. Particularly men of good breeding and wealthy backgrounds, like Sundra was and like she pretended to be. Her so-called brother had gotten the brunt of it, though, in part because he'd been careful to shield her and in part because his natural elegance and charm had rubbed Udayin the wrong way right from the start.

Though she rarely wished ill on anyone, Ruhi couldn't find it in herself to mourn the fact that the young raja was now dead. But Sundra was right, walking through the empty house was eerie. Especially since it had the feel of a place hastily abandoned—they passed rooms with furniture knocked to the floor, tapestries and curtains askew, and, in the dining hall, food still molding on the table. The house had felt cold and unfriendly before, but it was twice as forbidding now.

After scanning the first-floor rooms, they climbed the stairs, the same ones Udayin had fatally fallen down, and went straight to the raja's former bedchamber. Neither of them had ever been in this room before, but Ruhi wasn't surprised to find it elegant to the point of being ostentatious, with marble tiles on the floor and carved columns and posts supporting a high, heavily beamed ceiling. Delicate arches pierced the walls, with small alcoves beneath several. A massive bed occupied most of one side, its frame handsomely carved and gold-lacquered wood. Unlike the rooms downstairs, these chambers bore only signs of mild disarray, as if their owner had risen earlier that day and no one had been by to tidy up after him yet.

Off to one side, an arch led to a sturdy door, which opened onto a second, smaller room with a black-and-white-tiled floor, similar arches along the far wall—and an enormous, gilt desk beneath a set of windows. Beautifully patterned rugs covered much of both rooms' floors.

"You won't find anything," Sundra remarked, settling onto the low divan against another wall as Ruhi sat at the desk, tugging over the large ledger filling much of its marble top.

"What do you mean?" she asked, flipping to the last marked page and beginning to scan the numbers there. "It's all right here."

But her "brother" shook his head. "It isn't," he corrected. "Udayin was way too sneaky—and way too greedy—to actually list what he had. Or to keep it here, the first place anyone would look."

He rose to his feet. "But go ahead. I'll be right back."

And with that he strode from the room.

Not sure what he was on about, Ruhi did return to the ledger. But after twenty minutes or so, she had to admit that Sundra was right. The accounts here were messy and disorganized, but everything was accounted for.

Or at least that's what she thought until Sundra set a small, beautifully carved, silver chest down on the desk in front of her.

"What—?" she started, her words and thoughts trailing off as he lifted the lid, revealing an overflowing pile of coins. Most of it gleamed gold, though she did catch the flash of silver here and there. She gaped at the small fortune, then up at her "brother," who was trying very hard not to grin.

"In the puja," he explained to her unasked question. "I thought to myself, 'If I was a greedy, nasty little coward like Udayin, and I wanted to hide all my precious money nearby so I could fondle it whenever I wanted while still keeping it safe, where would I put it?'" He shrugged, trying desperately to seem nonchalant and failing badly. "And it occurred to me," he continued with a smirk, "that the best place to hide money is the one place you figure no one will ever look. Because doing so could offend the gods." He tapped the little box with his finger. "It was tucked under the altar, behind the candles and incense. Which, in this place, nobody ever used."

"Well done," Ruhi told him, and smothered a laugh as he preened at the compliment. "I'd say this was more than enough reason for people to try stealing, kidnapping, and all the other madness."

"Sadly, I'd say you're right," he agreed, hefting the little chest for a minute before placing it back on the desk. "But the question is, did anyone but Udayin himself know about this? I'm guessing no, not even Shivaji—if he had, the big brute would've taken it the minute Udayin fell over dead."

That made sense—the powerful pirate had been almost fanatically loyal to Udayin, but once the raja was dead, he would have been torn between a desire for revenge and the need to look out for himself. If he'd known about this wealth, he would have claimed it immediately as his due. Yet here it was.

"I think I know where some of this came from, too," she revealed, flipping to an earlier page in the ledger. "It looks like Udayin's family had its own khet as well, and a durga—but he sold them off years ago."

"And probably only listed part of the sale price there," Sundra guessed. "The rest went into this emergency stockpile." His gaze flicked to the treasure once more. "You know, just a few of those coins and we'd be rid of these cursed bracelets, free to choose our own paths."

But Ruhi shook her head. "Kosala would know, somehow," she pointed out. "And then we'd be in even worse shape."

Her brother sighed. "I suppose you're right. It's just, it's all right here!"

To forestall any further agonizing, Ruhi rose to her feet. "Put it back where you found it," she advised, handing Sundra the little metal chest. "We'll let Kosala know. The rest is out of our hands."

He nodded and exited the room, leaving Ruhi alone with her thoughts and a collection of overly gaudy and impractical furnishings. Clearly Udayin had possessed as little style as compassion or kindness, though she'd already known the former from his clothes and the latter from his treatment.

⬟ ⬟ ⬟

Vihaan's house was, as always, a study in contrasts to Udayin's. Where their vicious former employer's home was lavish and overdone, a display of wealth and power and poor taste, Vihaan's was cleaner and more classic, with its gold dome, white columns, and flat, railed roof. Guards stood at its front doors as well, and more blocked the back door through which they'd once entered the place, but their writ again earned them passage, and soon Ruhi found herself standing in yet another murdered raja's home—and utterly stunned. The interior was just as distinct from the last one as the exterior, but for very different reasons.

"Wow," Sundra muttered beside her. "Are we sure nobody broke in when the guards weren't looking? Or that the Parishad hasn't already sold everything off?"

His question wasn't completely nonsensical, because, from where they stood, the entire house looked bare. Stripped clean, in fact: no rugs or hangings, no sculptures or lamps, no curtains or ornaments, only bare tile floors, clean white walls, enameled ceilings, and stained glass windows, offset by the one or two pieces of furniture too large and heavy to have been removed.

It was more than the absence of art and ornament, however. "Look," Ruhi said, pointing at and then leading the way into the kitchen. When they'd been here before, even though the house's owner had already been dead the place had been a hive of activity, with cooks baking roti and roasting meat and vegetables and cooking rice. Now the hearths were cold and the room empty.

Very empty. Too empty. Pots and pans were gone, ladles and serving forks missing, plates and dishes absent. The entire place had been cleaned out, thoroughly and completely. Even the pantry was bare, no sign of flour or meal or spices left. Such things weren't worth much, certainly not enough to attract the Parishad's interest—but she could think of some people who would absolutely not want to leave them behind.

"They packed up and left," she said, turning toward Sundra. "Vihaan's staff, his people. He must have left instructions, taught them what to do if anything ever happened to him." Which, as a pirate lord, would be a reasonable concern—and an accurate one, as it turned out.

"After he died and those men attacked us and Chetan here, they must have cleared out." She shook her head, more in admiration than anything.

Though they'd only met the young raja once or twice, he'd seemed a good sort, and this proved it. He'd made sure his people were taken care of. "I'll bet we won't find a single coin here." He'd have given them all to his staff or told them where to find the money if they needed it.

Sundra started to argue, then stopped. "You're right," he agreed, leaning against a column. "He'd have had a stash put aside for emergencies, he was too smart not to, but he'd have told his staff where it was. They took it and left." He scuffed his boot tip on the tile floor. "Makes it easy to tally everything up, I guess."

"Very." She looked around, just in case, but every glimpse confirmed her earlier assessment. "Let's head back. Kosala wanted us ready to go to the Parishad with her."

"Right." Her so-called brother grinned. "And this meeting's one I really don't want to miss."

CHAPTER TWENTY-SEVEN

RUHI

They made it back in plenty of time and accompanied Kosala and Sanga to the Council Hall yet again. When they arrived, however, there was one very notable absence.

"It's not like Koliya to miss a session if he's in port," Jasleen commented, scowling at the empty seat the big man usually filled to capacity and beyond. "Has anyone spoken to him recently?"

Beside her, Ehsaan cleared his throat. "I saw him making haste out to sea a few days back," he answered, his voice as soft as ever, forcing Ruhi to strain to hear him. "I have not yet seen him return." Of course their houses were near one another, and both along the docks, so Ehsaan was in a perfect place to observe such comings and goings—no doubt a deliberate choice, given how careful the man seemed.

Chetan frowned. "Well, he's not here, but we still have a quorum. Shall we?" He turned his attention to the tall, slim man supposedly presiding over this meeting, and dipped his head. "Nayak."

Girish Malhotra bowed back. "Raja. Rajas. As host to the Council, I, Nayak Malhotra, hereby call this meeting of the Parishad to order."

They were clearly observing all the proper formalities today because this was a full meeting, with not only the rajas but many of the town's more prosperous merchants and tradesmen present, as well as possibly representatives from various guilds and even other strongholds and plantations.

The tall, sober-looking governor cleared his throat. "Before we turn to other matters, as this is my first time participating as governor, I have a few items I would like to put forward for the Council's consideration, matters concerning Surpakat and its current and future prosperity." He had several pages in front of him and consulted them before launching into a detailed explanation of one such matter, the one involving docks and how many should be allowed to each resident.

Ruhi was watching the rajas throughout this conversation. She had no doubt that if Koliya had been here, the burly pirate would have opened his mouth even as Malhotra wound down, to speak in favor of this proposal and call for an immediate vote on it. But he wasn't here to push in that direction. Instead, someone else opened the remarks. Someone a good deal better at negotiations— and subtle manipulations.

"I fail to see," Kosala stated loudly, leaning back in her chair and toying with the goblet before her, "how reducing the number of docks one person may own makes any sense. If I have the money to build and maintain six docks, and space along my property to put them without either encroaching on others or placing my own ships or others at risk, whose business is that but my own? And, since the town already collects taxes on each and every dock owned, wouldn't limiting those reduce the amount of revenue to the town itself?" She scratched at her nose. "That doesn't sound as if it would benefit anyone."

"Too right," Jasleen said, banging her cane on the table for emphasis. "Bunch of rot and nonsense."

Chetan, Ehsaan, and Falguni all nodded, and after a moment Tarabai did the same. With Koliya absent, that made the decision unanimous.

"Very well," the governor said. "The proposal is hereby rejected." He did not seem at all upset about this, but then Ruhi knew he had not devised that plan. "Moving on," he continued, "I would like to propose a change to the way unclaimed properties within city limits are handled. I suggest the city take ownership of such places and sell them off to interested parties, starting with those who have already expressed interest or even put in potential bids. The resulting money would then be split between the city and the Parishad." He nodded to the assembled rajas. "Surpakat's portion of the money would allow us to make repairs to our roads, our walls, our docks, and our buildings, as well as paying our guards and funding any other necessary projects and improvements."

This time Jasleen Lal got there first. "More rot," she declared, her words accompanied by the thud of her cane. "Stop trying to steal what's ours. This city's only here on our sufferance," she warned, pointing at the governor. "Don't get uppity."

Tarabai nodded. "Yes, even though none of us controls Surpakat, that's because we've all agreed to share it equally," she offered. "So those unclaimed properties revert to us, as they should."

Falguni was nodding and seemed ready to weigh in as well, but Chetan beat her to it. "We don't cover the city's expenses," the rough-edged raja began. "So it should reap some benefit from such properties. I have no problem with it laying claim to them or selling them off as it sees fit—as long as half of what it gets still goes to us. I don't know about this idea of putting in bids, though. If I could state now that I want Kosala's house if she dies, that's another way of me saying I'm going to kill her so I can take it."

He grinned at Ruhi's employer, who offered a "go ahead and try it" smirk in return as a few of the assemblage chuckled.

"It's a fair point," Ehsaan agreed. "No one should be allowed to lay claim to a place before it becomes available, and all should be able to try for it, if so desired. In fact, auctioning those properties would most likely earn you far more money and be considerably fairer, besides." That was well thought out and well stated, and confirmed what Ruhi had heard about the raja—he was extremely clever, extremely quiet, and extremely careful. A dangerous combination.

"That can't be allowed to affect the current situation, though," Jasleen Lal insisted. "Those are the Parishad's responsibility. Any properties that go unclaimed after today, those can be handled by the city—and we get our cut."

The others all nodded, and the amended proposal was passed unanimously.

"Thank you, Rajas," the governor said, bowing once more. "I will enter an updated version of the proposal into the town's records, and its passage will be recorded here by my lieutenant, to take effect as of dawn tomorrow." He gestured to a woman who sat just behind him, taking notes in a large, thick book, and Ruhi realized that this must be the infamous Chennama Macola. She studied the woman, having only seen her from a distance before.

Chennama was neither ugly nor beautiful, falling solidly midway between the two extremes, as most people did. She had strong, thick brows, a straight nose, and a wide, full mouth, but her face was too round and too soft to make the most of such powerful features. Her hair was pulled back in a simple knot, and she wore very little jewelry, her sari and ghagra made of plain, serviceable cloth, though at least her dupatta was bright-blue silk. She was gritting her teeth now, even as she nodded and continued her work. So she was not pleased that her first proposal had been shot down so completely and her second had been gutted.

Ruhi, on the other hand, was thrilled. They'd been lucky to catch Chetan at home the day before, and even luckier that he'd been willing to listen as they'd explained about the government proposals. He had promised to stop or at least defang this one, while Kosala had assured them she would kill the other. And they had both done admirably—even if Koliya had been here to protest, he would have been overwhelmingly outvoted. Ruhi thought it an especially nice touch for her boss, one of the rajas who lived the farthest from the water and the docks lining them, to argue against altering the waterfront, while Chetan, who showed no interest in purchasing more properties here, had just been instrumental in disarming the proposal regarding local properties. No one could accuse the two of them of opposing the proposals for personal gain, and of course no one would ever dare suggest that Kosala and Chetan could be working—and plotting—together.

"Speaking of properties," Tarabai stated quietly once things had settled again, "we still need to deal with Udayin and Vihaan's. I would like to again request that I be granted at least some of their former ships, to bolster my own barely adequate fleet."

Jasleen Lal actually sneered at that. "You want ships, go out and win them properly," the old pirate stated. "Spoils to the victor! If we're going by sheer strength, those ships are mine!"

"Koliya would disagree," Falguni cut in sharply. "And do any of us want to see his fleet get even bigger?"

That brought mutterings all around as the meeting devolved into yet another round of demands and accusations and pleas regarding Udayin and Vihaan's former property. Someone among the audience called out to ask when the Parishad would make its final ruling on distribution, and was treated to responses ranging from "Soon, dear, soon"—from Tarabai—to "Shove off!"—from Chetan—and everything in between. But there clearly wasn't a consensus yet on what they should do with all those resources, and Ruhi suspected her employer was in for some long nights dealing with haggling, bargaining, and outright demanding.

She was very, very glad, as the governor declared the meeting over and people began to rise and file out of the second-floor room, that she did not have to be present for any of those conversations. She just hoped the rajas would continue to enforce their rule of no weapons in this chamber, otherwise those meetings could potentially turn very violent and very dangerous.

CHAPTER TWENTY-EIGHT

SUNDRA

Sundra woke late the next day. It was the staff's day off again, so he didn't technically have any chores, though of course he intended to stop in and visit the horses regardless. He'd tried arguing that, since they'd been at sea and thus had missed several of the previous days off, he and Ruhi and Meera should get an extra day or two, but unsurprisingly that hadn't gone anywhere. He hadn't really expected it to, but had figured it was worth a try. As it was, he enjoyed being able to stretch out in bed and just lay there for a bit, admiring the way the late-morning sun slanted through the window and edged its way across the floor.

His roommate was long gone, of course, but Sundra didn't think anything of it until he was already up, washed, dressed, and heading to the kitchen. Then he remembered the last time they'd had liberty, how Ruhi had completely disappeared for the day, and frowned. Surely she wouldn't be so foolish as to do so again? Things had been quiet the last time, but now, with both the missing mages and, more particularly here, all the contention over Udayin and Vihaan's former possessions, it was a bad time for one person to go wandering around Surpakat alone.

Especially someone as ill-equipped to defend herself as his supposed older brother.

But sure enough, when Sundra reached the kitchen, Laila teased him about being such a late riser compared to his brother. "Off before dawn, that one was," the cook declared. "Guess he was kind enough not to wake you, hmm?"

Sundra feigned smiles and laughter at the joke, all the while fuming inside. How could Ruhi be so stupid?

Over fresh-made idlis and mango chutney, however, he realized that his anger was just a mask for something else entirely: fear. He was worried about her. In many ways, Ruhi was smarter than him and more worldly, having grown up working in a warehouse while he'd been sheltered on his family's estates. But his education had included politics, both taught and seen first-hand, and Sundra felt that made him a better judge of certain risks than her, who had always been the boss's daughter. Plus, he was simply better able to defend himself if something should happen.

He had to find her and make sure she was safe.

The question was, how? Sanga might know where she'd gone, but Sundra shied away from asking the rangy pirate for a variety of reasons, not least of which that he knew Ruhi would murder him if he embarrassed her like that. Besides, it was a lot harder to justify worrying over his older brother Rawal being off somewhere alone than his female friend Ruhi, and that was definitely *not* a conversation he planned to have with Sanga!

But there was someone else who might know Ruhi's whereabouts and who already knew her secret. Accordingly, after doing his best to enjoy brunch and then checking on the horses, Sundra set out for the Quiet Fire.

The place was bustling today, as it was still lunch time, so much so that Padmini had brought in some additional help, a tall, slender young woman in a deep-green dupatta over a more muted blue-green sari. The proprietress saw his glance when she sat him and smirked, but Sundra wasn't in the mood for flirtation at the moment and focused on the menu once he was seated, knowing from past experience that the tavern owner wouldn't deign to speak with him until after he'd ordered and eaten anyway.

Besides, her food was always excellent, and he'd not had much appetite for breakfast, so his stomach was already growling at the rich smells emanating from the kitchen.

"What can I get you?" The voice that asked wasn't Padmini's but was still somehow familiar, and Sundra glanced up at the young server—and froze, staring as he took in her unlined face, strong brow and nose, and firm chin, all paling behind dark, thoughtful eyes he saw every single day.

It was Ruhi.

"What are you doing here?" she hissed, leaning in to refill his water from the pitcher she carried.

"What are *you* doing here, with everything that's been going on?" he countered, lowering his voice when she shushed him. "I was worried about you!"

She must have seen the truth of that in his face, because her anger abated, her own brow smoothing. "I'll be back," she promised, and moved away to help some of the other tables. Her hair had been cleverly pulled back into a thick knot at the nape of her neck, he saw, disguising the fact that it wasn't long enough for a full braid. Padmini's work, no doubt, which explained her smirk. Of course she'd known where Ruhi was the whole time.

And at least she hadn't been out wandering the streets, looking for answers on her own, Sundra reminded himself, sipping his water and nibbling one of the fresh roti she'd set down for him. She'd been here, under their friend's watchful eye, in about the safest place she could have been outside of Kosala's home.

Particularly since no one would recognize her as Rawal Chera in her current state.

A few minutes later, she returned, bearing two bowls of fragrant, steaming stew and a plate of samosas, their golden exteriors still crackling from the fire. Placing those on the table, Ruhi sat down, setting the serving platter against her chair leg.

"I'm on break," she explained, snatching one of the samosas

and cracking it open so the smell of fried meat and potatoes wafted out.

"So this is what you do on your days off?" Sundra asked, taking one himself and biting down, enjoying the crispness of the fried dough against the juice and spice of the filling. "You leave work so you can work?"

She shook her head, taking a sip of lassi from the cup she'd brought herself. "It's not about the work," she explained, "though I'm glad to help Padmini out. It's about…" She trailed off, looking away and biting her lip. Was she embarrassed?

Or was it just that she expected him to tease her about it? But Sundra understood.

"It's a chance to be yourself again," he finished for her, stirring his stew with its spoon as he spoke though his eyes were on his friend. "Ruhi, not Rawal. I can't even imagine what it's like for you, always having to be someone—something—you're not. So you come here, where you know your secret is safe, and Padmini helps you be Ruhi again, at least for a day." He nodded. "I'm glad you can have that."

Her eyes were bright as she regarded him, but not as bright as her smile. "Thank you." She glanced down at her hands. "I'm sorry I didn't tell you. I thought…"

"I know," he said, sparing her having to say it. "But even if most of the time I have to be your little brother, Ruhi, I'm always your friend." It actually hurt a little that she hadn't felt she could confide in him, but he did understand why.

Ruhi nodded. "You are. Thank you." They ate in silence for a bit after that, before she added, "You're right, though. I wasn't thinking about everything else that's been happening. If that isn't all resolved before our next day off, maybe I'll just stick to the compound that time, instead."

Sundra took a sip of lassi, the cool yogurt drink helping to clear away some of the spice from the samosa and the stew. "That'd probably be best." Then he grinned. "Unless I come with you, to watch your back. Or maybe bring a few of the others, to be safe.

Like Sanga. I'm sure he'd love to see this place—and its pretty new server."

Truth be told, Ruhi wasn't really his type. Sundra preferred women a little shorter and a bit more rounded. But it wasn't *his* preference that mattered here, and the way she blushed, his friend knew it.

"Shut up," she told him, balling up a piece of rhoti and tossing it at his head.

Sundra laughed, ducking the small missile. He noted, however, that she hadn't forbade him from bringing Sanga here, where he could see her as she really was.

That might be something to think about, once all this other mess had been cleaned up.

CHAPTER TWENTY-NINE

RUHI

The next morning, back in her now-familiar garb and beard, Ruhi found herself and her "brother" summoned to their employer's office at daybreak.

"Stop scratching at it," Sundra whispered as they followed Ilan down the hall.

"I can't," she muttered back. "It itches!" This had happened the last time too, and the first time as well. She knew she'd get used to the fake facial hair again soon enough, but after her cheeks and chin being blissfully bare for a day, re-adhering the woven piece to her skin tickled and chafed like mad. But she knotted her hands into fists, bunching them at her sides to keep from scratching as they reached Kosala's office and were shown inside.

The raja was lounging at her desk, turned sideways in her chair with one leg thrown over the arm, her back against the other. As usual, she wore a choli and gharara, the former gold-edged black today and the latter a muted, almost coppery gold, and at the moment her black-and-red sherwani hung from the coat stand by the door, so that her tanned, well-muscled arms were on full display. She had a small, sharp dagger and was carving paper-thin slices from the mango in her other hand, eating them right off the blade.

"Well?" she said once they were standing before her, side by side like a pair of errant schoolboys. "What have you learned so far?"

It took Ruhi a second to realize their employer was asking for an update on their investigation. "Not much," she admitted once she had. "We know several of the thalakurioi have gone missing, and more continue to do so. We know some of those were malcontents, though not all. We know they figured out a way to remove their bracelets." She rubbed at her own. "And that's about it."

Kosala grunted. "Not much at all," she agreed, and her tone was disapproving, as was her stern gaze. "I promised the others your help," she reminded them both. "It won't reflect well on me if you cannot deliver an answer to this riddle."

They both nodded, and Sundra opened his mouth to speak but was interrupted by a quick, sharp knock on the door. Ilan opened it without being called, sticking his head in.

"Sorry, Raja," he burst out, "but you'd best come quick. There's trouble."

She was on her feet in an instant, grabbing her talwar where it rested against the chair's side and sliding it through her belt as she strode toward the door, snagging her coat and tugging that on along the way. Ruhi exchanged a glance with Sundra, and without a word they hurried after.

Three people were waiting on the front porch, with three more standing guard just beyond, and only one of them was familiar. Pillai didn't look at all pleased, even less so than usual, but for once her irritation was not directed at them, nor even at Kosala. Rather, the guard captain was glaring at the two men who stood to either side and who were busy scowling at each other. Both were well-dressed, in flamboyant, lightweight clothing clearly never intended for an ocean voyage or, indeed, for any sort of manual labor, and their elegant mustaches and beards and ostentatious jewelry proclaimed them both to be men of wealth and substance.

"Sorry to disturb you all," Pillai began, and banged her spear on the porch's polished, wooden floor when the men started arguing and interrupting. "But," she continued, raising her voice to be heard until they finally subsided into sulks, "we have a small confusion I'm hoping you can clear up." She gestured to the man on her left. "Shri Tejas here insists that you, Raja, have granted him the home formerly belonging to the Raja Udayin." She held up a rolled document, which the man tried to grab but which she quickly twisted away and raised to move out of reach. "This is your writ, granting him such."

She offered the paper to Kosala, who took it with a sniff, unrolling it to scan the page quickly. "I don't know you," she said once she looked back up, speaking to the man, "and we both know I didn't write this. Nor does it have my signature, or my seal." She wadded it up and tossed it at his chest.

"There!" the second man sneered as the first dropped to the ground, snatching up the discarded page. "I told you!"

He subsided at another stamp from Pillai's spear. "And Shri Veer, here," she went on, "argues that you ceded him that same property, and also comes bearing written proof." She offered a second scroll.

Kosala took this one and glanced it over as well, but her fierce glower told the truth before she even stated, "This is no more real than the last one," and crumpled that up as well. "Even if the property were mine to dispose of, instead of the Parishad's as a whole, I have not and would not sign it away to a pair of merchants I don't even know."

The second man—Shri Veer—was evidently less willing to cut his losses. "But you must remember!" he insisted instead. "We discussed it just the other day, and you agreed! You even had your boy serve us tea!" He pointed at Sundra. "You remember, don't you?" Kosala raised an eyebrow, Sundra chuckled, but the man doggedly continued, "And you couldn't find your seal, that's why you didn't use it!"

Kosala held up her gloved left hand—showing off the thick silver signet ring that adorned her first finger, her seal taking up the entirety of the piece's broad front. The man paled and fell silent at last, though Ruhi had to give him credit for persistence, if not for knowing when to quit.

"I thought as much," Pillai told them all, and at a gesture her guards approached and took the two men into custody. "Thank you."

She started to turn away, but Sundra stopped her. "Has there been a lot of that?" he asked, nodding toward the two merchants. "Just outright lying and hoping they can bluster their way through?"

The guard commander sighed, leaning a little on her spear. "You have no idea," she admitted, more quietly than her earlier declarations. "We've had people saying you and your brother gave them the land, people saying you did"—that was directed at Kosala—"some even saying all three of you did. There are people claiming you owe them money and promised them the former rajas' possessions in payment. Others saying the rajas themselves owed them money for various goods and services. We had one the other day who argued the wood for Udayin's ships had come from trees on his land, and therefore the boats were his by right." She laughed without humor. "It's been an absolute madhouse."

Kosala had been listening to all of this, her face still set in a deep scowl, but before she could reply a guard appeared at the end of the lane. "Captain!" the guard called out, and Pillai hurried over. The raja chose to join her, summoning Sanga from just inside with a snap of her fingers—and, since no one had said not to, Ruhi decided to follow, with Sundra easily keeping pace.

"There's a problem at the docks," the guard was explaining, visibly out of breath from having run here, but Pillai was already sprinting past, back in that direction. The rest of them followed her, making an odd group but an effective one, as residents scattered before them like small birds making way for a herd of cats.

In moments the water came into view, and Ruhi found herself approaching a set of docks well below the ones used by the Parishad. Several boats sat here, some with activity flowing over them, some still—and one in the act of being backed away from the mooring posts. Several figures lay sprawled upon the dock beside it, and she could make out the glint of helms and spears and armor among them. Ruhi was reminded of a previous encounter, though these guards had obviously not surrendered without a fight.

"Stop!" Kosala shouted, putting on a burst of speed as she sprinted for the boat. Sanga took off after her but soon shot past, his long legs eating up the distance down the dock. A man was just coiling the mooring rope, preparing to toss it back on board, when the tall pirate plowed into him, knocking the man to the ground. The rope went flying—and Kosala lunged forward, catching hold of it before it could slip beyond reach.

"Here!" she shouted, and Ruhi hurried forward along with Sundra and even Pillai, the three of them grabbing hold and helping tug. The boat was drifting slightly, but its sails had yet to catch the wind, and it had not cleared the dock yet, leaving enough slack on the rope for them to loop it back around a pylon and secure the vessel once more.

"Get down from there!" Pillai demanded once the boat was tied off. "At once!" The men on board jeered at her, and one raised a bow, sighting along the arrow nocked there—but froze when a dagger thudded into the railing inches below his chest.

"Loose it and die," Sanga warned, his quiet, calm voice carrying clear menace across the distance, and the archer gulped, weighing his chances. Ruhi saw that Sanga had drawn a second dagger from his belt and was holding it down at his side by the blade instead of the handle, fingers loosely pinched and ready to lift and release, sending the weapon hurtling forward the way he had the one before it. The bowman must have seen the same and recognized how close he stood to becoming a corpse, because a second later he lowered his weapon, releasing the string and lifting the arrow clear.

"Gangplank!" Kosala snapped, and after a second, the long wooden plank was extended from the ship to the dock. "Down here, now!" she ordered next, and the archer was the first to obey, stepping onto the gangplank and hustling down to them, the wood bowing and swaying with each step.

Others soon followed, and a few minutes later ten men were standing before them, some glowering and others fidgeting, some silent and others cursing.

"Whose idiot idea was this?" Kosala asked, the steel clear in her voice. There was much shuffling and muttering, but eventually they all turned to look at one in their midst.

He wasn't tall or powerfully built, nor gloriously handsome either, and his clothes were no better than the rest. Yet the others all deferred to him, in the same way Ruhi remembered seeing her family's warehouse workers behave toward Ganath, their foreman. Yes, this was the one in charge.

Kosala had noticed it as well. "What's your name?" she demanded in a tone that did not leave room to forgo an answer.

"Fardeen," the pirate replied, lifting his chin in a display of bravado Ruhi could tell would avail him nothing.

"And, what—you just thought you'd knock out my guards and steal this ship, Fardeen?" That had been Pillai, who was now up in the man's face. "We don't steal from each other! It's part of the code!"

He glared back at her. "I wasn't stealing it from nobody!" he insisted. "'Cause it don't belong to nobody! Not yet! So taking it's fair and square!"

"This was your big plan?" Kosala asked, drawing a dagger and waving it about as she talked, pacing back and forth. "You'd steal it and then, what, we'd just let you keep it?"

He wilted a little under her gaze—as who wouldn't, Ruhi thought—but still held his ground. "Why not? If I've already got it, who's gonna stop me?"

It did make a certain amount of sense, and both Kosala and Pillai were nodding grudgingly. "There's just one problem with all that," Kosala told him, leaning in close, her voice dropping as if she were sharing a secret, though she still spoke loud enough for everyone on the dock to hear. "These boats *do* belong to someone. They're property of the Parishad until we decide otherwise. Which means you just tried stealing from the Council of Rajas."

Fardeen flushed, then paled. "No," he insisted, backing up a step. "I didn't—I would never! I meant no disrespect!" The rest of the would-be crew were mostly on their knees now, hands up as they begged for mercy.

Pillai's other guards had followed, albeit at a slower pace, and they arrived to this scene. The would-be, and now very regretful, boat thieves were soon taken away, and the unconscious guards revived and helped back to headquarters, leaving a moment of quiet once more.

"Tell me you're going to do something about all this, and soon," Pillai stated, looking to Kosala. "Because it's only going to get worse otherwise."

"We will," Ruhi's employer replied. "And soon. This all should have been cleared up sooner, but for various disputes delaying us." She tugged at her gloves. "Meantime, I promise you that neither I nor either of them will sign anything giving anyone any of these belongings, or granting anyone any special privileges toward them." Ruhi nodded quickly, as did Sundra. "That should save you the trouble of having to ask us again, anyway."

Pillai frowned but nodded. "Fair enough." She bowed sharply. "Thank you for your help."

Kosala acknowledged that with a faint dip of her chin, then she turned on her heel and led the way back home. Sanga moved to walk beside her as usual, and Ruhi and Sundra followed along.

None of them said much, each lost in their own thoughts. Ruhi only felt shock at the lengths people would go to claim that which wasn't theirs—and no small amount of awe at the way both Kosala and Pillai carried themselves.

Neither of them ever had to worry about their fake beard itching!

CHAPTER THIRTY

SUNDRA

The Parishad had called another meeting, and Kosola had brought Sundra and Ruhi with her, saying that this session in particular would directly involve them. But they'd barely settled into their chairs, seated in the front row of the gallery filling one side of the big council meeting room, before the largest of the rajas jumped to his feet, pounding a big fist on the polished table.

"I want to know who thought it'd be a good idea to mess with me!" Koliya bellowed. "Because when I catch them, they're gonna wish they were dead!"

He glared around the room and particularly at his fellow rajas but none of them seemed cowed by his bold statement.

Finally Falguni made a show of yawning. "I, for one, don't have a clue what you're talking about," the sharp-featured pirate lord replied. "Care to enlighten us, or did you just want to make more idle threats?"

Koliya scowled down at her, his whole face red with rage. "Somebody sent word my stronghold was under attack," he rumbled, sweeping his eyes over his peers once more. "But we'd barely got out to sea before I found out it wasn't true." He bared his teeth within his thick beard. "I'd have been traveling for days, and for no good reason!"

Sundra wasn't sure how any of that could be the case. He'd seen the maps and knew that Sharan was roughly the same distance from here as Enkar Bindu—if you were a bird. If not, you'd have to go around the island that held Bahut Saare, Suraksha, and Phasal Kaatana, which would add at least another day's travel in each direction. So four days there and four days back, yet here Koliya was, only five days later? Had he really "got word" while at sea? If so, how? Carrier pigeons, perhaps, but how would anyone at his stronghold know to send one saying everything was fine there?

Whatever the explanation, the massive pirate lord hadn't spared him and Ruhi more than a cursory glance, so at least it seemed they weren't suspected of any involvement. Which was definitely for the best, considering the man's temper.

Kosala merely laughed, meanwhile leaning back in her own chair. "I'd have thought you'd enjoy that, Koliya," she remarked. "We are pirates, after all. Being at sea is in our blood." The others all nodded or muttered agreements, as did much of the room.

That only made the big pirate even angrier. "I *do* love being at sea!" he insisted. "Just not being tricked into going on a wild goose chase!"

"It doesn't seem to have hurt you any," Chetan pointed out, drumming his thick fingers on the tabletop. "And you're back, so no harm done. Can we get on with this?"

The others all nodded, and Malhotra quickly called the session formally to order before sitting back down. He didn't have any papers with him today, nor was Chennama here to take notes or provide additional materials, which told Sundra this meeting was all about the rajas and their agenda rather than the governor and his plans.

Sure enough, no sooner had Surpakat's leading official sat back down, than Jasleen Lal, with a glance around at her peers, rapped her cane on the table.

"Listen up!" she called, making sure she had everyone's attention. "Everyone's been on a tear trying to find out what's going to happen with Vihaan and Udayin's former properties, ships, monies, and so on. I've heard some of the stunts people've been pulling, and its utter madness. That needs to stop right now!" She glared around the room as if daring anyone to contradict her, but everyone stayed silent, save for a few murmurs of assent. Not that agreement here in this chamber would stop the people beyond it from continuing with their reckless plans—or even those who were here, though this lot might be more circumspect about such things in future.

"Good," the aging pirate queen continued. "Now, we're still discussing things. Don't want to make a hasty decision we'll regret later. But we *are* talking, and we're nearing the end of that. So we'll convene again in four days' time to announce how those possessions'll be distributed, and to whom."

Four days! That sounded both still very far away—so much time for others to cause mischief and mayhem—and extremely close—only four more days and this would all be over!

But Tarabai cleared her throat. "As long as it's safe to do so," the raja added, causing Jasleen to turn that sharp gaze on her. It was so strange seeing Tarabai shrink back under that glare, remembering how fierce and dominant she'd been at Riyaasat. But of course there she was the utter master of all. Here she was practically a guest. And Jasleen Lal commanded respect from even the hardest of pirates—save her own daughters, he recalled.

"Safe?" the elderly raja was barking now. "What's that supposed to mean? You afraid they're going to come for you, for us, to force us to give 'em those things? Let 'em try!" She shook her cane at the world in general, and Sundra, seated close, didn't miss the faint rattle it made. Ah, he'd wondered if that might be the case. No true pirate would go around without a proper blade, especially not one of such deadly reputation, and that was indeed the case here. The impressive walking stick was a sword cane. And either the guards—and the other rajas—didn't realize that or, more likely, they looked the other way in deference to Jasleen's age and authority.

Meanwhile, Tarabai was shaking her head and shooting entreating glances at the other pirate lords. "No no," she insisted, "that's not what I mean at all! Only, there's a big storm coming, and it may not be safe for us to meet here during the worst of it."

Chetan harrumphed, arms folded across his thick chest as usual. "When has a little wind and rain ever stopped a proper pirate?" he grumbled, but Sundra thought the protest was merely for show.

He knew Chetan was too pragmatic not to seek shelter in a fierce storm like the one they'd faced on their way to Dveep Kile. That was at sea, of course, where you faced dangers like capsizing, but even here on solid ground, if there was thunder and lightning all around, Tarabai was right, it might make sense to delay the next meeting until after such threats had passed. Especially considering this chamber had those tall, glass doors leading out onto that nice, broad balcony. All it would take was a good, sharp gust from a gale to turn those handsome barriers into a maelstrom of razor-sharp glass.

Falguni and Ehsaan were both nodding, and even Kosala dipped her head in agreement. "Fine," Jasleen stated, though she released the word in a huff. "If that happens, we'll meet soon as the storm's passed. Happy?" Tarabai nodded gratefully. "Anything else anyone needs to say?" No one replied, and the silver-haired raja turned to Malhotra, who obligingly rose to his feet and ended the session. That had been quick!

Sundra didn't bother to move yet—Kosala didn't look to be in a hurry either, lingering to speak with some of the other rajas, and there was no point heading back before she was ready. Particularly since some of the other attendees had glanced his and Ruhi's way a few times. The last thing he wanted was to have to fend off more pleading or bribing or threatening, right here in front of the rajas. The presence of town guards was having a quelling effect on people's enthusiasm, though, and no one had yet had the courage to approach. So he was surprised when he felt a hand on his arm, though less so since he quickly recognized the touch.

Sure enough, Ruhi leaned in close. "Let Kosala or Sanga know we'll be back shortly," she told him, keeping her voice down so it wouldn't be heard over the tumult of others leaving. "I have an idea we need to test out."

He glanced her way, trying to discern what she was thinking or goad her into revealing more, but she only smiled enigmatically behind her beard. A part of him wanted to protest, to dig in his heels and refuse to budge until she explained, but somehow he found himself standing and making his way toward their employer and her second instead.

Since Kosala was still speaking to Falguni, he headed for Sanga instead. The tall pirate was leaning against one of the pillars as usual, watching the room, his fingers twitching as if they were desperately wanting to reach for a knife that wasn't there.

"Rawal's got an idea we need to check out," he said, and Sanga studied him a second before nodding. "We'll return home soon as we can."

"Be careful," the pirate warned him as he turned to go. "You saw what was going on last night."

Sundra nodded. "I will." He almost added that he'd make sure to keep Ruhi—Rawal—safe, but stopped himself in time. After all, his "big brother" should be able to take care of himself!

He hadn't missed the way Sanga's eyes had flicked toward Ruhi when he'd urged caution, though. Something was definitely going on there, though he doubted either of them really knew what, exactly. Of course, Ruhi's disguise wasn't lending itself to clarity.

They'd figure it out, though. Sundra just hoped it wouldn't be *too* quick, or that it'd somehow prevent him from poking fun at his "brother" along the way.

"All set," he told her now as they met back up and headed for the doors back out toward the stairs. Most of the other attendees had left already, only a few of the rajas and their immediate crew remaining, along with the guards. "So, where're we headed?"

"Back to the docks," Ruhi answered, tugging the door open and slipping through, with Sundra right behind her. "I just hope the *Kalinga*'s in port at the moment." That mysterious smile was back. "I've got a few questions for our good friend Nalan."

CHAPTER THIRTY-ONE

RUHI

Chhavi smirked upon seeing them, her dark eyes flashing. "Just can't stay away, can you?" Her gaze and her smile were directed right at Ruhi, and if not for the fact she knew the female pirate could see through her disguise, Ruhi might have thought the other woman was flirting with her.

Luck had been with them, and the *Kalinga* was indeed back in Surpakat, moored only one dock over from where they'd found it the first time. And, just as then, they'd approached the pirate ship, only to find the woman who'd once captured them sitting by the gangplank, nibbling slices from a piece of fruit she was carving up.

"Always good to see you as well," Sundra replied, dipping into a perfect bow, and not for the first time Ruhi envied her so-called brother's ease and charm. Was the man ever tongue-tied or shocked into silence, even once? "But I'm afraid we're here for that thalakurios of yours. Nalan."

"Oh, you're not here for me? I'm crushed!" Chhavi fell back against the mooring post she'd been leaning against, raising one hand to flutter at her face like some silly maiden from the old tales. Then, hoisting herself up off the ground, she shouted at the ship,

"Nalan! Get your sorry butt out here! You've got visitors! Again!"

Several heads popped up over the railing to see what all the fuss was about, including one whose bald pate caught the sunlight. "You again?" Nalan called down. "What do you want now?"

"Just a few questions, shouldn't take long," Ruhi replied, and the mage grunted but, after staring for a moment, finally made his way to the gangplank. As before, he didn't descend all the way to the docks but stood balancing on the wooden expanse a few feet above.

"All right, make it quick," he snapped, hands on his hips. "I've got things to do."

Sundra bristled visibly at the mage's tone. "This would go a lot faster if you were down here with us," he suggested before pausing as if surprised. "Oh, wait, that's right, you can't, can you? Because you're not allowed to set foot in this city." He shook his head. "That can't be fun, never being able to leave the ship while all your crewmates get to come ashore and drink and carouse and just feel solid ground beneath their feet." His gaze had flicked to Chhaya, who shrugged, trying to look nonchalant, but couldn't resist the mocking little smile that had blossomed on her lips.

Yes, Sundra was good at this indeed.

Then again, Ruhi reasoned, she wasn't without her own Gifts either. Like now, as she crossed the dock and reached up to grasp the mage's bare upper arm. "Please," she entreated. "I know you're a busy man, but it would be such a big help."

He frowned, but couldn't manage a full scowl. "Fine," he declared at last, crossing his arms over his bare chest, his angavastra fluttering behind him like a small flag.

"What do you want to know this time? Because I still haven't seen or heard from Makiya." His mustache fluttered as well, stirring above his lip with each word.

"This actually isn't about him," Ruhi promised, earning a raised eyebrow from the surly mage. "It's more a general question. Well, a question for an expert. Like you." She still had her hand on his arm and could see her Gift working, reducing his resistance, mollifying him, making him more pliable. Of course, the outright flattery probably didn't hurt, either.

"Expert?" he repeated, stroking his mustache with one hand. "Well, if it's about weather or ships or magic, yes, that's true enough. All right, what is it?" He didn't sound nearly as annoyed now, though.

Ruhi had thought about this on the way over, or at least the notion had been bouncing around inside her head. She had to be careful not to spook him, however. So she started out slow.

"There's a big announcement coming from the rajas in a few days," she explained, not bothering to lower her voice but not raising it either. If those on the ship wanted to learn what she'd said they'd either have to come down themselves or ask someone like Chhavi who already was. "About those two who died recently."

"Aye, we heard," Nalan said. "So they're finally settling the matter?" He harrumphed. "Divvying up their goods like hyenas fighting over a carcass."

She shrugged. "Sure. But it has to be done, otherwise there'll be fighting, real fighting. Thing is, they're worried they may have to postpone, the Parishad. There's a big storm coming, really big, and it could swing this way instead of passing us by."

"You're right," the pirate mage admitted. "I've sensed the conditions for it, out at sea. If those keep up we'll get a storm, all right. And it'll be a big one, real nasty." He looked back fondly at the *Kalinga*. "Good thing she's sturdy, and that we're safe at harbor here."

"What if you weren't, though?" Ruhi asked, pressing her point. "What if you were out to sea and the storm hit? You could stop it, couldn't you? Use your weather magic to calm the wind and clear the sky?"

But Nalan was already shaking his head. "It's not that easy," he explained.

He shifted his stance, forcing her to pull back her hand, but Ruhi wasn't too worried. After that much extended contact, he should still be willing to listen to her for at least a few minutes, maybe longer. Besides which, it looked like the man was beginning to warm to his lecture.

"This isn't like stopping a kid who's running past, or halting a spooked sheep."

Out of the corner of her eye, Ruhi saw Sundra raise an eyebrow and mouth the words "Spooked sheep?" but she did her best to keep her attention on Nalan and her expression engaged and curious.

"What do you mean?" she asked now. "How's it any different?"

The pirate mage let out a strangled gasp. "Have you no eyes?" he demanded. "Can you even imagine the sheer force a storm like that generates, just minute to minute? It would be like trying to bail the ocean, one spoonful at a time. Can't be done."

Sundra had been listening intently. "So you couldn't stop a storm like that?" he asked now, his tone making it clear that there was a "then what good are you?" tacked on at the end but never spoken aloud.

And Nalan heard it as well, because he bristled. "Of course I could stop it!" he all but shouted at them now. "I'm thalakurios! I can beat any storm!" At the last second he lowered his head and mumbled something Ruhi almost didn't catch. "Given enough time."

"What does time have to do with anything?" she asked now, still looking as vacuous as she felt such a pose required.

Nalan sighed. "Working storms is a slow, gradual process," he admitted to them. "Just like building 'em, only in some ways it's worse because everyone assumes the storm is gonna take a while, follow its own course, and break some things along the way, so as long as you manage to create the darn thing, it's a success. Calming one, especially if you're in its path, there's no margin for error. You've gotta get it right, first time out of the bay. That's not something you can just do all at once, or do entirely on your own."

Sundra was enjoying himself now as well. "You can do magic with someone else? What, like pooling your talents? You take the left side of the storm and your friend takes the right?"

"Something like that," Nalan agreed. "More like weaving your magic together, but the important thing is, the bigger the effect, the longer it takes to create and the more people you need working on it. Stopping a storm cold?" He shrugged. "I'd need at least two others, three or even four to be safe." He lifted his chin. "Now, if a storm's about to wash over us, I can nudge it out of the way all on my own, push it to one side so it misses us completely. That I could do in a hurry. Maybe even split it so it goes around us, though that's harder. Looks impressive, though."

Ruhi nodded. "So you can't stop a storm all at once, especially not by yourself," she reiterated. "You can move one, and you can make a storm bigger or smaller, stronger or weaker, but you can't just create one, at least not quickly. Is that right?" He nodded, and she eyed him closely, focusing on his face. "What about stopping one from moving, like anchoring it to a particular place?"

The stocky weather mage frowned—but right before he did, his eyes widened, then looked away.

Gotcha.

"I don't have time to play word games," he snapped, pivoting to march back up the gangplank. "Stop wasting my time and your own." Then he was gone.

Chhavi had been there for the entire conversation, of course. Now she shrugged. "Sorry. Still not exactly warm and cuddly." She grinned, and winked at Ruhi. "I could be, though."

Ruhi felt her cheeks warm, and the blush only intensified when the pirate laughed at her.

"Good to know, thanks," Ruhi managed to mutter, glaring at Sundra, who was giggling right along with her tormentor. He was supposed to be on *her* side! "We'd better get back, though." She started edging away, away from the water, the ship, and the troublesome pirate woman.

"Well, don't be a stranger!" Chhavi called as Ruhi turned and hurried off the docks at a quick walk. "We're here only a few more days this time, hate to have you miss out!"

Sundra was still chuckling, but at least he'd taken the hint and hurried after her, catching up and settling in alongside by the time the ground under her feet changed from the worn wooden planks of the dock to the equally worn cobblestones of Surpakat proper.

She couldn't be too angry, though. Not when she'd got what she came for. Nalan definitely knew more than he was saying, and now she had a pretty good idea what that was.

That confirmation didn't put her any closer to knowing who was behind all this trouble with the thalakurioi, or what they were up to, exactly.

But it just might put her closer to finding the answers, both literally and metaphorically.

CHAPTER THIRTY-TWO

SUNDRA

Sundra waited until they were all the way back at Kosala's house, just a few paces from the front porch, before he lengthened his stride to get out in front and turned, cutting Ruhi off completely.

"All right," he said, folding his arms over his chest. "I've been remarkably patient, I think. So explain. What was the point of that little interrogation, and why've you looked so darn pleased with yourself ever since?"

Ruhi laughed and reached out to pat him on the cheek, but he pushed her hand away. Both because he didn't feel like being mollified or treated like some annoying little brother, but also because he was starting to have his suspicions. He'd noticed how Nalan's attitude had changed toward them, the mage becoming far more amenable to both conversation and questioning—and how that had occurred immediately after Ruhi'd laid her hand on the man's arm. There had been other times, too, when people had relaxed noticeably under Ruhi's touch. Including him.

Yes, he was starting to think perhaps he wasn't the only brother who had a Gift. And that his "big brother" had been rather free with the use of his.

"Talk," he insisted, and she sighed but nodded.

"I think I know where the missing mages are," she explained. "But I need the map. If that's all right with you?"

Grudgingly he shifted to the side, letting her sidle past, then followed her back into the house and to the office that she now used for her bookkeeping—and the large map of the Areyat Islands there on the wall. They both stared at it a second, but even when Ruhi shouted, "Yes! That's it!" Sundra had no idea what she'd found.

Fortunately, this time she wasn't so secretive. "Remember when we were out on the *Shikra*?" she asked, turning to lean on the desk and face him. "And we ran into that storm?"

He couldn't help chuckling. "Which one? There were three of them!"

But his "brother" shook her head. "It felt that way," she corrected, "but there were only two, actually. And that's the key." She saw his frown and continued, "The first one, that was down near Riyaasat." She shuddered a little at the memory, nor could Sundra blame her. That had been a rough time. "But then there was that second one, right?"

"Sure." He remembered it clearly. "It was sort of in our way to Dveep Kile, but that turned out fine 'cause we turned and went to Ooncha Need first anyway." He tapped his chin, recalling their recent travels. "But there was a third one, we detoured around it on our way back."

"It wasn't a different storm, though," Ruhi told him triumphantly. "That was the same one, we just ran across it coming and going."

"Uh…" He studied her to see if she were joking, or crazed, but neither looked to be the case. "We were there long enough for that first storm to have moved past already." Then he put the pieces together, combining those incidents with what Nalan had said. "Unless some stormer was keeping it in place!"

"Exactly." But he barely noticed her agreeing because his gaze had gone past her, back to the map. And there it was. A small island, little more than a speck, below and between Dveep Kile and Ooncha Need. In fact, the three formed an uneven triangle, with the unnamed land mass at the lowest point.

"You think they're holed up there, whoever's behind this—and that it's gotta be one of the weather mages themselves."

But he could already tell she was right. It all fit. The island was close enough to both those locations and not all that far from here or anywhere else on the islands, but it didn't have a durga or khet, which meant it was unclaimed and ostensibly unoccupied. And with a storm fixed around it like a magical fence, nobody was getting in or out without the thalakurioi's permission. Most people would never even know the place was there, since they'd detour around the storm. Exactly as the *Shikra* had. And if enough time passed before they returned that way, they'd assume it was a different storm the second time, same as he'd just done. He hadn't been thinking about the fact that they were looking for people who could literally control such weather. Only Ruhi had made that connection.

Which brought him to the next question. "Let's say you're right," he started, and held up a hand to forestall her protests. "Which I think you are, mind. So what do we do now? Tell the Parishad? Half of them would storm the place and try taking it by force—and lock any mages they find in chains and collars, punish them for trying to get free. They'd be even worse off than they were before, and I'm not exactly thrilled with their previous treatment."

That made her slump a little, dimming the joy at her victory. "Damn. I don't want to see them go back to that, either. Hells, if this is about being treated the way they were, I'm more on their side than the rajas." She grimaced. "But we can't not tell them, and we can't let whoever's doing this keep stealing people away. It's one thing if they're being freed and another if they're being kidnapped. Which it sounds like at least a few of them are."

Sundra nodded, considering. "We're going to have to go check it out ourselves," he pointed out. "Which means we have to tell Kosala. But nobody else, for now. Not until we know exactly what's going on."

Ruhi straightened, moving away from the desk. "That works. We'd have to tell her anyway, since we can't exactly go without her permission."

She raised her hand, the indenture bracelet jangling from the movement, and Sundra recalled that the mages had apparently found a way to break free of those too. Not that *he* had that kind of power. Nor, fortunately, as rough a time as some of them clearly had. Still, useful to know.

Knocking on the raja's study door produced no response, but before they could despair, Sundra heard her deep voice from down the hall, approaching the front door. Sure enough, a few seconds later, she and Sanga entered. Evidently they'd lingered after the council meeting.

"—the bribes are beyond belief," Kosala was saying. "If she wanted a ship that badly, she could've bought one off a few of us for a lot less. I see why, but still—" She stopped when she saw them waiting for her. "Yes? Any luck with that idea, whatever it was?"

"We think so, yes," Ruhi answered from just behind him. "We can show you."

A minute later, they were back by the map, and she was explaining her theory.

"Makes sense," Sanga agreed. "I mean, if you believe a mage can do that to a storm. But I've seen and heard some stories, so maybe they can. It'd make a perfect hiding place."

Kosala was fingering her daggers, her brow lowered in concentration. "It would," she agreed. "All right, let's say you've found them. What now?"

Ruhi glanced at Sundra, and he took over. "That's what we wanted to talk with you about," he started. "We still don't know exactly who's doing this or how many there are or what kind of defenses they have or anything other than where they are—if they really are there." He shrugged. "We want to go see for ourselves before we bring this to the Parishad."

Their employer's gaze was as direct as ever. "You could just tell everyone now and be done with it," she pointed out. "Then whatever we find and whatever happens, it's not your problem. So why're you delaying, really?" Somehow she always saw through them.

Since that was the case, Sundra dispensed with any hint of subtlety. "Have you seen how these mages are treated?" he asked instead. "They live like prisoners! Bracelets! Bars! Chains! I know it's called a contract and employment and whatever, but it sure looks like slavery to me."

For a second, he thought he'd overstepped, as the raja's eyes flashed, her lips compressed into a flat line and her expression hard. Then she nodded, once.

"I haven't looked too closely at how my fellow rajas treat their employees," she admitted. "Maybe because I didn't want to know. But with all this, we don't have much choice, and neither do they—they made the stormers a matter for the whole Parishad, and that means we'll decide how to proceed as a whole." She scowled. "And I don't like slavery any better than you do."

That was reassuring, as was the fact that Sundra suspected Chetan would feel the same. Whether they'd be able to convince the others, especially Jasleen, Tarabai, and Ehsaan, he didn't know. It was something, at least.

Sanga stirred from where he'd been standing, arms crossed. "If they're organized, this could turn into an even bigger problem than it's been," he pointed out. "I think these two're right. We need to know what we're dealing with first."

Sundra didn't miss the "we"—or the way Ruhi had brightened upon hearing that word. He'd have to tease her about that later.

For now, he was more focused on Kosala, who turned and departed without a word. She was back a few minutes later, however, and handed Sanga a pair of rolled-up documents.

"Their papers," she explained, more to Sundra and Ruhi, as her second accepted the parchments and stuck them inside his vest for safekeeping. "This way, you three can go together." Now she pointed a finger at each of them in turn. "Look, find out, and come back. That's it. None of you would be a match for a storm mage throwing lightning."

They all nodded, and she moved on to her next question. "How are you going to get there, anyway? I'd give you command of the *Shikra*"—that was to Sanga, of course—"but there's no way you're sailing my ship straight into some magic-powered superstorm."

Sundra was already turning to his so-called brother, guessing what she had in mind, just as Ruhi spoke up. "We won't need the *Shikra*, thanks," she explained. "But we are going to need a thalakurios to get us through." She grinned. "Fortunately, we know exactly where to find one, and there's even a ship that comes with him."

All of which was true. The problem, Sundra knew, was going to be convincing Nalan to help them.

And then convincing Khandereo to let them take the *Kalinga* to go look for some missing mages. The pirate captain had never struck him as the sort to make selfless acts or to risk himself, his crew, and his ship without a compelling reason—and some clear gain to be had from such efforts.

CHAPTER THIRTY-THREE

RUHI

Though the sky had darkened, heavy clouds beginning to gather overhead and promising a deluge soon, Chhavi was still sitting in the same spot as before, making Ruhi wonder if the female pirate did any work at all when they were in port. Then again, what was there for her to do? Ruhi still didn't know much about boats—when they were docked, didn't that mean the crew was at liberty? Although, if so, why did Chhavi choose to spend hers lounging on the docks instead of in the city carousing and doing whatever else pirates did on their days off?

Of course, the female pirate grinned at her as they approached for the second time that day, sparing a glance and a nod at Sanga before returning her attention to Ruhi. "Back so soon?" She sat up and leaned forward, her leather vest flapping open with the motion, her simple choli doing little to hide her cleavage. "Decided to take me up on my offer?" she asked, her eyes boring holes into Ruhi.

"I'm up for it if my brother isn't," Sundra offered, but the pirate only waved him off.

"Sorry, pretty boy," she told him, never even glancing his way.

"I like 'em tall, grim, and bearded." The words were almost serious, but her eyes danced with laughter, knowing full well that Ruhi was only one of those things. Still, she felt her cheeks flush at the attention, and the interest.

"Thanks, but unfortunately we don't have a lot of time for dalliance," Ruhi replied. "Nalan!" That shout was directed up at the ship, and the weather mage appeared a few seconds later. Almost as if he'd been waiting for them.

"What now?" he demanded. "I'm dealing with this storm," the mage continued. "It shouldn't be here yet, or be this focused. Something's off about it." But there was something different about his tone and his stance. Almost like a child who'd been caught misbehaving, Ruhi thought.

Or lying.

"We know where your friends are," Sundra shouted at the man. "But then you already knew that, didn't you? Because you've known where they were all along."

The mage glared at them both for a full minute—before hanging his head. "Not the whole time, no," he admitted more quietly, his words barely trickling down to them. "But later, yes."

"Come down here where we can hear you properly," Sanga demanded, speaking up for the first time, and Nalan looked at him in surprise, clearly not sure who this newcomer was. There was no mistaking the authority behind the tall pirate's order, however, and a moment later the thalakurios had descended to his customary spot near the base of the gangplank.

"Talk to us," Ruhi insisted, approaching him, though she didn't feel she could lay a hand on him the way she had last time, not with Sanga watching. "Tell us what's really going on here."

Her request was all but drowned out by a strange crackling in the air and the odd sensation of hair standing on end. Ruhi frowned, not sure what to make of it, but Sundra shouted, "Get down!" and dove to the ground. At the same time, Nalan straightened, sudden anger suffusing his features.

"NO!" he bellowed, hands leaping up over his head in fists,

wrists crossed. Power burst from him like the glow from a fire suddenly catching light, a wave of energy Ruhi could actually see spilling outward, a strong, warm wind emanating from the mage and pushing her back several steps.

That aura turned to a full-on ripple as lightning struck the storm mage, his protective bubble flaring so bright she flinched, black spots dancing before her eyes.

When her vision cleared enough for her to see again, she gasped. Nalan still stood there, unharmed—but the lightning now danced around him, crawling over his arms and shoulders and head and chest, crackling as it moved. His eyes were blindingly bright as well, trails of energy flickering at their edges as he peered into the darkness of the storm.

"Where are you?" Nalan demanded, and his words rolled with thunder. "Show yourself, you cowards!"

Lightning struck again, in clear response to his call, aimed not at him but at the *Kalinga*'s hull—but the bolt swerved at the last second, drawn to the already energy-wrapped mage, and was absorbed into that flow that washed over him like a living cloak.

And in the flash, Ruhi caught sight of something small and dark out on the water between the *Kalinga* and the next dock over.

"There!" she shouted, pointing, and all eyes turned toward the small ship, which is what it was. And the two figures standing in it, hands raised and aglow with energies of their own.

Nalan laughed, then. "Tara. Ojas. You thought you could stand against me? Even together, you're no match!"

As Ruhi watched, he brought his hands down, pointing one at each of the two rival thalakurioi—the same two the older mage Puvanti had mentioned, she recalled. They were clearly very much alive and unharmed, though Ruhi didn't know how much longer those conditions would last as glowing blue-white bolts leapt from Nalan's hands toward his foes, exactly as if lightning had been captured, harnessed, and fashioned into spears. The two other mages staggered back from the blows, and one toppled, sitting down hard in the little boat. The other managed to retain her feet, but she looked stunned from the impact.

That is, until an arrow took her in the throat. Her eyes went wide with surprise before she also fell, keeling over sideways and hitting the dark, roiling water with a dull splash. She did not resurface.

"No!" Nalan shouted, glaring up at the pirate who'd fired, but the man simply shrugged—and readied another arrow. "Ojas, surrender now, while you can!"

The rival stormer glared at him, but after a quick glance at the archer and the other pirates barely restraining themselves, he nodded. "Fine." He reached up—carefully—and adjusted his little boat's single small sail. There was enough of a breeze to carry the small craft the remaining distance to the docks.

Sanga was waiting. He leaned out over the water—and punched the mage full in the face. The man slumped, and Sanga hauled the unconscious thalakurios onto the docks. "Seemed the safest option," he explained as he tied the man's hands behind his back.

"I can't believe he sent them to kill me," Nalan was muttering, still from his place on the gangplank. "I told him I would not stand in his way, nor reveal his secrets!"

"Who?" Ruhi asked quickly, taking advantage of the mage's obvious sense of betrayal. "Is it Makiya? Is he behind all this? Is he the one masking that island?"

Nalan surprised her by laughing, but then he did answer. "That weakling? Not a chance—he can barely whistle up a wind, much less fix a storm in place like that!" He shook his bald head, his mustache swinging with the motion. "No, it's not Makiya." With a sigh, and a slump of his shoulders, the mage continued, "It's Yilai."

"Yilai?" Sundra frowned. "Wasn't he the one who died? The one who worked for Ehsaan?"

"He didn't die," the mage corrected, crossing his arms. "He escaped! Faked his own death to do it too. It was the only way out. Do you have any idea how most of us are treated?"

He glanced fondly at the ship beside him. "I'm the lucky one—I found a place here, and Khandereo's more interested in having me as a partner than a slave." Then his expression darkened. "It's not like that for most of us, though. We're too dangerous to be left to our own devices, they say. Too valuable to not be protected—what they mean is guarded and controlled. Yilai was like that. Never allowed a moment's freedom. So, when he got the chance, he took it." He scowled down at them, daring them to disagree. "I, for one, am glad he was able to."

Ruhi took a step closer, though pressure from the surrounding storm made the very air resist. "So am I," she promised, willing him to see the sincerity in her gaze and hear it in her voice. "We both are," she amended, gesturing at Sundra, who nodded. "You forget, we're indentured ourselves. And, like you, we're in a good place now, but we weren't always." She could see her so-called brother scowling at the reminder. "Our first post here, it was awful. We were slaves in all but name and mistreated horribly. So believe me, I hate what I've seen about how most of your friends are treated. And if Yilai got out of that, good for him."

"But what about the rest?" Sundra asked. "Are they just escaping, too? To an island no one can get to? What's the point?" The way he asked the question, angling his head as he did, made Ruhi think he already knew the answer but just wanted to hear it.

Fortunately, Nalan obliged. Apparently being attacked by his own friends had put him in a talkative mood. "They're not running away," he replied, chuckling at Sundra's apparent naivete. "They're gathering. Organizing. Yilai's got them working together—the storm's proof of that. He couldn't have done that all by himself, even as strong as he is. Once he's got everybody out, he's going to confront the rajas."

Now the mage's chin came up, pride suffusing his features. "He's going to force them to grant our kind their freedom. No more slavery! No more chains and bracelets and bindings! We work for who we want, and we get paid appropriately! Thalakurioi solidarity!"

It was the same thing that one mage, Utama, had shouted when he'd been trying to escape Dveep Kile, Ruhi recalled. Which meant

Nalan had definitely been in communication with the escaped mages since. He really had been lying to them all along. Still, she couldn't entirely blame him—he'd had no reason to trust them, and every reason to protect his friends.

"That's good," Sundra commented, rubbing his chin. "And I, for one, support the idea that you and the other thalakurioi will be able to bargain for freedom, better working conditions, better pay, all of that. You deserve it. But what about the ones who weren't interested in running away? The ones who didn't want to join this new collective or whatever it is? Ones like Farah? Or Utaya? Or the one who shared quarters with Yilai—the one who didn't want to go and had to be dragged away by him and the other one there?"

Ah! Ruhi straightened as those words penetrated and connected several dots that had been floating fuzzily around the edges of these questions. Of course! That was why, at Ooncha Need, two of the rooms had been neat and the other messy—as if one of the occupants had been forced to leave in a hurry, while the other two had time to prepare. Sundra had seen that and put the pieces together. And now, watching Nalan's face twist, the scowl fighting with a concerned furrow, she could see that her "brother" wasn't the only one to notice the difference in how some of the mages had left.

But the scowl won out, in the end. "They're fine," Nalan insisted, though he glanced down as he said it, at the worn planks of the dock, rather than at them. "But in order to force the rajas' hands, Yilai needs everyone to be onboard. Solidarity, that's the key."

"So he's, what, taken anyone who didn't agree to join his cause and hidden them away somewhere?" Ruhi asked, and by the way he stiffened, she could see she'd got it right. "These are your friends!" she reminded him. "How can you sit by and let him do that to them, even if it's supposedly for a good cause? How is that any better than the way they were treated before?"

That had the mage glaring at her, and she felt the pressure increase and the space around them darken further as those clouds began to mass again overhead, looming down like angry giants. Maybe pissing off a weather mage wasn't such a good idea. For now, at least, he was only replying in words, though there was a bite to those as well.

"He wouldn't hurt them!" Nalan insisted. "It's just so they won't interfere or make it look like we're not all together in this, and only until the rajas agree to his conditions! Then they'll be free, just like the rest of us!"

A chuckle cut off any further tirade—from Sundra, who was slowly shaking his head. "Are you really that naive?" he asked, his tone utterly patronizing, for that instant becoming every bit the high-born noble speaking down to some ignorant worker. "Yilai can't ever let them loose after this. They'll undermine his authority if he does—and make any new thalakurioi doubt whether he can be trusted to lead them and bind them together as a group."

He sighed. "No, there's no way he can have any of you around if you even hint that you accepted the previous state of things, or that you don't fully support him. He'll wait until he gets what he wants, so he doesn't lose the rest of you—but as soon as he does? He'll kill them, make it look like an accident or blame the rajas somehow, but they'll be dead all the same."

Nalan was staring at him, eyes wide, face gone pale, and Ruhi suspected she was the same. "He wouldn't," the mage whispered, but it was mere horror at the thought, rather than true negation. He didn't believe that himself, not at all. And, sadly, Ruhi knew Sundra was right. Judging by how both Chhavi and Sanga were nodding, they all did.

"And speaking of non-joiners," Sundra continued, "how is it you're still here?"

The mage, still pale, recovered enough to manage a weak smirk. "He asked," he replied simply. "I said I didn't want any part of it. I'm good where I am. But I support what he's doing." He frowned. "Or at least I did."

Even Sanga was shaking his head now. "Clearly that wasn't enough," the rangy pirate pointed out. "No wonder he sent those two after you. He can't risk you telling anyone what he's up to—like you are right now."

"And if he's going to come after you, when you're at least sympathetic," Sundra added, "what will he do to the ones who actively oppose him?"

The terror returned to the storm mage's face as that reality sank in.

"We can save them," Ruhi promised impulsively, closing the distance and clasping his hand, but for once not attempting to use her Gift. She didn't need to. "Help us. Get us to the island, help us free your friends and confront Yilai. We'll bring all of this to the Parishad—including current conditions. Not all the rajas support that, and with it in front of them all, out in the open, we can make things better. But only if you help us. We can't do this without you."

Sundra had stepped forward as well, joining them. "And no one else can save your friends," he urged. "They'll die unless we get to them first. Unless you do."

The mage stared at his hand in Ruhi's before finally raising his head to meet their gaze. The horror was still there, but his mouth was a firm line beneath his mustache, and his jaw was set. "All right," he agreed. "I'll help. What do you need me to do?"

Ruhi let out the breath she'd been holding, retreating a pace so she had room to think. "We need to get there, first," she said. "Can you get us through the storm?" He nodded. "Good. Let's go—there isn't any time to waste."

But a new shadow fell upon her as someone else stepped out onto the top of the gangplank, blocking their intended path. Someone tall and slim, in a long, heavily embroidered coat.

"Well, now," Khandereo, captain of the *Kalinga*, drawled. "Let's discuss that, shall we?"

CHAPTER THIRTY-FOUR

SUNDRA

This is Parishad business," Sanga declared, using his own long legs to hop up onto the gangplank just above Nalan and step quickly toward the top, where he could confront the pirate captain eye to eye. And they were equally matched in height, Sundra saw. Neither was terribly bulky, but both had the taut muscles of men who toiled at rope and sail for a living—and both bore enough scars to show they had been in plenty of fights, but all minor enough to show they could handle themselves. If it ever did come to blows between the two, he had no idea who would win.

In this case, however, there was no contest, as Khandereo folded his arms over his bare chest and peered down at Sanga, who was still several paces below him.

"That's as may be," he stated, his voice as calm and clear as ever, "but this is my ship. And I don't work for the Parishad, singly or together." He glanced to the left, where Sundra could just make out the top of the *Shikra*'s mast. "Go take one of your own ships, why don't you?"

The real reason they weren't was that Kosala wasn't willing to risk her own ship on such an expedition, and none of the other rajas were aware of this latest development yet. But of course they couldn't say that. Instead, Sundra called up, "Because Nalan is your shipmate. He knows the *Kalinga* best, which means it'll be easiest for him to use his magic on."

He was relieved when the mage nodded. "Aye, true enough," the man informed his captain. "And you know I'd never put the ship—or any of you—at risk if it weren't needed."

But Khandereo wasn't sold. "I understand you wish to save your friends," he told his storm mage, speaking around Sanga, who still glared at him from only a few feet away. "And that's noble and all. But we aren't nobles. We're pirates. And you *are* talking about putting my ship and crew at risk. Or did I misunderstand the part about a storm being held in place so we'd have no choice but to cut through it?"

"There's cutting through and there's cutting through," Ruhi argued. "You said you could bend a storm around a ship, right? So the *Kalinga* wouldn't even get wet."

Nalan grimaced. "Don't know as I'd go that far," he admitted. "There'd still be some spray, some castoff. But it wouldn't be the brunt of the storm, no."

"And once we're through?" his captain asked, unrelenting. "What then? You were talking about storm mages massing on this island, looking to win their freedom. You really want us to sail into that? Armed with swords and clubs and spears?" He shook his head, his thick braid swaying behind him. "Sounds like a death sentence to me."

"Like the death sentence they just tried to pass on Nalan?" Sundra asked quickly. "He's part of your crew, will you really let them get away with that?"

Khandereo glared at him. "Normally, no," he replied with just a touch of heat. "I'd carve the liver from any man or woman who threatened one of mine. But this is mage business. I trust Nalan to handle it. Get in the middle of that, just so I can feel superior about sticking up for my crew—even while I'm dooming them all at the hands of a living storm? No thanks."

He started turning away, and Sundra knew if the man left the gangplank it was all over. They might be able to talk Nalan into accompanying them anyway, and maybe sway Kosala into giving them one of her other ships, but that would take a good deal more time, and who was to say how much they had?

Desperately, he cast about, looking for something, anything that might change Khandereo's mind. His gaze swept to Chhavi— and the female pirate held it with her own, but there was no mirth in her eyes now, nor any flirtation as she nodded toward the ship and then extended the first two fingers of her right hand, where it hung at her side. Then she winked at him.

Clearly, that was a message of some sort. But what? Sundra puzzled over it, looking from the ship to her to her fingers and back again. And then he understood.

"It *is* a fine ship," he shouted, and Khandereo stopped, glancing down at him. "I'd hate to see anything happen to it either. But it's just one ship, after all." He rubbed his chin as if in thought. "Now, if you had two…"

"What are you doing?" Ruhi hissed at him, but Sundra waved her off.

"Negotiating," he whispered back. "Watch."

Sure enough, the *Kalinga*'s captain had turned back, resuming his former post. "Two ships would be nice," he agreed mildly, as if they were discussing what to order for lunch. "Of course, if anything happened to either, I'd be back down to only one again. Now, if I had three, say…"

Sundra frowned. "That seems an awful lot to ask for a short, simple boat ride," he argued. "And with no cargo, nothing but the three of us, and only a few days each way. I'd think one additional ship more than adequate compensation for all that."

"And you'd be right," Khandereo agreed easily. "If you weren't asking us to wade into a whole nest of riled-up storm mages. That's worth at least another ship. Maybe more."

Sanga was glaring down at him. "Those ships aren't yours to give," he pointed out.

"True," Sundra agreed. "But, as I keep being told, my word and my brother's counts for something here. So if we were to say that the captain here deserved one or even two of those ships for helping us resolve this whole stormer situation, I'd think the rajas might listen. Don't you?"

"He's right," Ruhi agreed, and he felt a wave of relief that she'd finally chosen to back him up. "They'd agree that was a fair price to pay. *If* we manage to solve this. Which means getting there as soon as possible."

Khandereo was eyeing them both now. "I want your word," he stated.

Sundra nodded at once, and Ruhi was right behind him. "You have it," he replied. "Mind you, I can't guarantee they'll give you a ship, but I promise that we will speak on your behalf, and argue you should have it."

"Them," the tall man corrected. "Have them. Two ships."

Sundra frowned, but in the end he knew he couldn't win this one. "Two ships," he echoed at last.

No one moved for a moment. Then Khandereo smiled. "Very well." He stepped back, swiveling to the side, and executed a deep bow well-suited to his fancy coat and fine turban. "Welcome aboard."

They hurried up the gangplank, Chhavi right behind them, and Sundra whispered, "Thanks!" to her as they clambered up the incline.

"Don't thank me too much," she told him, not bothering to lower her own voice. He could hear the grin in her words. "I'm aiming to be captain of one of those new ships."

He had to laugh at that, but why not? Khandereo would need to install someone he could trust to handle those ships and still follow his lead. The sensible choice was someone from his current crew, and it certainly seemed that Chhavi had his trust.

Of course, if she became a captain her flirting with Ruhi might increase dramatically, and he chuckled at the thought—and at picturing Sanga's reaction to the same.

Yes, he saw nothing wrong with any of this.

Khandereo had already begun shouting orders, and the crew scurried this way and that, loosing the mooring rope, retrieving the gangplank, and raising the sails. They'd also hailed a worker on a nearby dock, sending him to notify the guards about the stunned stormer they'd left trussed at their side.

Meanwhile, Nalan had moved to the ship's stern, downing a small vial of some strange, vividly blue liquid as he went, and was standing at the broad, raised railing there, hands spread wide, eyes closed, not moving.

But a moment later, Sundra swore he could feel the first tickling of a breeze.

It increased, ruffling his hair, then tugging at his shirt and vest, and above them, the ship's mainsail began to fill, angled aft so that the wind pushed them away from the dock and out into the bay. The crew swung the sail about, pivoting the ship, and suddenly the wind was at their back instead, their prow aimed toward the open water beyond.

The *Kalinga* was off!

CHAPTER THIRTY-FIVE

RUHI

R uhi had not been on the *Kalinga* before. She and Sundra had been captured on the *Aden Star*, a bigger ship, and, rather than bring all his prisoners across, Khandereo had simply put Chhavi and a few of his other crewmembers— including the burly pair Jayant and Rohan, who she now learned were brothers—onto the *Star*, sailing the captured vessel along beside them until they could bring it to Surpakat. As a result, she hadn't realized just how small and narrow the pirate ship really was—until she was forced to squeeze onto it with not only its regular crew but Sundra and Sanga besides.

There was only one cabin below, at the rear, and that was reserved for the captain himself. Everyone else slept either up on the deck or in hammocks in the central hold. That included Chhavi, and Ruhi had been shocked when, a few hours out from the city, the female pirate had casually strolled to the ship's stern, dropped her pants, perched on the rear railing facing forward, and peed over the back. None of the men had paid her any attention—except for Sundra, who'd resolutely turned away in a surprisingly gallant gesture—and Ruhi had done likewise, but not before Chhavi had winked at her. What in the heavens?

After she'd finished, Chhavi calmly straightened and pulled up her trousers. As she passed Ruhi, she whispered, "I'm on watch at dusk. You can go then. Promise I won't look."

That was more or less how Ruhi had managed on the way to the pirate islands, only with Sundra serving as her lookout. It was a relief to know she might have two people protecting her secret here, but the complete lack of privacy on this boat still made her uneasy.

Of course, there was another problem. She hadn't thought to ask Kosala or Sanga about the wristlet she'd worn before, the one that had helped keep any nausea or seasickness at bay. Fortunately, the rangy pirate had, and handed her the slim bracelet as they were casting off.

But, while it definitely still helped, it seemed the bracelet's innate properties just couldn't compete with the speed and choppy motion of a ship being powered at regular intervals by a storm mage.

"How fast are we going?" she managed at one point, clinging to one of the ropes for dear life, her braid whipping about her. This felt much like when they'd suffered through that first storm, only without any rain or thunder and lightning.

Sundra, swinging from a nearby rope and looking completely at ease even as his own loose hair streamed out behind him, grinned. "Would it make any sense if I told you?" he replied, having to shout for her to hear him over the strong winds. "A whole lot faster than we should be able to manage, though!"

One of the sailors, strolling past with that odd rolling gait only seasoned boaters had, laughed and clapped them each on a shoulder. "That's right!" he declared. "Ol' Nalan's really in a hurry this time! Must be, way he's using those elixirs of his! Worth more'n gold, those are!"

The stormer had fallen into a deep sleep right after they'd left Surpakat, but had awakened a few hours later to eat a hefty meal of liver and dried meat and then whip the wind into a frenzy again.

He'd gone back to sleep after that, only to start the whole cycle all over again.

To take her mind off their speed, Ruhi studied the ship's two sails, which had been lowered so that only their top sections were up catching the wind, and which had also been pulled taut, their surfaces nearly flat. "Why are they like that?" she asked, yelling.

It was Sanga who answered, the tall pirate leaning on the railing near them in an effort to stay out of the actual crew's way. "You can't run too much sail in a wind like this," he explained, not raising his voice but somehow making himself heard. "You see a lot of novices try that. Snaps the mast or shreds the sail—or both. You want to reef much of it, so you can better control the rest. And you want your sail tight and almost flat for the same reason. We'd be a little faster if we didn't do either, but only until we lost a sail or capsized or something worse."

He studied the *Kalinga*'s crew, who were all moving about constantly, not in any sort of panic but clearly busy, each with their assigned tasks and each managing to stay out of each other's way, and nodded in approval. "Good crew," he offered.

Ruhi nodded, but her attention was still on not getting sick. She tried leaning out over the rail a little, just enough to feel the sea spray on her face, but then her eyes were drawn to the water rushing by below. And it *was* rushing, no question—staring just at the water, she felt like they were flying across it, although more accurately it was flying along with them. She wasn't even sure how that was possible, or how it worked with the winds.

"Nalan's got the winds at our back, driving us forward," Sundra explained when she asked him, not wanting Sanga to think her any dumber or more ignorant than he already did. "But that's only half what he's doing. Normally, we'd be running with the wind but going against the current, or at best cutting across it side to side." He shook his head, swaying to the sound of the waves striking again. "Somehow he's got it so there's this narrow little channel around us, and in this one small patch he's got the entire Ekiladitar flowing northeast. We're just getting carried right along with all that. The sails are a bonus."

Khandereo happened to be strolling past when he said that and paused to respond. "He's really taken your warning about his friends to heart," the tall pirate captain told them. "Only other time we've ever gone this fast is when we were ducking a trio of heavy baghala, all filled with soldiers looking to put us down." He squinted up at the sky, taking its measure. "We'll reach your little island day after next," he stated finally. "If he doesn't collapse or tear my poor ship apart first." He left them with that cheery thought, continuing on his way toward the rear and the pirate he had stationed at the tiller there.

"Don't worry," Sundra assured Ruhi as soon as the man was gone. "That won't happen. Nalan knows he won't do anyone any good if he gets us all killed, himself included."

That wasn't as much comfort as he probably thought, but Ruhi clung to it nonetheless, the same way she clung to the railing—and to Khandereo's estimate. Two days, he'd said. She could survive that. She could survive anything for two days.

Two days later, she wasn't so sure. She'd barely slept either night, the constant, rapid motion and the intensity of both wave and wind making her too anxious to do more than doze fitfully. Her stomach hurt, as did her head and sides. Her legs ached from trying to keep her balance, and her hands, arms, shoulders, and neck from clutching railing or rope nonstop. Plus the added stress of trying to keep her gender hidden when surrounded by men—including Sanga—had all left Ruhi a complete mess.

Sundra, who didn't seem to be feeling any of that, had passed it off as severe seasickness. And, fortunately, the others had all seemed willing to go along with that. Especially after Chhavi had backed him up.

Even so, Ruhi felt a pang of relief when one of the pirates at the boat's sleek, raised prow called back, "Storm ahead!" While not

the emotion one would normally experience upon sighting fear-
some weather, she knew it meant they were closing in on their
destination.

Now they just had to reach it safely.

"Is that the right one?" Sanga asked, leaning his weight against
a rope as he peered ahead. "Or are we just running up against a
different, completely normal storm?"

The other man at the ship's prow turned, his bald head shin-
ing from reflected sunlight—and sweat. Nalan had kept to his
rigid schedule, hurling his focus and his magic at the waves and
wind when he was awake, eating vast quantities and then sleeping
like the dead in between, and so both gaze and voice were under-
standably terse as he snapped, "There's nothing normal about that
storm. That is our destination."

"Best put this on," Chhavi offered, handing Ruhi a storm coat
like the one she'd already shrugged on herself. She passed one to
Sundra and another to Sanga, then left the three of them to tie
themselves to the rail.

"Feels oddly familiar," Sundra quipped. "But hopefully it'll be
over a lot quicker."

"As long as it's not all over for us in general," Sanga replied
from her other side, and despite her discomfort and fatigue, Ruhi
raised an eyebrow, making the tall pirate shrug, though his lips still
quirked in a smile. Had that been a joke? If so, it was the first such
she'd heard from him. And, even though it maybe hadn't been the
best, it still showed a slightly softer side to the normally fierce and
closemouthed pirate.

Ruhi thought she liked it.

She forgot about all that, however, as the *Kalinga* continued to
race forward—straight toward what now looked like a solid wall of
dark-gray clouds occasionally lit by lightning within. Pirates reefed
the sails completely, nothing but the current and the magic driving
them on, but their pace didn't slacken in the least.

"Hold on!" Nalan shouted, raising his hands high. They were
nearly to the storm, close enough to feel its wind cutting across

the gale of their passage and taste the rain it sprayed in their direction. Just as the *Kalinga*'s prow closed with that storm wall, Nalan shouted a wordless cry that echoed all around them—

—and the clouds parted like a thick, fuzzy curtain, letting the ship pass through unmolested.

Or nearly so. They didn't split apart completely, more like the storm thinned around them as they entered it, rain and wind weakening as if they were passing through a screen so fine as to be nearly invisible. Ruhi still found herself pummeled by a downpour flung in her face, but it was a summer storm versus a deadly hurricane.

The bubble shielding them from the worst of the storm traveled forward as they did, the storm sealing back in behind them so that now the ship was surrounded on all sides, nothing visible beyond its railings besides gray clouds, even the water below hidden from view. They were sailing blind, but Khandereo held the tiller steady, pointing them straight ahead.

And, just as Ruhi started to fear they'd be trapped in the storm forever, it ended, the ship bursting out the other side, gray falling away behind and nothing but clear, blue sky overhead—

—and a small, rocky island directly before them, so close the pirates quickly grabbed long poles to keep the ship from running up onto the rocks. A walled structure rose along the near edge, with a short, cylindrical white tower poking up behind that.

They had arrived.

CHAPTER THIRTY-SIX

SUNDRA

Ah! Giants' teeth!" Sanga muttered, staring out at the strange place along with the rest of them. "I know this place!"

"You do?" Sundra turned, fixing the tall pirate with a raised eyebrow. "And you didn't think to mention that before?"

The other man waved off the comment and the implied criticism, though he didn't seem angry about it. But then, Sanga was almost always calm and collected.

"I don't mean I've been here or anything," he explained, still studying the high brick-and-stone walls. A smaller, rounded spur jutted out into the water. The thick, stubby tower stood in the distance. "But I've heard of it. Shaant Sthaan—it has to be."

At the tiller, Khandereo nodded. "Aye, that makes sense," the pirate captain agreed. "Huh. Forgot all about the tales of this place." He and much of his crew were eyeing the island with contemplative, almost awed looks now.

"Anyone care to enlighten those of us who weren't born and raised as pirates?" Ruhi asked, scowling, and Sundra would have laughed if he didn't currently share her frustration.

Fortunately, Sanga came to their rescue. "It's an old, old fortress," he explained. "From back when these isles were first home to our kind. Before Jasleen Lal, even."

He gestured up at the white tower. "That's a lighthouse. Those stationed here only lit it when they saw the right signal from an approaching ship. Otherwise, the tower stayed dark and ships would crash into the rocks or miss the island completely." He shook his head. "It was a safe haven for any pirate fleeing pursuit—for a price."

"Ah." Sundra nodded, tapping his chin. Yes, he could see how those early ships would've paid a pretty penny for a safe berth. Clever racket for whoever built and maintained the place—all they had to do was sit here, keep watch, occasionally light the signal fire, and collect their pay. "What happened?"

Sanga grimaced. "The usual. People got greedy, someone decided not to pay, fight broke out, place got sacked. By that point, Surpakat and a few others were being established, so no one needed to come all the way out here anymore." He shook his head. "Totally forgot it was here."

"Looks like Yilai took full advantage of that," Ruhi commented, pointing toward the tower—and the lights they could see through its windows. "Guess we've lost any chance at sneaking up on them now."

"I doubt we'd have had much luck with that anyway," Sundra replied, studying the layout. "Guessing the only ways in are from this one extended dock or from sally ports along the back. We're going in the front door, whether we like it or not."

Nalan, who had left the *Kalinga*'s prow to join them midship, scowled at the fortress. "I'll blow the entire place to bits if that's what it takes to free my friends," he vowed.

"Good attitude, but probably safest for them—and us—if you just make a door instead," Sundra answered, gingerly patting the mage on the back.

The mustachioed man bristled a little, but let it go, which was a relief. After that display back at Surpakat, Sundra definitely didn't want the stormer angry at him.

The dock in question projected out from that one spur, and they moored quickly, tying the *Kalinga* tightly but with knots they could slip in a hurry. The thick stone-and-brick wall faced them, its only visible opening a heavy iron door.

"Stand back," Nalan warned, downing another elixir before raising one hand, and the wind came whistling in around him, whipping at their hair and clothes until the mage stood at the center of a tiny, focused gale. He brought his fist down with a snap, aimed at the door, and the wind hurtled forward, smashing into the barrier so hard it buckled the thick iron, crumpling it inward. Then edges of that tempest snuck in at the edges, wrapped around the sturdy door—and pulled.

With the groan of distressed wood and the shriek of torn metal, the door was ripped from its hinges and flung out to sea, well clear of their docked ship. Now the doorway stood empty, yawning wide and dark beyond.

"Expect anyone we meet's a mage," Nalan warned as they advanced in a tight clump.

Most of the crew had remained behind on the ship, only Chhavi and the brothers Jayant and Rohan joining them on this expedition. Sundra had initially wondered if this was cowardice on Khandereo's part—not that he'd ever dare suggest such to the pirate captain's face!—but quickly realized it was merely caution, and a desire to both protect ship and crew and also keep ready for an urgent escape if needed.

"Knocking them out fast is your best defense." Nalan sighed before pleading, "Try not to kill them, if you can." He looked exhausted, like he could barely keep his feet, but his eyes were almost too bright, and his speech and movements were rapid and jerky.

"No promises," Chhavi warned, sword in hand, and the others all nodded. Hefting the slim blade he'd borrowed from the *Kalinga*, Sundra understood and respected the mage's concern for his friends, but the female pirate was right. If they had to defend themselves, he wasn't going to worry about pulling his punches.

The passage beyond the door was wide and stayed dark only a short while, as barred windows punctured its sides past a certain point. There didn't seem to be much else here, however. Until Chhavi, ranging ahead, spotted the staircase leading down and another angling up.

"Up will just put us atop the defenses," she pointed out. "If this place has a jail, it'll be below." That made sense, and they all followed along as she descended to a lower level with thick doors set at intervals on both sides. Small openings, covered in a thick, metal grille, allowed some light to spill through from the windows beyond. The place looked every inch a prison, and a sturdy one at that.

As the last of them shifted from the stairs to the brick floor, a rustling came from behind one of the nearby doors. Then the light was blocked by a silhouette.

"Who's there?" a woman demanded.

Nalan gasped and hurried over. "Farah, is that you?" He frowned at the door. "I can try to tear it free, but there's no wind down here."

Ruhi smirked and shouldered him aside, drawing the knife Sanga had loaned her and a long, slim-handled metal comb.

"Allow me." Crouching down, she worked her own brand of magic with the two, and a second later, the door clicked open. "Old lock, nice and simple," she explained as she straightened and stepped aside to let the mage tug it open.

He did, and a woman tumbled out and into his arms. "Nalan!" she cried as she hugged him. "What are you doing here? I didn't think you'd let yourself get caught in this mess!"

"I'm here for you and the others," he answered, returning the embrace before leaning back to study her. "Are you all right?"

"Fine," she answered, wiping at her face and brushing back her long hair. She didn't look harmed, Sundra thought. Just tired and dirty. And angry, as her eyes swept over the rest of them. "Who's this?"

"Friends," Nalan replied. "Here to help. Let's find everyone else and get all of you out here." His face darkened, visible even in the dim light. "Then I'll deal with Yilai."

The woman started to say something, but Nalan had already moved past to the next cell. A man answered his call, and Ruhi hurried over to unlock the door for them.

"Handy fellow to keep around, your brother," Chhavi commented to Sundra with a grin. Beyond her, the remark produced a scowl from Sanga.

"Very," Sundra agreed, amused despite their current circumstances.

They found six other thalakurioi and freed them all. The rescued mages were in bad shape, however, so at Nalan's request, Chhavi and the brothers led the mages back up and out through the empty doorway to the *Kalinga*. Nalan himself ventured up to the top level, with Sanga, Ruhi, and Sundra trailing after him.

"Time to end this," the mage muttered as he visibly forced his feet forward.

The upper level was open to the sky, though the walls were still above their heads. Sundra could see that those barriers curved away once they left the beach, forming a large diamond. The tower sat at the back corner. A handful of men and women stood near the outer wall, arms raised and eyes focused toward the storm beyond. They were still as statues, and Sundra guessed they were the ones currently maintaining the concealing weather.

No one else was in sight, which didn't stop Nalan from shouting, "Yilai!" as loud as he could. The storm surged closer in response as the wind lifted and amplified the call until it echoed throughout the fortress.

In answer, a door at the top of the tower swung open, and a man emerged. From here, all Sundra could tell was that he wasn't terribly tall or particularly thin, that he had a short beard and wore a pale turban, and that his angavastra was the same stormy blue-green as Nalan's.

"Nalan," the man replied, stepping up to the railing around the tower's upper edge and peering down at them. "How dare you invade our stronghold? And with outsiders, no less!" His contemptuous gaze swept over them all, as the sky darkened overhead.

"How dare *you* imprison our friends!" Nalan shot back, still marching forward. "Or try to kill me!"

Others had begun to appear from doors at the tower's base and along the fortress walls behind it. A buzz rose from them at that last comment.

Nor was the *Kalinga*'s mage slow to notice. "That's right!" he continued. "I told Yilai I wouldn't join whatever this is, but that I supported him and you and would not stand in his way or share his secrets. But evidently that wasn't enough, so he sent Tara and Ojas to end me!"

He'd reached the middle of the wide square before the tower now and stopped there, hands going to his hips as he glared up at Yilai. All his attention was focused on the other mage, though his words were clearly meant for their audience as a whole.

"Is this your idea of solidarity?" he demanded beneath the gathering clouds. "To kill anyone who doesn't fall immediately in line?"

If he thought he'd cow Yilai, however, he was mistaken, as the other mage sneered. "I knew you'd talk," he hollered down. "And clearly you did!" He pointed an accusing finger at the rest of them. "Else why are you here with these interlopers? You've betrayed us to the Parishad!" That brought an angry muttering from the crowd now assembled. Sundra counted at least a dozen, maybe more. That wasn't good. Not good at all.

They couldn't back down, though. Not now. "He didn't betray you, you turned on him!" Sundra shouted, stepping forward to join the verbal fray. "And then he realized you meant to kill the others who wouldn't join, too! That's not the mark of a leader—it's the sign of a tyrant!"

"What do you know about anything?" Yilai taunted. "You're not one of us."

Now Ruhi moved to stand beside him. "We may not be mages," she called out, "but we know what it's like to be forced to serve."

She raised her hand over her head, so the bracelet on her wrist could catch the light. "We promised Nalan we'd speak to the Parishad on all your behalf, force them to see how wrong your treatment has been."

More murmuring, but to Sundra's ears it didn't sound as fierce now. More thoughtful. Most of these thalakurioi were scared and angry, he realized, but not necessarily hateful or aggressive. They'd welcome a peaceful solution.

Not Yilai, though. "Kill them!" he screamed, waving at their small group. "Kill them all!" He followed the command by calling lightning from the clouds and hurling it down from the tower, and the battle was joined.

Sundra ducked, not sure what else he could do against mages, when a hand landed on his shoulder. It was Sanga. "Come on," the tall pirate urged. "Quick!" He'd tapped Ruhi as well, and led them both at a run across the courtyard, directly toward the tower.

Several mages stood there but hesitated upon seeing the trio charging them. Sanga flung a dagger, taking one in the stomach, and the others bolted out of the way, leaving the door at the building's base open and unguarded.

"Can't fight magic," the rangy man gasped as he hurried up a set of stairs built around the tower's inner wall, curving upward toward the top. "But maybe we can even the odds some."

Sundra nodded, conserving his breath. He could already guess what the pirate had in mind.

Sure enough, when they reached the top, Sanga stopped to listen. Then he stepped outside, moving with surprising stealth for such a tall man. Sundra and Ruhi followed, doing their best to keep quiet as well.

Whether they succeeded or the raging battle was simply so loud as to mask any sounds they made, they exited onto the tower's rooftop balcony without the one mage there turning around. Yilai was too busy exchanging bolts with Nalan. At the same time, several figures were busy clubbing any mage who resisted. It seemed the *Kalinga*'s crew had joined the fray after all.

Creeping forward, Sanga edged to one side of the rebellious storm mage, gesturing for Sundra and Ruhi to take the other. When they were nearly to the railing, and only a foot behind Yilai, the pirate shouted, "Now!"

Together, the three of them lunged forward. Sanga had a dagger in hand and raised it high, bashing Yilai in the back of the head with the heavy pommel. At the same time, Sundra slammed his own sword hilt into the mage's gut, and Ruhi wedged a foot between the man's, tripping him.

The result was immediate and gratifying. Their target groaned in surprise and pain, doubling over and tipping sideways, then stiffened as Sanga connected. By the time he hit the balcony floor, Yilai was unconscious.

For an instant, the fortress fell silent, as the other mages stopped their attacks, staring up at the place where their leader had stood. Then Sundra gathered his voice and shouted down, "We have Yilai! It's over!"

The other mages stirred—until a voice cut through the tumult. "Nothing is over!" One of them pushed through to confront Nalan, sparing only a quick glare upward before spinning to face the rest. "Not until *I* say it's over!"

"Makiya!" Nalan snapped, breathing hard from the previous fight but appearing unharmed. "I didn't think Yilai had the brains to put all this together on his own!"

That made the new mage—Makiya, the one Jasleen Lal had tasked them to find in the first place—laugh as if it were the funniest thing ever. "That idiot?" he scoffed, turning toward Nalan again, hands on his hips. "Not a chance!" He raised his voice. "But you know what he did have? Bruises! All over! And do you know why? Because he'd been beaten—by his own crew!"

Everyone else had gone dead silent, allowing the angry storm mage's words to carry easily as he went on. "That's right! He didn't get attacked by rivals or have to fend off soldiers or guards or anything like that. His own crew beat him! Why? Because they'd gone after a fat merchant ship, and it had got away. They blamed Yilai, told him his kind—*our* kind—were only good for one thing, and he couldn't even do that right. So they attacked him." He scowled at everyone assembled and the world at large, folding thick arms over a thicker chest.

"He was stunned, and scared. These were his own shipmates! When one of them landed a lucky blow, though, he acted on reflex—and blasted the man with lightning. Killed him instantly— and blew a hole in the ship's hull. It sank like a stone. Only Yilai survived."

"So he played dead, like he'd gone down with the ship and the rest," Nalan guessed.

Makiya nodded. "Exactly. Funny thing, though—that lightning strike? Fried his bracelet. He was free!" He laughed again, mockingly. "Poor fool didn't know what to do with it! Fortunately, he came looking for his old pal Makiya for help. And I knew what to do right away."

Sundra had already guessed. "You saw your chance, not just to escape, but to free everyone," he said, only having to raise his voice a little to be heard in the silence, even from that distance. "But you didn't think they'd listen to you. Yilai and his tragedy, though, that'd get them all up in arms, make them agree it was time to act."

The mage did look up at him now, and Sundra almost shrank back from the naked hatred plain on the man's broad face. "That's right! Finally, they all saw what I already had—how your kind has always hated us! How you'll never leave us alone! How we can never be free—not unless we take that freedom for ourselves!"

The crowd was shifting again, shuffling their feet, but the noises were growing louder, more impassioned, more aggressive. His ranting was stirring them back up. If he convinced the others he was still in the right, they could be in trouble.

"So were you behind trying to kill your fellow mages, too?" That was Ruhi, moving to the railing as well, and her words froze everyone in place. "How does that fit into your claims of wanting freedom, if you only want it for those who do what you say? That's not freedom, it's just another form of slavery, only with you as the slaver, dominating your own friends. That's worse than anything else."

Makiya's eyes flashed, and Sundra tensed, prepared to pull his friend back if the mage began throwing lightning up at them. But for the moment, the stormer was too enraged to even conjure such an attack.

"Shut up!" he screamed instead, his face purpling. "You don't get to speak here! You're nothing but a lap dog for those idiot rajas and all the other fools who serve them! I am in charge here! Only me!"

"Enough!" The voice was Nalan's, the single word like a thunderclap. "You have gone mad with power," the *Kalinga*'s mage continued, his own face red but set and stern beneath his mustache. "You have put your own thoughts of revenge and your own lust for control above the needs of our fellows. You are not fit to lead them or anyone. And your would-be reign ends here and now." Nalan strode forward, closing the distance to Makiya.

But the other storm mage had recovered from his initial shock and stood his ground. "You don't get to tell me what to do!" he retorted, his own aura beginning to brighten in response. "You turned your back on our friends! Go back to your little ship and mind your own business!"

"This *is* my business, and all of ours!" Nalan shot back. "You made sure of that! The Parishad will outlaw us all, kill us, exile us, whatever it takes—because you drove them to it! Unless we stand down and hope they can still be made to see reason." He was within reach of the other man now. "And if that means you must pay for your crimes, so be it."

Makiya opened his mouth to reply, but Nalan didn't give him the chance. Instead the bald mage's fist shot out. His punch landed squarely across his rival's jaw, snapping Makiya's head back, the blow resounding like a hammer against stone. Sundra watched from up above as the rebel mage was lifted off his feet by the impact, his eyes already fluttering shut, crashing to the ground several paces away in a senseless heap.

As the echoes faded, the other mages began to move around, to approach a tottering but still resolute Nalan—but hesitantly, hands out and open, without any sign of malice or renewed assault.

It was over.

CHAPTER THIRTY-SEVEN

RUHI

Sailing to Shaant Sthaan had been bad.

Sailing back to Surpakat was ten times worse.

Not because of how fast they were going, though that was still a factor. Sanga had explained to Nalan that they would need to get back in time for the meeting of the Parishad, otherwise who knew how long it would be before they could get the entire Council convened again to hear about the thalakurioi? Especially when there were several rajas who might prefer that the topic of the storm mages' treatment not be raised so publicly.

Despite his obvious fatigue, the *Kalinga*'s mage had nodded, his mustache swaying in the breeze, and soon there was a wind to propel them back to town and a wave to carry them along.

That was made far easier—and, Ruhi suspected, faster—by the fact that he had considerable help this time around.

And that was the real issue. The *Kalinga* was not a large ship, not like the *Aden Star* had been. It was smaller and leaner, perfect for a small crew of pirates relying upon speed. Khandereo had only nine manning the ship, including himself, Chhavi, and Nalan. Ruhi had felt that even just adding herself, Sanga, and

Sundra had filled the narrow ship to capacity.

And now they had picked up an additional twenty people.

The mages had two small ships of their own, as it happened. One of those Tara and Ojas had used when they'd come after Nalan—at Makiya's order, the others confirmed. The second was still at Shaant Sthaan, tucked away in a small hidden dock accessed by a concealed door at the base of the outer wall. But it was as tiny as the first had been, with a single mast and space for perhaps five, six at most, and no cabins or belowdecks at all. Such a boat was perfect for a quick jaunt, but for anything longer than an afternoon it would be unbearable.

Besides which, even though Farah and the other rescued mages had promised to keep watch over Makiya and Yilai and stop them from causing any mischief, Ruhi didn't trust them and knew she was not alone in that concern. Especially since most of the other thalakurioi had quickly surrendered once Makiya had been defeated, and apologized for ever following him, claiming they'd not known the extremes he would take and then were too scared to argue. That all sounded very convenient, though, and so Ruhi and her friends weren't inclined to trust them, either.

Which all meant they'd had no choice but to squeeze everyone onto the *Kalinga*.

As many as could be fit were shoved belowdecks. The rest slept out in the open, and during the day they crowded the rails, trying to keep clear of the pirates, ropes, and sails.

It was less than ideal. Ruhi was actually glad they were making such haste to return home, if only so she could get off this boat and back to Kosala's, where she only had to share quarters with Sundra. And where she could bathe properly, and relieve herself properly, without having to worry about being discovered.

Along the way, partially to keep her mind off their current close quarters and partially to avoid thinking about the speed with which they were flying over the water, Ruhi discussed plans with Sundra and Sanga. It was helpful having the rangy pirate there, since he knew Kosala far better and could, to some degree, predict what she might do.

For one thing, he assured them both, and Nalan as well, that their employer would fully support relief for the mages.

"Kosala despises slavery," Sanga explained, the scowl on his face confirming that she was not the only one. "It's why she's never used your services herself. But she had no idea how bad things were for your friends. Once she does, she'll do everything she can to make sure that never happens again."

Chetan, they all agreed, would feel the same way. It was one of the areas where he and Kosala would absolutely see eye to eye.

That was only two out of seven, however. And most of the others would not be nearly so happy about seeing the thalakurioi freed.

"Koliya doesn't use mages," Sundra pointed out on the eve of that first day, as the sun was beginning to sink beneath the water off in the distance, sending its last rays across the ocean like a spill of liquid fire. "And weakening the others is good for him, so he'll support it. Right?"

"Probably," Ruhi agreed. "Especially since he can act all high and mighty about it. But that still leaves it four to three." She tapped her fingers on the railing as she thought. "Tarabai, Ehsaan, Falguni, and Jasleen Lal. All of them had thalakurioi. All of them won't want to give that up."

Sanga nodded from where he was perched on the railing, feet dangling above the deck. Seeing him sit like that made Ruhi nervous, but the tall pirate acted completely relaxed there.

"Tarabai's a coward," he said. "She won't dare stand up to the others, so if Kosala and Chetan can gain the advantage, she'll go along without a fuss."

"Falguni can probably be reasoned with," Ruhi said, recalling their recent meeting with the lady raja. "She's smart enough to know when to push and when not. Besides which, she won't want Kosala as an enemy. And at least one of her mages has already said she'll go back willingly." That was Farah, who had proven to be as friendly and desirous to help as Falguni had claimed.

"That just leaves Ehsaan and Jasleen Lal, then," Sundra summed up. He frowned, fingers splayed along his chin, and Ruhi wondered if he even realized he was posing. Probably not—it just seemed to come naturally to him. At least this time they didn't have Meera along to swoon over him. "Ehsaan's too careful to oppose everyone else. He'll agree, or at least not fight it. But Jasleen—"

There were sighs and nods all around. Jasleen Lal was not only the oldest of the rajas and the most experienced, she was also arguably the toughest—and the most stubborn. She wouldn't give up her mages without a fight.

Of course, they weren't really hers anymore, were they, Ruhi thought. Not exactly. "I have an idea how we might get through to her," she told the others, and explained what she was thinking.

"That might actually work," Sanga commented once she was done, giving her an approving glance that made her feel suddenly warm all over. "But you could wind up making an enemy of Antara, if she hears you're the one who brought it up. And sooner or later, she's going to be raja in Jasleen's place."

Ruhi exchanged glances with Sundra, who looked worried but still shrugged. "We'll deal with that if it comes to it," he stated, putting on a bold front. "Right now, the important thing is to make sure Farah and the others are protected."

They were all agreed, then. The only question now was, would they get back in time to put their plans in motion? And would those same plans be enough to win the rajas over?

❦ ❦ ❦

They reached Surpakat shortly after dawn the next day, having sailed on through the night, with Nalan, Farah, and others rotating duty whenever needed to ensure they maintained their unbelievable speed. Ruhi wished she could just flop down on the docks or, even better, on the cobblestones past them and luxuriate in the feel of solid ground beneath her whole body.

But there was no time. The Parishad were gathering today, and they needed to catch the rajas before the council meeting ended and they lost any hope of an audience.

Accordingly, after Khandereo had expertly slipped the *Kalinga* through a surprising number of ships in the harbor, she, Sundra, and Sanga charged down the gangplank. Nalan and Farah and a few other mages accompanied them and dragged Makiya and Yilai along as well.

Those two had not caused any additional trouble on the trip back, scowling at everyone and occasionally berating their fellow thalakurioi for betraying them but clearly realizing they were badly outnumbered and that trying anything would only get them knocked out again. Thus, it was with the pair in tow that they set foot on the docks—and suddenly found themselves surrounded by a crew of tough-looking men and women all armed with clubs and staves.

"These two come with us!" a big, bearded man in front roared, pointing a thick wooden cudgel at Ruhi and Sundra. "The rest of you, back off if you want to live!"

Ruhi groaned, and beside her Sundra actually rolled his eyes. "This again?" he complained. "We're in a hurry, here."

Then Farah nudged them aside. "No problem," the storm mage promised and flicked her hand at the crowd as if brushing away flies. A powerful gust of wind sprang up around her—and slammed the thugs out of their way, toppling the ones on the left to the ground and banging the ones on the right against the *Kalinga*'s sturdy hull. "Let's go."

"You're a useful woman to have around," Sundra commented as they continued on past the stunned crew.

"Thanks, but I won't be able to do that again in a hurry," she replied. "It did feel good, though." Beside her, Nalan smirked beneath his mustache, but made no other reply.

Nothing else slowed their progress, and scant moments later, Ruhi burst into the first-floor taproom of the Council building and made for the stairs, Sundra at her side and Sanga leading the way with those long legs of his.

"Weapons!" the tall pirate announced, all but flinging down his sword and dagger on the table. The guards there raised an eyebrow but let him pass. They frowned and blocked the way, however, when they saw the men and women in blue-green.

"Stormers are forbidden to set foot in Surpakat!" one of the guards, a stout older man, declared. "You're all under arrest!"

"They are here on order of the Parishad itself!" Ruhi countered, holding up her writ. The guard stared at that, but the seals on it were plain to see and eventually he nodded and grudgingly moved aside to let them all pass.

The crowd beyond was already astir, having heard at least some of the commotion outside, and everyone watched silently as Ruhi and Sundra approached the rajas' table. All seven were seated there, and it was Jasleen Lal who reacted first, leaping to her feet.

"Makiya!" the aging pirate queen shouted, gesturing toward the man with her cane. "You found him! Oh, well done, you two! I knew I could count on you!"

"Found him, yes," Sundra replied, sweeping into one of his elegant bows without ever slowing his steps. "And all the other missing mages besides. But yours was no victim. He and this one, Yilai, were behind the entire thing."

Gasps broke out around the room, though everyone quieted again to listen as Sundra explained, with occasional interjections from Ruhi. Fortunately, her "brother" could be eloquent when he chose, and his explanation of the mages' standard treatment was impassioned and instantly sympathetic.

"While Makiya and Yilai's actions are reprehensible," he concluded finally, "surely no one can blame them, or any of the others, for wishing to be treated with respect and dignity, as befits any person, instead of being caged and shackled like some sort of trained beasts."

Jasleen's face had gone from sunny relief to fierce thunderclouds as she'd listened. "I would never treat anyone that way!" she snapped once Sundra was done. "You prove your worth, I treat you as such."

It was the perfect opening, and Ruhi didn't hesitate for a second. "We know you wouldn't," she agreed at once, making sure to speak up so everyone could hear her. "But you haven't been back to Dveep Kile in some time, have you?"

The seed had been planted and took only an instant to sprout, the comprehension dawning on the old woman's face. "No, I haven't," she agreed slowly. "And it seems things have gone astray in my absence. I will be correcting that, I can assure you." She focused on Makiya and dipped her head. "I'm sorry you suffered at my hands or the hands of those who profess to carry out my will," she stated formally.

The mage's lips curled in a sneer, but he did not deign to respond. Which was just as well.

Ehsaan had been following the conversation closely and now rose to his feet as well. "I, too, must offer my apologies," he stated softly, his face blank but his eyes sharp as ever. "I did not know there was such animosity toward you at Ooncha Need, Yilai. The violence you faced should never have happened."

Kosala stood next. "I think it's clear that things must change with regard to the thalakurioi," she declared, her words ringing out across the room. "They have valuable talents and should be respected for those, and compensated for them properly as well. I urge my fellow rajas to join with me in establishing rules to protect them and to punish any who would mistreat them."

Chetan nodded, though he stayed seated. "I agree," he called out, his voice rough. "They have been slaves in all but name, and any form of slavery is unacceptable in the Isles."

There was a strong murmur of agreement to that, and all the other rajas nodded quickly as well, including Falguni and Tarabai. Ruhi felt a wave of relief wash over her. They'd done it!

The rajas were not finished, however. "That's all fine for the rest," Jasleen Lal stated sharply, but what about those two?" She pointed her cane at Makiya and Yilai. "They started this little uprising. That's treason. They should be put to death!"

Everyone started talking at once, and Ruhi felt the shift as

Nalan and the other mages closed ranks around the two former leaders—and as the air grew taut, like right before a storm. The pair might have put everyone at risk, but they were still thalakurioi, and it was clear the storm mages meant to protect their own.

"I know a mine that could use a few more workers," Falguni offered, her tone mild but her eyes sharp as ever. "No wind or water for them to play with there." But no one was fooled—it was still a death sentence, if a slower one and committed out of sight.

Kosala was still standing and banged a fist on the table to draw the room's attention. "I think we can all understand why they did it," she began, "and can appreciate their frustration and anger. In their place, would we have had the courage to act so defiantly? But"—and here her pointed gaze speared Makiya and Yilai—"I cannot condone kidnapping your fellow mages. That is no better than your own treatment. I move that you both be allowed to live, since your motives ultimately were noble, but that you be exiled from the Areyat Isles, never to return upon pain of death." The others nodded, accepting the compromise, with Koliya and Jasleen pounding on the table.

"For the rest of you, however," Kosala went on, glancing at Farah and Nalan and the handful of other storm mages who'd accompanied them, "I vote that we pardon you all of any involvement you had in this. You were acting in self-defense, and it was only your two apparent leaders who took things too far."

Ruhi recalled Tara and Ojas, who hadn't shown any qualms about killing Nalan and anyone else who stood with him, but kept quiet. Now was not the time to muddy the waters, and she suspected Nalan would make sure Ojas paid for what he'd done.

"Thank you, Raja," the *Kalinga*'s storm mage replied now, stepping forward slightly to speak and dipping into a rough but serviceable bow. "All the rest of us want is a chance to live our lives and wield our magic as we choose, and to be treated fairly for that in return."

Jasleen pounded her cane on the table. "All right, all right," the aging raja said, lowering herself carefully into her chair once more.

"That's all settled, then. We'll work out the finer details after, but you can be sure they will be fair." She nodded to Ruhi and Sundra. "And, again, well done, you two."

Chetan grinned at them. "I believe the reward the last time they solved something for us was one dinar apiece, to be put toward their indenture?" he reminded the others. "I feel that would be appropriate here as well."

Kosala agreed at once, of course, and Jasleen nodded. "That is indeed fair," the silver-haired raja declared. "And with the Parishad's thanks." If she was still displeased with the results of their investigation, she did not show it. Besides, they *had* found her missing mage and determined where he had gone and why, exactly as promised.

Koliya had not said anything during all of this, letting everyone else speak, but now the big raja stirred. "If we're done with all this storm mage nonsense," he grumbled, "can we get on with what we really came here for? To determine, once and for all, who gets Udayin and Vihaan's ships, lands, and goods."

A ripple of excitement flowed through the room as the other rajas also returned to their seats, and Ruhi stepped back to one side with Sundra and the others. Their report was over, it seemed. And she had to admit, she was as curious as everyone else what would be decided about the two dead rajas' former belongings.

Before the Council could begin discussion, however, the doors from the hall opened, and someone slipped in. It was a woman, not tall but slim and fit, wearing the tapering helmet and scaled breastplate of the town guard, her expression as stern as ever.

Pillai crossed the room, stopping close to where Ruhi had just stood a moment ago, facing the assembled Parishad. "My apologies for the interruption," the guard commander began, banging the butt of her spear on the floor to quiet any other conversation. "But I bring ill news regarding some of the very items you are here to discuss." Her keen eyes swept the rajas. "There appears to be some trouble at the docks."

CHAPTER THIRTY-EIGHT

SUNDRA

That caused an immediate tumult of noise, rising until Sundra couldn't hear himself think. It was only alleviated by Pillai's spear on the floor and Jasleen Lal's cane on the desk, both rapping loudly for attention. When things finally quieted down, however, it was Chetan who took charge.

"What kind of trouble?" the burly raja demanded, glaring at Pillai as if any disturbance was her fault. Sundra knew that was just the big pirate's way, however, and the guard commander was not shaken in the least.

"Several docked ships have been blockaded," she replied in a clear, firm voice, speaking to the crowd as much as the rajas. "Specifically, those belonging to the late rajas." She held up her hand for quiet as the whispers started again. "From what we can see, these new ships—which fly no flag or insignia—have archers lining the railings. With fire arrows at the ready."

There was no holding back the noise then, as the whole room buzzed. Sundra frowned, thinking over the situation. Fire arrows? So whoever had sent those new ships wanted the others burned out and sunk rather than captured or claimed? Why? Why not try taking them instead?

Unless whoever it was knew they wouldn't be getting those ships themselves—and worried about who might. He could see the tactical advantage to getting rid of the ships then. Maintain the current power balance.

That only favored those who were in positions of strength, however. Particularly when it came to ships. He scanned the rajas quickly. Tarabai was white as a sheet. Of course she would be the most worried—she desperately needed those ships. Falguni looked troubled, Ehsaan pensive, Jasleen Lal, Chetan, and Kosala all enraged.

And Koliya sat back, smirking.

"You!" Kosala rounded on her massive peer. "You did this!"

"I have no idea what you're talking about," Koliya protested, though the words rang hollow since he was still smirking when he pronounced them. "Why would I want to destroy perfectly good ships?"

"Because you have the largest fleet of any of us," Ehsaan answered quietly. "But you know that could change, depending upon what we decide here today."

Sundra felt a nudge at his elbow. It was Ruhi. "I can see him doing that, sure," she whispered when he leaned his head in her direction. "But it wasn't the ships he really wanted, remember?"

She was right, and the minute he realized that Sundra surged forward. Not toward the rajas at their table, however. Instead, he hurried over to Pillai.

"You need to have your men check the houses," he told her hurriedly. "Udayin's and Vihaan's. Those were what Koliya really wanted."

She gave him a sharp glance but not an angry one, followed by a quick nod. Then she gestured to the guards stationed by the doors and began issuing orders, her words soft enough not to reach anyone else. The two saluted and rushed away, exiting the room.

Something else had occurred to Sundra, but it wasn't anything he could share with the town guard. Instead, he approached Sanga, who had been watching the chaos, arms crossed, body tensed, ready to step to Kosala's aid in an instant if need be.

"I have an idea," Sundra told the tall pirate, and explained his thinking. The man surprised him with a grin and a short laugh before clapping him on the shoulder.

"That's brilliant!" Sanga told him, keeping his own voice down. "I'll see to it at once." And, with a quick nod to Kosala, he slipped out after the guards.

"What was that all about?" Ruhi asked when Sundra rejoined her.

He just smiled. "A little insurance." But he didn't want to say anything more. Too many people were listening.

The rajas were all shouting at each other—well, Koliya and Kosala were shouting at each other, with Chetan and Jasleen Lal joining in against the big raja. The other three were watching but seemed hesitant to interfere.

This continued for so long that they were still at it when the pair of guards returned. They made straight for Pillai, whispering something to her that made her straighten, her scowl deepening. She had to bang her spear on the floor several times before the rajas quieted enough for everyone to hear her.

"My guards have just reported that both Udayin's and Vihaan's homes have been broken into," she announced, her volume increased by clear anger. "The guards I left at each have been beaten and tied up, though not killed, for which whoever did this should be grateful. But both homes have been barricaded against further entry, and those within appear to be armed with torches and casks of oil."

"Are you mad?" That was Falguni, her words aimed at Koliya. "You mean to burn down the homes as well?"

He shrugged but his smirk was gone, now replaced with the petulant look of a pouting child. "I know nothing about that," he declared with a harrumph. "But if they did burn down, I wouldn't mind. At least that way no one else gets them." He folded his powerful arms over his chest and eyed his fellow rulers closely, clearly awaiting their next move.

Just then, the doors to the hall opened again. This time it was Sanga returning, and he nodded to Sundra as he did, then approached one of the guards. Excellent!

Sundra watched, struggling to restrain his own rising excitement, as the guard then marched over to Pillai and whispered something to her. Whatever he said brought a big grin to the guard commander's face, one of the first times Sundra had ever seen such an expression on her.

"It seems," she declared, having to shout to be heard over all the chaos, "that there is another location currently at risk of fire." The look she leveled at Koliya could only be called triumphant. "Your docks."

"What?" The massive pirate leaped to his feet. "What are you talking about? Who would dare?" His eyes landed upon Sanga, now back leaning against the same column as before, then jumped to Sundra before he swiveled around to loom over Kosala. "You! You did this!"

Naturally, the female raja was completely uncowed by the big man. "I have no idea what you're talking about," she told him bluntly—and completely truthfully, as it happened. "But I would suggest you back up a step or two and sit down, before I give you cause to regret it." That last was said in a lower tone, the threat unmistakable, and despite her lack of weapons and much smaller size it was Koliya who looked away first.

"I need those docks!" he muttered, half entreaty and half reminder. "Without them, my ships are useless!"

"True," Ehsaan said. "And, if they did burn, and someone else were to claim that space and build docks of their own there instead..." He let the threat hang in the air, Koliya's face purpling as he realized just how vulnerable his position was.

Which Sundra had known, of course, when he suggested Sanga send men to threaten those docks. The fact that Koliya had only the two made that even easier.

Falguni spoke. "Perhaps, then, all torches and arrows and the like should be set aside, all together," she suggested sharply. "All crews withdrawn, all blockades and barricades lifted." She was staring daggers at Koliya, as were the other rajas, and the big man finally hung his head, nodding glumly. He waved over a man who'd been standing off to one side of his chair.

"I might be able to convince whoever's behind this to back away," Koliya stated loudly, and the man nodded before making for the door.

"I suggest we call a short recess," Ehsaan proposed. "Until such time as we may proceed without danger to any ship, dock, or home."

The other rajas concurred, Pillai saluted and left, and people began standing, milling about and talking as everyone waited for the danger to pass.

"That was you?" Ruhi asked. "Smart."

Sundra dipped his head. "Thanks. I figured it was the one thing that might make him back down."

"You realize we've just made a serious enemy," she pointed out. "He didn't like us before, but now he's got real reason to hate us."

"I know. But it was the only way." He managed a small smile. "Thank you for saying 'us,' though. This was all on me."

She shrugged, not without a tiny smile of her own. "We're brothers, right? We stick together."

Sundra laughed and bumped her with his hip. "We do indeed." He sighed again. "Now I suppose *we* had better tell Kosala that we've promised she'd give two ships to Khandereo."

That got a full laugh from his "brother." "Oh, no," she protested, giving him a playful shove in the raja's direction. "For that one, you're on your own."

✦ ✦ ✦

At last Pillai returned. "The blockades have been lifted," she reported, "the houses cleared out and placed under guard again, and the docks also freed."

"Very good, thank you, Commander," Ehsaan said. He turned to his fellow rajas. "Perhaps now we can properly take up our original topic for today's meeting? The distribution of our former, fallen fellows' belongings?"

Kosala cleared her throat and stood. "Before we get to that," she stated, "there is another, related matter. That of Bahut Saare." Several gasps suggested that some in the room had forgotten about the plantation and its current ownerless state. "As the person most targeted by its former owner," she continued over the noise, "I have the strongest claim to the property. And I request—that we give it to the Raja Falguni."

There were more gasps, and Sundra noted that the other rajas looked surprised as well. All except the one in question, who merely nodded.

"Falguni, your stronghold is the farthest from here," Kosala told her. "Having Bahut Saare will give you a much closer base, making it far easier for you to attend these meetings. I think you will find the plantation already in good order and its current over-seer someone you can work with."

That was a clear hint, and Falguni bowed her head in acknowl-edgment. "Thank you, Kosala," she replied. "I would be honored to accept Bahut Saare, if the rest of the Parishad approves, and only too happy to lean upon the experienced staff already in place."

No one objected, and in seconds it was done. Sundra wasn't entirely clear on the why yet, but he'd worked for Kosala long enough now to know that the raja never did anything with-out a clear plan. He suspected he would learn the answer soon enough.

And, in fact, it was only seconds later that Falguni leaned forward. "On the matter of ships," she announced, "I propose Vihaan's be given to the Raja Kosala who, again, suffered the most in the machinations that led to Vihaan's death." The two women smiled at each other, and Sundra nodded. That had clearly been arranged beforehand and made sense—Kosala wouldn't have wanted responsibility for Bahut Saare anyway, and this gave her a noticeable increase in her fleet.

Chetan nodded. "Agreed."

Kosala bowed in her seat. "I would happily accept those ships," she answered. "Although two will go to the Captain Khandereo, as payment for his assistance in resolving the matter of the thalaku-rioi. And three I offer to my sister raja, Tarabai, to bolster her own fleet."

That startled Tarabai, but she was quick to respond with a grateful smile. "Thank you, Kosala," she said sweetly. "That is truly generous of you. I approve Kosala receiving those ships as well."

With four in favor, the motion would carry, but both Ehsaan and Jasleen approved it nonetheless. Koliya pouted and refused to vote either way.

Chetan spoke next. "Regarding Udayin's ships," he said, laying his hands flat upon the table. "His former second, Shivaji, has requested them. I do not feel he has enough experience or patience to become a raja." There were many nods and murmurs of agreement on that. "In view of his long service, however, I would propose we give him eight of those ships. Then let us see how he handles them—and himself."

That was a wise choice, Sundra felt, both because it would appease the big pirate and because it would let them see whether he was really fit to become the next raja. The others agreed, and that motion was swiftly passed.

"For the rest of the ships," Ehsaan suggested, "perhaps we could divide them amongst us. It is only one or two apiece, I believe."

It was, and that proved agreeable to all as well. Tarabai was especially pleased—between those and the three from Kosala, her position would be far more stable now. Even Koliya couldn't argue about getting two additional ships for his fleet.

Kosala took up the conversation again next. "Regarding money, there isn't much," she reported. "Udayin had some, but he also had many creditors who should be paid off first. I doubt there will be any left after those debts. Vihaan had none on hand, it seems." She was too experienced to wink at Sundra and Ruhi, but he could tell she wanted to. "That just leaves their homes."

She frowned, though only for an instant. "I suggest we give Udayin's to Shivaji—it was his home as well, after all, and if we're gifting him those ships he will need a base here." No one argued, so she continued, "For Vihaan's home, I think we should give it to—Nalan on behalf of his fellow thalakurioi."

That brought a wave of surprise, confusion, and possibly even consternation from the audience as well as the other rajas. Except for Chetan, who pounded the table with one fist.

"Yes!" the weather-beaten raja declared. "Let it be a symbol of our decision to improve their lot, and to address past injustice!"

"But they're forbidden in Surpakat—" Tarabai offered hesitantly, looking at Governor Malhotra, who had remained silent throughout, only to have that objection waved aside.

"No longer," Chetan stated, glaring at Malhotra as if daring the man to disagree. "How can we expect to treat them with any respect if they cannot even come here to live, to work—and to bring us any grievances? No, I am with Kosala on this. We lift that ridiculous ban and we give them the house so that they have a place of their own."

Now Malhotra did respond. "I am only too happy to lift that ban," he stated in his clear, deep voice. "I agree, Surpakat should be open to all residents of the Isles equally."

Everyone turned toward Nalan, who looked stunned. "I— thank you," he finally managed, bowing, his mustache quivering and his face red. "I am honored, and gratified. I will make the house a home for all my fellow thalakurioi, a place where we can gather and live and a place where any can find us with offers of fair work."

That seemed to settle the matter. Kosala and Chetan enthusiastically voted in favor, of course. Koliya, after his initial disappointment at not getting either house for himself, also joined them, apparently taking some solace in the notion that this would seriously annoy the remaining rajas. Falguni and Ehsaan approved it as well, no doubt wishing to seem reasonable and supportive, as did Tarabai. Jasleen harrumphed but finally agreed, making it unanimous.

It felt as if it had been hours by the time Governor Malhotra stood and ritually declared that this meeting of the Parishad was now concluded, and Sundra found he was exhausted. But pleased. All had gone well.

But, seeing Pillai stationed near the doors, he remembered that there was still one last problem they had to solve. Hopefully that would go as smoothly.

CHAPTER THIRTY-NINE

RUHI

Ruhi sighed as Sundra glanced her way, then over at Pillai, then back at her. "Ready?" he asked.

"Not really," she replied, but stayed alongside him as they headed over to the guard commander. Might as well get this over with.

It appeared that Pillai had had much the same thoughts, since her face was set in a slight grimace. "I know what you're going to say," she told them, shaking her head. "I was hoping it wouldn't come to this."

But Sundra, at least, stood firm. "That would have been nice," he agreed, "but we all knew it probably would. And there's no time like the present."

She nodded and led them back over to the Council's grand meeting table. Several of the rajas had already departed but a few lingered—as did the town's governor, currently engaged in conversation with Chetan and Ehsaan.

"Nayak Malhotra," Pillai stated once she'd stopped just a few feet from the three men. "Might I have a moment of your time?"

Malhotra greeted her with just the hint of a smile, and a nod.

"Of course, Captain. If you will excuse me, Rajas?" The two pirate lords tipped their heads and moved away, leaving the governor with the three of them. "What can I do for you?" His gaze took in Ruhi and Sundra, and one eyebrow quirked, but he gave no other outward indication of curiosity. Ruhi found him extremely difficult to read in general.

"I'm sorry to have to go to you with this," Pillai began, her hand tightening upon the spear's haft the only visible sign of her anxiety. "But it's come to my attention that your lieutenant governor, Chennama, has been displaying partiality toward certain others, even so far as slanting legislation in their favor."

For a moment, no one spoke. Then the governor shifted, facing her fully.

"That is a weighty accusation, Captain," he said, his voice as grave as his manner. "I trust you have proof to back this up?"

She nodded, but her eyes darted to the side, pleading silently for help. Help Ruhi found she couldn't refuse.

"The two recent proposals you brought to the Parishad, sir," she stated, drawing the governor's attention. "Both of those were authored by Chennama, were they not?"

He nodded slowly. "I believe so. Or at least she presented them to me, whether they were originally her creation or someone else's. That is not unusual, however—I wrote several proposals for Nayak Laghari, in my time."

Ruhi nodded quickly. "Of course. But in this case, both were designed to aid one person, and one person only—Raja Koliya." She explained how both would have helped him gain more property and weaken his rivals, and the governor listened carefully, which she appreciated. At least he was not dismissing their accusation out of hand.

When she had finished, however, he merely nodded, less in agreement than in thought, she felt. "I can see where those would seem to favor the raja," he commented slowly. "But there are others who might have profited from those proposals, now and in future. Do you have other evidence to support this?"

Sundra started to open his mouth beside her, then stopped. Ruhi knew exactly why. He'd been about to relate the incident where they'd sent Koliya off on a fool's errand by telling Chennama the raja's stronghold was in danger. But that would only prove that the lieutenant governor had informed one of the ruling council about a threat to his property, which was perfectly reasonable and even expected of someone in authority. It also painted them in a bad light for spreading false stories.

"Nothing concrete, no," Pillai was forced to admit after a telling pause.

Malhotra frowned. "Very well. I see only one way to resolve this." Straightening, he peered past them, raising his voice. "Chennama!"

Turning, Ruhi saw the very woman standing over near the doors. Upon hearing her name, she hurried over. "Yes, Nayak?" The woman dipped her head to the three of them. "Captain Pillai. And I don't believe I've had the pleasure, but of course I know who you are—the brothers Chera."

They all bowed back, as Malhotra cleared his throat. "Chennama, there has been some question of impropriety and favoritism," he explained. "Specifically, from you toward the raja Koliya. Apparently there are concerns that the recent proposals you gave me were designed entirely to aid him."

"What?" The woman reeled back as if struck, eyes wide. She was certainly acting surprised and insulted. "But that's preposterous, sir! I would never do such a thing!"

"So I said," the governor assured her quickly. "But perhaps you can speak to these claims, nonetheless."

Nodding, she visibly forced herself toward calm, taking slow, deep breaths. "Of course."

Turning, Chennama faced the three of them, though she did keep glancing back at her employer. "Both bills were designed to aid the city, not any one person. The first, regarding dock space, was to prevent overcrowding in the bay and to make a more equitable use of the remaining space among all our residents. The second was intended to help provide city funding for much-needed projects, as well as giving us some measure of control over the distribution of wealth within city limits. Nothing more." She allowed herself a slight smile. "You are correct that the raja might have benefited from both, but that was purely coincidental, not the intent behind the proposals."

"It *is* a notable coincidence," Malhotra commented, folding his long arms over his chest. If not quite disapproving, his tone was at least concerned. "As city officials, we must strive at all times to remain objective and to keep all our actions free of even a hint of partiality. Otherwise we damage the dignity of our office and others' trust in us and our decisions."

Chennama bowed her head. "Of course, sir," she agreed. "I was not thinking the matter through clearly. I apologize."

He nodded. "Such things happen," he said magnanimously. "Please make sure to be more careful in future, however."

Then he turned his gaze toward the three of them. "Thank you for bringing this to my attention," he said. "It is best to nip such rumors and concerns in the bud, before they can spread and cause further damage."

They all nodded, because what else could they do? This was obviously as far as he was willing to believe them for the moment, and all he was prepared to require of Chennama in response.

"Thank you for your time and for all that you do, sir," Sundra declared, bowing. He backed away then, and Ruhi followed—but not before she caught a glimpse of Chennama's face.

The lieutenant governor was glaring at them both, the fury in her eyes at odds with the faint smirk upon her lips. She caught Ruhi looking and winked, but it was far from a friendly gesture. No, this was the look of someone saying, "Yes, I bested you here. And I will do so again. But you have angered me, and you will pay for that."

Ruhi tried not to shudder as she looked away, nor to rush too much as they headed for the exit.

"Well, that went poorly," Pillai commented as they reached the doors and the other guards waiting there. "Thank you for trying, however."

"We'll keep our eyes open," Sundra promised. "She's bound to slip up eventually."

"I wouldn't be so sure," Ruhi replied. She forced herself not to glance back. "She knows we're on to her now, so she'll be twice as careful. And she's going to be after us in return, for bringing this to Malhotra's attention."

Pillai scowled. "You'll have to watch out for Koliya as well," she warned softly. "Chennama's sure to tell him, and he's not known for letting his grudges sit idly. He may not be able to move against you openly while you're under Kosala's protection, but that won't stop him from trying something if he gets riled up enough."

"Great, another reason for him to hate us," Sundra muttered.

Kosala and Sanga were approaching, though, so he mustered something of a smile. "We'll be careful," he promised Pillai. "And we'll talk again soon, I'm sure."

One last bow and they were leaving with their employer, following the raja down the stairs and outside. It felt good to be in the open air again, and Ruhi breathed a little more freely as they walked back toward home.

Still, she knew they had made enemies that day. Pillai was right, they'd have to be more careful in future.

That was a problem for another day, however. For today, Ruhi was determined to instead be happy they'd solved the matter the Parishad had put before them, and that the question of Vihaan and Udayin's goods had finally been settled.

Perhaps they'd be allowed some peace and quiet now.

CHAPTER FORTY

SUNDRA

Pillai studied their surroundings as they stepped inside. "Can't say I've ever been in here before," she admitted, examining the high ceilings, dark floors, and sturdy columns interspersed among the tables. For once the guard commander was not wearing her customary mail shirt and metal cap, nor did she have her spear, though her sword was still there at her side. Without the armor, she looked like a whole different person—less rigid, even a bit less fierce.

"Me either," Sanga agreed, looking more nervous than Sundra could ever recall. "I typically stay above the Line—don't usually feel all that welcome this far south."

Sundra snorted, and Ruhi actually elbowed the tall pirate in the ribs. "We're barely below it!" she protested. "It's not like we brought you all the way down to the Governor's Hall or anything."

Any further retorts were cut off as Padmini appeared before them. "Six, is it?" she asked, though of course her sharp eyes had already confirmed that.

Ruhi nodded, and the stocky proprietress spun on her heel, leading them to one of the larger, rectangular tables set near the front, just below a window. "This way."

They all followed, Ruhi leading, Sanga just behind her, then Meera and Naaz. Sundra tried to bring up the rear, as a gentleman, but Pillai gave him a look, and he ceded that position without a fight. At the table, he found himself seated against the wall, Ruhi beside him—Sanga had claimed the end and Meera and Naaz the opposite side, leaving Pillai the other end, facing the door. Everyone seemed satisfied with the arrangement, even more so when Padmini returned bearing a tray of fresh roti, dhal, various dipping sauces, and pitchers of both lassi and water.

"This is Padmini, the owner, and the best cook you'll ever meet," Sundra told the others.

Padmini laughed, but the color in her cheeks showed she was pleased by the compliment. "Whatever you recommend," Sundra added, handing back his menu, and she managed a creditable curtsey in return.

"I just made a prawn coconut curry this afternoon," Padmini answered, addressing the table. "I should have enough left for six bowls."

Everyone nodded, and she retreated, though not before patting Ruhi's shoulder.

"How'd you find this place?" Meera asked, tearing off a piece of flatbread and dipping it into mango chutney. "It smells amazing!"

"We literally stumbled onto it," Ruhi answered, taking up the first pitcher and pouring lassi for them all. "Now we come back whenever we can."

"If the rest of the food is this good, I can see why," Sanga commented, stuffing a piece of dhal-coated roti into his mouth.

Everyone laughed, including him, and Sundra raised his cup.

"Thank you for coming along," he told them all. "My brother and I appreciate it. We just wanted to celebrate solving another mystery—and the reward that came with it."

The others all nodded, lifting their cups to clink with his and Ruhi's. "A whole dinar each!" Naaz marveled, her voice so soft it was almost impossible to hear her over the sounds of the half-full tavern. "I can't even imagine!"

Sundra smiled at her, but it was Sanga who said, "Believe me, they earned it!" He toasted them with his cup. "At this rate, you'll be out of indenture within the month!"

That's the idea, Sundra thought but didn't say aloud. After all, once they were free, it would beg the question of what to do next. They'd be able to leave Surpakat, even leave the Isles altogether if they wanted. But would they? Or would they stay with Kosala, but as full employees rather than indentured servants? Or find some other opportunity here? And, whatever they chose, would it be separately or together? Would he even still have a "brother" at that point?

He didn't want to think about all of that. For now, he just wanted to enjoy the fact that he was here with his friends and that he and Ruhi had not only survived the strangeness of the past month but triumphed. That was worth celebrating!

As if on cue, Padmini chose that moment to return, bearing another tray, this one covered in bowls from which an enticing scent rose. Sundra's nose twitched at the smell of tamarind, peppercorns, mustard, and chilis, all mixed with coconut, rice, and of course prawns. His mouth started watering, and Ruhi slapped his arm as she rose to help hand around dishes.

Meera helped as well, and soon they all had fragrant, steaming bowls before them. Padmini had whisked away with her empty tray before they could invite her to join them, but the table was full as it was.

When he'd suggested they have dinner here to mark the occasion, Sundra hadn't necessarily meant for it to be anyone but himself, Ruhi, and Padmini. But then his so-called brother had suggested they bring Meera and Sanga along as well.

"That would look an awful lot like a romantic dinner for each of us, don't you think?" Sundra had teased her, and she'd gone a deep, dark red at the thought. "Not that I'd mind," he'd added, but she was already shaking her head at the thought, looking so panicked he took pity on her.

"Why don't we invite Naaz as well?" he'd offered. "And maybe Pillai? Then it's just a group of friends eating together."

Ruhi had grasped at the notion like it was a rope and she was drowning, and they'd promptly sent word to the town guard headquarters, then rounded up the others. Everyone was amenable, and now here they were.

It was interesting being together outside Kosala's house, Sundra thought, sitting back to watch a bit as he ate the deliciously spicy, sour dish. Naaz was even more shy whenever she realized there were other people around or when she glanced at Pillai, but relaxed if she was concentrating on Meera, himself, Ruhi, or even Sanga. Sanga and Pillai had initially bristled at each other, pirate versus guard, but had quickly found common ground in giving Sundra trouble and also in sizing up possible dangers. Meera was so friendly she'd had no trouble incorporating Pillai into their conversation or drawing Naaz out of her shell.

As for Ruhi? Well, it was entertaining watching her flounder around Sanga—and the usually calm pirate being equally flustered in return. Sundra wasn't the only one to notice, as he and Meera shared a knowing grin, and at one point, he saw Pillai's eyebrow rise while watching the pair.

Of course, if there was genuine interest there it would eventually lead to an awkward conversation about Ruhi's true nature, which might complicate matters for in general. Sundra suspected Kosala wouldn't care much, but some of the others might wonder and talk about what a young man and young woman were doing traveling together and sharing a room. He had no idea how Sanga would react, especially since he wasn't sure if the rangy pirate was normally attracted to men, women, or both.

Yes, this could definitely get tricky. Fortunately, for the moment, that too was in the future. Right now, Sundra dug into his food, laughed at something Ruhi had just said, teased Naaz about something, and then groaned at Sanga's jibe in response. Why worry about possible futures all the time, after all? It was important sometimes to just relax and enjoy the moment—and this particular moment was a good one.

❡ ❡ ❡

They stayed at the Quiet Fire for hours, following their curry with kozhukkattai, the sweet, rice-flour dumplings pairing nicely with cups of hot chai.

Afterward, as they rose to go, Pillai paused. "Thank you for including me," she told them, much of her usual sternness erased after so much good food and good conversation. "This was... nice." She nodded to everyone in turn, thanked Padmini for a spectacular meal, and took her leave.

"It was," Naaz agreed softly, smiling at Sundra and Ruhi and managing to maintain eye contact a full ten seconds before looking away. "Thank you."

"Thank you for coming with us," Sundra told her, and meant it. It had been an excellent evening, all in all. He reached for his coin pouch, but Sanga stopped him.

"I've got this," the pirate insisted, setting a few coins on the table. "Best meal I've had in ages, and the company was every bit as good."

He was looking everywhere but at Ruhi as he said this, which was for the best, since she'd turned red again. Meera laughed silently, and even Naaz giggled, while Sundra filed it away for teasing his so-called brother later.

They all headed back together and only lowered their voices as they reached the front porch, since it was late and many of the windows were already dark. But as they entered, Kosala opened the door to her study and stepped out.

"There you all are," the raja declared, and something in her tone gave Sundra pause. Not annoyance, exactly, but there was a terseness there that warned him it was more than an idle observation. "I trust you had a good evening?" Everyone nodded. "Good. Sundra, Rawal, if I might have a word? The rest of you, good night."

Meera and Naaz quickly said good night and hurried off toward their rooms. Sanga lingered, frowning, but a slight headshake from their employer kept him from following as Kosala ushered Sundra and Ruhi into the room—and then shut the door behind them.

"We need to talk," she stated, crossing to her desk and seating herself at it, and now there was no mistaking the seriousness in her tone or her look. "It's about your father."

"Our father?" Ruhi managed, but the look Kosala shot her way shut her up instantly.

"Not yours, young lady," the raja corrected sharply, returning her gaze to Sundra alone. "Just yours… Kunwar Sundra Aruvar."

GLOSSARY

Achkan: a knee-length open jacket with buttons all the way down

Alleppy Meen: a curry made with fresh fish simmered in spiced coconut gravy with raw mango

Angavastra: a man's shoulder cloth or stole, often with decorative borders. It can be worn over a kurta or against bare skin.

Ayya: an honorific meaning "noble" or "worthy"

Baglah: a large, deep-sea ship, typically with three masts

Badan: a small boat with a flat bottom, good for shallow creeks and canals

Chettiar: a landowner or merchant

Choli: a fitted, midriff-baring bodice, worn by women under sari or sadri

Churidar: tight pants

Daniq: a smaller gold coin, six to a dinar

Dhangi: a smaller deep-sea ship, usually with two masts

Dhoti: embroidered, silk sarongs tied to resemble loose trousers

Dinar: a heavy gold coin

Dirham: a silver coin, twenty to a dinar, roughly three and change to a daniq

Dupatta: an embroidered shawl that can be draped around both shoulders and over the head or across the chest or in several other ways

Durga: a stronghold

Fals (plural Falus): a copper coin, ten to a dirham, two hundred to a dinar

Gekurios: an elemental mage. Plural is gekurioi.

Ghagra: pleated skirts worn under a sari

Gharara: wide-legged, silk, brocade pants that flare out dramatically at the knees

Idlis: steamed rice-dough pancakes

Jal dvaar: "water gate," a chain strung across the mouth of a harbor to keep out unwanted ships

Kameez: a long, loose shirt or tunic

Khet: an estate or plantation

Kolossoi: the mythic Giants

Kotia: a deep-sea ship similar to a baglah in size but more slender with an additional foresail

Kozhukkattai: a dessert of sweet, rice-flour dumplings, usually filled with shredded coconut and jaggery and sometimes other bits of dried fruit

Kunwar: the son (or Kunwari, daughter) of a Sirdar, essentially a prince

Kurta: a loose cotton shirt

Mekhela: an elaborately beaded or linked belt

Nayak: a governor

Nilavilakku: a traditional oil lamp, typically tall and slim like a candlestick and made of brass or bronze. They are often found at the entrances to homes, and lighting them is considered good luck.

Pagri: a traditional headdress made of a single long cloth wound around the top of the head; also called a turban

Parishad: council or assembly, the Pirate Council that rules the islands

The Pirate Line: a wall running across Surpakat and effectively dividing the older, pirate-run portion of the town ("above the Line") from the newer, more respectable section for business and government ("below the Line")

Puja: a small alcove or room used solely for meditation and prayer

Pujari: A holy man or priest who performs important rituals

Raja: "king," a Pirate Lord

Rampini: a small, narrow, unmasted boat, propelled by oar

Rishi: A holy man or sage who dispenses wisdom and knowledge

Sadhu: An ascetic holy man who engages in meditation

Sadri: a vest, often embroidered

Sari: a long strip of cloth, often beautifully woven, women wear wrapped around them

Sasaka: captain

Shalwar: drawstring trousers, loose at the top and cuffed at the bottom

Sherwani: a longer, heavier jacket, often embroidered or made of brocade

Shikra: a small, fast bird of prey. Also Kosala's ship. The name means "hunter."

Shri: a polite form of address equivalent to "Mr." or "Ms."

Sirdar: a nobleman of the highest rank, a chieftain

Stanapatta: a band worn over the breasts

Talwar: a long, slim sword with a curved, single-edged blade, a one-piece, metal handle and cross guard (and often knuckle bow), and a disc-shaped pommel.

Tegha: a sword with a wide, double-edged blade that curves and widens toward the tip.

Thakur: a minor nobleman

Thalakurios: a mage who specializes in sea magic, the power of wind and water and storm. Plural: thalakurioi. Also known as "stormers" or "storm mages."

Vaidya: a practitioner of the Ayurvedic healing arts; a doctor

Places:

Bahut Saare ("plenty"): the largest plantation in the Islands, close to Surpakat, formerly held by Bhadra Khatri

Dveep Kile ("island fortress"): the stronghold of the Raja Jasleen Lal

Enkar Bindu ("anchor point"): a stronghold where the Raja Kosala holds sway

Harit Maarg ("greenway"): an island, home to Bahut Saare, Suraksha, and Phasal Kaatana

Khajaana ("treasure"): a stronghold near the far north end of the Islands, controlled by the Raja Falguni

Khet Parivar ("family farm"): a plantation controlled by the Raja Jasleen Lal and her family, on the same island as Dveep Kile

Ooncha Need ("high nest"): the stronghold of the Raja Ehsaan

Phasal Kaatana ("harvest"): the plantation formerly (and quietly) held by the Raja Vihaan

Riyaasat ("homestead"): a stronghold ruled by the Raja Tarabai Banerjee—her docile husband Zubin Banerjee is governor

Shaant Sthaan ("A place of rest," "resting place"): a small island near the northeast edge of the Areyat Isles

Sharan ("refuge"): the Raja Koliya's stronghold, little more than a safehouse

Suraksha ("safety"): the stronghold formerly held by the Raja Vihaan, modest and not necessarily known to be associated with him

Surpakat: the Areyat Isles' capital and main stronghold, guaranteed independence by the Parishad

ABOUT THE AUTHOR

AARON ROSENBERG is the author of the best-selling DuckBob
SF comedy series, the Relicant Chronicles epic fantasy series, the
Dread Remora space-opera series, the Areyat Isles pirate fantasy
series, and, with David Niall Wilson, the O.C.L.T. occult thriller
series. His tie-in work contains novels for *Star Trek*, *Warhammer*,
World of WarCraft, *Stargate: Atlantis*, *Shadowrun*, and *Eureka*. He has
written children's books (including the award-winning *Bandslam:
The Junior Novel* and the #1 best-selling *42: The Jackie Robinson Story*),
educational books, and roleplaying games (including the Origins
Award-winning *Gamemastering Secrets*).

Aaron lives in New York. You can follow him online at
gryphonrose.com, at facebook.com/gryphonrose, and on X (formerly
known as Twitter) @gryphonrose.

If You Liked...

If you enjoyed this novel and the world it's set in, then the creators of the Eldros Legacy would like to encourage you to don thy traveling pack and journey deeper into the mysteries of the world Eldros and all the myriad adventures set therein.

The mortal world of Eldros is coming apart. The Giants, who once ruled its five continents with draconian malice have set their mighty designs on a return to power. Mortals across the globe must be victorious against insurmountable odds or die.

Come join us as the Eldros Legacy unfolds in a growing library of novels and short stories.

You can find all the novels at:
www.EldrosLegacy.com/books

Our website is, of course:
EldrosLegacy.com

The Books by Series
Legacy of Shadows
by Todd Fahnestock
Khyven the Unkillable
Lorelle of the Dark
Rhenn the Traveler

Legacy of Deceit
by Quincy J. Allen
Seeds of Dominion
Demons of Veynkal

WHEN MAGIC DIES,
ONLY THE DEAD HOLD MAGIC.

Once, the empire of Ritakhou was full of magic. But since the Schism, the realm, renamed Rimbaku, is a pale whisper of its former majesty. Now the only magic is the Relicant Touch, a power allowing talents to be drawn from *aishone*, relic bones that are jealously guarded and widely coveted.

Kagiri and Noniki leave their tiny village with a few aishone and all the hope they can muster, but the world is a larger, more dangerous place than they ever dreamed. Forced into a dark bargain that may cost them not only their lives but their souls, their fates intertwine with an emperor, a warrior, a graverobber, and a killer in ways none of them ever imagined, ways that could reshape the Relicant Empire forever.

This is the first book in The Relicant Chronicles, the Anime-esque epic fantasy series from international bestselling author Aaron Rosenberg.

AARON ROSENBERG

BONES *of* EMPIRE

BOOK ONE OF
THE RELICANT CHRONICLES

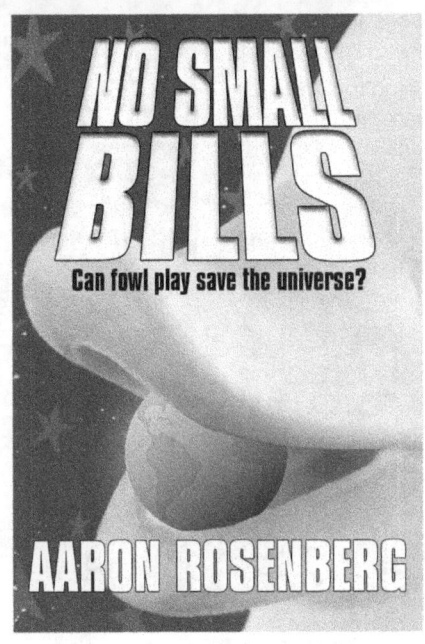

www.ingramcontent.com/pod-product-compliance
Lightning Source LLC
Chambersburg PA
CBHW072108020726
47501CB00003B/765